The Beltane Choice

C000092835

Celtic Fervour Series
Book One

Nancy Jardine

Ocelot Press

Second Edition Nancy Jardine with Ocelot Press 2018

"*The historical side is meticulously researched (it is set in Northern Britain in 71 AD, against the background of the Roman invasion) and has, at its heart the paradox of a conflict between conflicts (on the one hand, the inter-tribal conflicts that had riven British societies for centuries and, on the other, the conflict with the Roman invader that requires those societies to come together). As such, it combines a very human and personal story with a very believable vision of Late Iron Age society in Northern Britain.*" Dr. Mark Patton, archaeologist

Find Nancy Jardine online: www.nancyjardineauthor.com
Join Nancy Jardine on Facebook
https://www.facebook.com/NancyJardinewrites
Follow Nancy Jardine's blog: https://nancyjardine.blogspot.co.uk/
Nancy loves to hear from her readers and can be contacted at nan_jar@btinternet.com or via her blog and website.

Dedication

I dedicate this novel to my lovely daughters, Fiona and Sheena, who have listened to my rambles about my writing, and who have always encouraged me every step of the way. It's utterly gratifying that they have continued our family tradition of being avid readers, and I'm extremely proud to be their mother.

Acknowledgements

A number of people helped me on the journey to the re-publication of this book, offering their valuable advice. I give especial thanks to my editor of this edition, Stephanie Patterson, for her continual encouragement and guidance.

I would also like to give huge thanks to my Cover Designer, Karen Barrett, who designed the coordinating covers for this re-publication of my *Celtic Fervour Series*. She has very patiently put up with my many requests for changes, and tweaking, during the design process – most of which occurred because I'm still a novice regarding cover design, and forgot to mention really important aspects during initial discussions.

I've had various people help me with the Gaelic terms included across the series, to give a hint of what would perhaps have been heard around the roundhouse fireplace. My thanks go especially to Facebook friends Seumas Gallacher and Leanne Ferguson.

About the Author

Nancy Jardine lives in the castle country of Aberdeenshire, Scotland and is so lucky that there's a wealth of history right on her doorstep – Neolithic long barrows; standing stone circles; Iron Age village remains; Ancient Roman marching camps. There's easy access to evidence of human occupation, and interaction, all the way through the centuries to the present day.

History was a favourite subject to teach during her primary teaching career: researching the Ancient Roman invasions of northern Britain, in particular, having filled many hours during the last decades. Keeping up with current archaeological excavations is utterly fascinating.

When not involved in historical research, or writing tasks, Nancy is a fair weather gardener, and a regular grandchild minder, which sometimes accounts for the creativity in the garden.

In addition to her Celtic Fervour Series of historical fiction, she's published contemporary mysteries, some with an ancestral connection, set in fantastic European cities and in other locations across the globe. Her time travel historical fiction is for the early teen market, though adults love reading it, too!

She's a member of the Romantic Novelists Association, the Scottish Association of Writers, the Federation of Writers Scotland and the Historical Novel Society.

Nominations

After Whorl: Bran Reborn (Book 2 Celtic Fervour Series) was accepted for THE WALTER SCOTT PRIZE FOR HISTORICAL FICTION 2014.

The Taexali Game, a time travel novel set in Roman 'Aberdeenshire' AD 210 achieved Second Place for Best Self Published Book in the SCOTTISH ASSOCIATION OF WRITERS BARBARA HAMMOND COMPETITION 2017.

Topaz Eyes, an ancestral based mystery thriller, was a Finalist for THE PEOPLE'S BOOK PRIZE FICTION 2014.

Table of Contents

The Beltane Choice

Characters in Book 1 - The Beltane Choice

A – Aanghos (guide from Garrigill); Ailin (Raeden warrior helping Cearnach); Agricola (Roman Governor of Britannia); Arian (1st son of Tully of Garrigill)

B -Beathan (son of Lorcan and Nara); Brennus (4th son of Tully of Garrigill)

C –Callan (Nara's father); Carn (Tully of Garrigill's carer); Cartimandua (Brigante Queen); Cearnach (Nara's Bodyguard; Cerialis (Roman Governor of Britannia)

D – Donnal (Carn's father)

E –Eachna (Nara's horse); Egan (of Owton)

F –Fionnah (wife to Gabrond); Fergal (Lorcan's war band); Frontinus (Roman Governor of Britannia)

G –Gabrond (3rd son of Tully of Garrigill)); Grond (son of Gyptus); Gyptus (chief of the Crannogs of Gyptus)

K – Keirnan (of Owton)

L - Lleia (daughter of Gyptus); Lorcan (2nd son of Tully of Garrigill)

N - Nara of the Selgovae; Niall (Nara's sickly brother);

R –Rigg of Raeden; Rowan (Cearnach's Roman horse); Struan (warrior of Gyptus)

S – Seamus (spearman to Gabrond); Shea of Ivegill (Carvetii); Soveran (Lorcan's war band)

T –Tully, chief of Garrigill

V – Venutius (Brigante King)

Tribal Map AD 71
Northern Britannia

Celtic Britain AD 71
Locations in The Beltane Choice

TARRAS ■   ■RAEDEN
              ■FORD OF SEQUANA
            ■CRANNOGS OF GYPTUS
            ■GARRIGILL

SKERNE ■

■ WHORL

EBORACUM■

Chapter One

Nettle-sharp tears of frustration reduced Nara's vision. She pressed her hand under her ribs to dull the pain and ploughed her way through the pitted undergrowth. Wrenching aside jagged gorse bushes dotted with yellow blossoms, the thorns scraped blood-red lines on her arms.

"You have my spear and my blade, but you will not have my life."

Gruelling breaths were snatched between curses. A glance over her shoulder caught the beast smashing on behind, scattering leaves and pinging twigs and branches. The folds of its hairy flesh quivered, its trotters pounding the earth, thudding minor tremors.

She scanned around for refuge. In the past, she had felled a boar, though never such a hefty beast, and this one exuded such vigour it would pursue her till she dropped if she could not climb out of its reach. The slight beech up ahead must suffice since the trees in the bush-strewn thicket were limited, all thin-limbed.

At the bole of the tree she wheeled round, a glint behind the bobbing animal snaring her attention. Her spear lay there on the ground, torn out of the boar's hide in its relentless drive through the spiny broom. Only paces away, yet how to reach it?

The trickle of blood seeping from the animal's wound made her cringe, her long knife still embedded in the beast's flank. She had no hope of using that blade a second time, and fingering the hilt of the small knife tucked in her waist pouch was futile. Though sharp enough, it was useless against the tough flesh of the beast lumbering closer.

"Your tusks will not be my future." Her hiss was stubborn. She may have been expunged from the *nemeton*, the island home of the priestesses where she'd lived for many years and now discarded like a broken loom, but there was still a life for her.

"Nara of Tarras entreats you, Rhianna. I put myself in your hands."

Startled by her outburst, the boar skittered to a halt, giving her time to use the flat of her foot. A mighty leap made, she grabbed the lowest branch, her legs swinging upwards as the frenzied boar thudded against the bark. Knees encircling the bough, she edged her way along to the trunk, her juddering thigh muscles clamping around it. Climbing higher, she selected the strongest join of bole and branch where she rested astride, hugging it tight. Exultant relief followed, her heartbeats ceased their frantic pump, and her breathing settled despite the boar continuing to hurtle its mass against the base.

"Sweet goddess, Rhianna, I thank you." Her words whiffed against bark. Safety was not assured but her bodyguard, Cearnach, would no doubt come to her aid before the animal uprooted the tree.

A smirk broke free in spite of her predicament. Life had changed drastically these last two moons, but the changes did not all have to be bad. Perhaps a handsome stranger would rescue her from the fearsome creature of the forest? Her grin widened. It was due time something exciting happened.

"Cearnach? Where are you?"

Impatience mounted, the pummelling below continued, her repeated cry ringing out over the copse while the beast yowled and squealed, its energy infinite. Small disturbed creatures scurried off, the fluttering and cheeping bird cry alerting the forest floor to danger.

"Woman! Be ready."

The rumbling holler came so suddenly Nara almost lost her grip on the trunk. It was not Cearnach; the tone was deeper, gruff and strangely disturbing. A search of the dense bush cover revealed no-one, yet a toying laugh reached her ears, its owner amused by her failure to spot him.

"Reveal yourself!" Nara's request echoed around the shadowy thicket. Below her the boar scratched and pawed the ground in frustration, circling around, alerted to the new presence but uncertain of which way to charge.

"Woman, heed me. I will help you kill this beast since it will take more than one weapon, now you have raised its hackles, but you know that already from your bungling attempt."

The implacable voice made Nara flinch in embarrassment, the burst of acerbic laughter that followed hurtful to her pride. Angry to be scorned in such a way, her resentment burned deep, yet the truth was his words were justifiable since she had been a poor huntress.

"I will distract it to reach your spear, but assure me only the boar will receive its death throw."

"And if I do not pledge?" Nara's words challenged, wondering why he set such terms.

The boar squealed, and the rumbling laugh rippled around. "You will be left with this creature, already livid enough to batter that immature tree down in a few more charges. Could you not have picked a stronger one?"

Indignation spewed. This was a greater insult than his chastisements. "Did I have a choice?"

"There is always a choice."

She bit back a scathing reply since, so far in her life, personal choice had been limited. The warrior's amusement incensed, but she was vulnerable. With no weapon at hand, the man's help was essential, as the beast was unrelenting.

Then nothing moved except for the faintest sough of the wind through the leaves above her. An unnatural stillness descended on the forest floor as the boar halted. Its snivelling snout twitched up, its ears tweaking before it emitted the eeriest of howls – something spooked the beast. A shiver of alarm rippled down Nara's back, superstitious fear replacing anger.

"Rhianna? Do not desert me."

3

"Woman, you invoke the help of Rhianna, but will the goddess save you from this creature baying for your life blood? Or…will I?"

Triumphant crowing made the hairs on Nara's neck bristle with apprehension. Was it a man alarming the boar, or something else?

"Are you Cernunnos, god of the forest?"

Cloaking fear from her voice was not possible, yet she prayed she did not reveal the horror which would result from a confirmation. Unlike her gentle goddess Rhianna, Cernunnos was well known for sadistically toying with humans. A capricious god, he was a deity not always kind to the people who invaded his territory. Visions of disembowelment, and other ghastly deeds attributed to Cernunnos, swamped her. Near silence wreathed the copse. The boar stood rigid, its breathing agitated, furious pricking of its ears matching the flickering black beads of its eyes, glistening as they did in the rays of sunlight shafting down through the trees.

"Are you Cernunnos shape-shifting? Disguised as the animal attacking this tree where I take refuge?"

"Nay, woman. I am Lorcan of Garrigill. I am no shape-shifter. Undoubtedly, Cernunnos is here in this forest, but I am not he."

Nara mulled over the reply. This had to be a real man. Relief flooded through her. The thought of it having been the fickle Celtic god of the forest was frightening.

"Woman? You tarry. Agree, or I leave."

An ear-splitting crack echoed around when the protesting branch splintered beneath Nara's thighs.

"By Rhianna, nay…" Her screech of dismay muffled into the bark. She plummeted down, her hands scrabbling for the nearest branch where she hung for long moments till she was able to grip her legs against the trunk. Chest heaving, she clung tight before resettling herself as the boar resumed its battering.

"My word is yours, Lorcan of Garrigill."

The next howling cry came from neither Nara, nor the boar, but the animal was the target of the vehemence when a

4

jagged stone slammed its rump. It whirled around, yowling in fury and charged off in the direction the sling-shot had come from. Close to Nara's tree, a lithe warrior surged from behind a dense clump of bushes to swoop up her spear.

"Catch!"

The spear hurtled up. She grasped it while the irate beast squealed its return. Lorcan's bloodthirsty cry boomed, and then his spear slashed through the air to spike the boar full in front.

"*Fóghnaidh mi dhut*!"

Nara's finishing thrust from above was a powerful one to its head. The animal keeled over and lay twitching and groaning.

She jumped down from the tree as he plunged his sword into the beast; the boar's writhing slowing to a halt. One foot balanced on the animal's belly, he yanked out her spear then straightened up, the muscles of his powerful shoulders stretching the material of his orange and brown checked woollen tunic.

Ill-tempered eyes confronted her, black brows puckered tight. Absorbing the warrior's dark scowl, Nara felt a strange rush of awareness sweep through her, despite that he looked angry. The trembling of her leg muscles was in reaction to her drop to the ground, but such an act did not normally make her quiver.

The glowering warrior in front of her caused it. She had endured two long lonely moons waiting for a response like this to happen, and now could not believe it had come to pass. Her mouth curved, delight widened her eyes, because this instinctive affinity with a man was what she needed to restore her spirit.

Her gaze lingered on the lime-spiked hair around the crown of his head, the rest of his black mane hanging free below his shoulders, a thin braid lying tight to each ear. Hazel eyes stared resentfully above a strong nose. A marked cleft in the chin shaved of hair sat below a full lower lip, the upper lip shrouded with full black whiskers that bearded down to his jaw line. It was an attractive countenance, compelling. A tiny

5

shiver beset her again. Her eyes dipped further...and she wished they had not.

"By Rhianna, nay."

Any elation she had just felt shrivelled like a decaying autumn leaf. How could Rhianna be so cruel? The blood-heat generated by his appeal turned to cool. A finely wrought gold torque, copper tipped at the terminals, encircled his throat. Wide bands of engraved copper adorned the muscles of one arm, his decoration proclaiming him a warrior of high status. High ranking was admirable but not the sign that lay above the armbands.

Why had a Brigante rescued her? Killing her, or leaving her to the ravaging boar, would have been customary since the small star confirmed he was Brigante, her enemy. She was even more vulnerable now than she had been when confronted by the tusks of the beast, and too late to understand his terms regarding the use of her spear.

Conventions had to be followed, though. She lifted her gaze to acknowledge his part in her rescue, even though her throat was dry as a parched field of emmer wheat in a summer drought.

"The deed was well done, warrior. I thank you for your intervention."

Lorcan stared, some of the antagonism leeching from his appraisal when he nodded a terse acceptance. Not trusting his movements while he removed her long knife and his own spear from the animal, she avoided the blood-flow leaking from the wounds.

"You claim to be a branded warrior-woman?"

His tone was contemptuous when he stared at the spear brand decorating her upper arm, though she wore no armbands below it. It was Nara's turn to scowl, exasperated by the aspersions he cast on her abilities. Though his glances were askance, the warrior considered her just as thoroughly as she did him. Two moons ago no man would have given her such frank assessment, but it was impossible to look away now. An instinctive tremor prickled her spine when the centre of his eyes darkened to cavernous black.

A conflict of sensations washed through her. She hated his superiority in the situation, detested his contempt but could not deny his stare made things happen – which no man had ever managed to do before. Quelling the stimulation seemed impossible. Yet, try she must.

His silent survey continued, sliding over her. A twitch came to his lips while his gaze lingered on her breasts heaving as they were against the wool of her dun-coloured tunic. Heat flared and rose up to her cheeks, a reaction she could not prevent but hoped was not visible to this supercilious warrior.

A wry grin flashed when his gaze halted at her empty scabbard which hung from the leather thong around her waist, then skated down to her legs covered by brown and green checked *braccae*, cross gartered with leather strips binding them firmly at the ankle. Her warrior clothes were well worn. When he had looked his fill, the arrogant Brigante held out her spear, angling the grip towards her.

Nara was not used to this scrutiny, or treatment. Men gave her a wide berth once they knew who she was.

"Your spear, warrior-woman. What name do you go by?" The Brigante's burr was infuriating.

Aware of his change of mood, Nara hastened for her weapon. Almost letting her grasp it, he tugged it from her reach, his chortle derisive. "Nay. I do not think so. Not yet, woman of the Selgovae, of the tribe who call themselves hunters."

Stung by his sneering attitude, Nara bristled. "You have saved me from the boar, Lorcan of Garrigill, but you may not toy with me, whatever you desire."

Half-hooded lids flickered, a dangerous gleam settling, before his brows lifted skywards. "You have no knowledge of what I desire." His amusement rippled. He paced around her setting off a surge of anticipation she did not understand. "And how do you think to stop me?" Sardonic humour permeated his gaze, which Nara did not appreciate when his head bent towards her.

"There is always a choice," she said, though her belief was not the same.

Her body tensed as she continued to challenge him, her tongue sharp. "Did you not just tell me that?"

The Brigante chuckled. His rugged face came closer, so close the drooping facial hair prickled her skin. She reached forward, though she would have sworn she had had no intention to move. Covering up her strange response, she spluttered, "Leave me be! My tribespeople lie close."

Her words rasped when she reared back. Her neck muscles strained her head out of his reach yet pressed her breasts forward as he leaned in. Nara could not match his strength. Defensive manoeuvres she had learned on the mock battle-field were unlikely to do him harm; the odds of height and might were all on his side.

Outrunning him was not a choice either. She had no knife or spear to aid her, but she would not give in without a struggle.

"They are not far away." A backwards stumble to stall his advance found her heels hitting tree roots, tripping her.

Her momentum halted, the warrior swooped. The heels of his hands clutched her upright. Drawing her into him, he imprisoned her.

"I think not, woman of no name."

The Brigante's mocking laugh deafened her, so close the warmth of it fanned her cheeks as a summer breeze would. Stunned by his physical handling, Nara gasped into his neck.

"My fellow warriors will make you pay for this."

His continued mockery affronted her. "You delude yourself, warrior-woman of the spear. My hearing is excellent."

Searching lips settled on her mouth, his whiskers a tickle. Only dimly did she register weapons tumbling to the ground behind her, his freed fingers clutching her properly. As his lips increased the pressure, an intense gleam widened his eyes to the blackness of night.

"Your man is dead." The dispassionate declaration came after he broke free for a moment. His teasing lips feathered her cheek and neck, his words filling her with dread. "If he is the warrior down by the ford?"

8

The blood drained from her face, his casual announcement whipping her out of the thrall he held her in. Wrenching herself from his grasping hands, her reaction was frantic. "Cearnach is dead? Who gave you the right to kill without reason? What was the challenge given?"

Lorcan seized her close. Resentment sparked in the gaze that condemned her, but she could not mistake the flash of pain he promptly suppressed. "My tribe has good reason to hate yours." He held her motionless for long moments, glaring down before he thrust her away. Tumbling back onto the fern-laden undergrowth, Nara grappled for a foothold and a more dignified position, confused by his actions.

The warrior's brows puckered as his foot lifted towards her. "My older brother, Arian, was a doughty warrior – not lost in battle – but in a petty raid on our outer territory."

She curled herself in tight, warding off the blow she felt sure was coming from his leather-swathed foot, but he merely tapped her leg, sidling her away from the pool of boar's blood. His anger abraded her ears while his body bent towards her, his words a snarl. "It was an unprovoked incursion, and you say I have no reason to hate your tribe?"

One strong arm reached down, gathered her at the neck and yanked her up with little effort. He shook her before clasping her tight against the length of his body, her feet dangling above ground.

"It could not have been Cearnach who killed your brother." Nara struggled to free herself, striking with her feet since her arms were caged fast against his chest.

Lorcan's gaze raked her, his hostility abating. A smile flickered at the edge of his mouth. "You defend your man well. He picked a fierce mate in you, but it is too bad he was not warrior enough to prevent his attackers from creeping up on him."

"Cearnach did not deserve your sword." Nara's hands beat an ineffective drum on his chest, her voice muffled against his tunic while she protested his treatment of her.

Derisive laughter burst from him, his breath whiffing her hair as his strong grip brought her face up on a level with his

9

own. "You think I wasted my own energy on him? Not true. It was one of my warriors you did not even know was around. Your feeble hillfort is too complacent, too ill-guarded that Brigantes can come close to your stronghold so easily."

"Raeden is not my hillfort. I assure you my own settlement has thorough defences against the likes of you." She spat at his face, her feet kicking out at his shins. "You would not sneak up on us unseen. You take too much for granted."

The warrior continued to berate, not yet done with his angry tirade. "You need teaching, one and all. That is why we are here, and I will be more than happy to teach your wayward tongue a thing or two. Who are you?"

Strong arms squeezed her. His callused hands returned to bracket her face, long fingers spread wide over the braids covering her ears. "We have already attacked the outskirts of Raeden, and now they round up their runaway animals. There is no one to come to your aid, woman of the harsh tongue. I have plenty of time for a little dalliance with you, but first I will know your name."

"I am Nara." Her cry muffled when his mouth covered hers.

Gripping fingers held her tight, his superior strength impossible for her to rally against. She was a whole head shorter than him and much weaker. With increasing confusion, she arched her head back breaking their lip contact.

"Leave me be, Lorcan of Garrigill!"

"Leave you be?" His flaring eyes scalded.

Nara cursed Rhianna. Why had the goddess put her into this invidious position? She did want to pick a mate who stirred her senses, but that mate could not be a Brigante enemy. Her thoughts whirled. Her fists pummelled his chest. "Nay!" Her hands pushed at his shoulders.

"Aye, Nara. Hold me like that."

It was irrational yet she took pleasure when he pressed her against the bark of the tree. The thought was sobering. "It cannot be."

With a soft thud they contacted the ground, Lorcan bearing the brunt of the impact before he rolled on top of her. She could not let it happen. Pushing him away, she slapped at his shoulder, too close to cause any real harm.

His grip relaxed, a soft grunt at the interruption escaping. "You little wildcat!" Though the warrior scolded her, his expression betrayed some measure of enjoyment.

"Leave me be. I take no pleasure in this."

Rolling away from him, she sidled herself upright. Unable to locate her weapons she used her feet, a swift kick that contacted his solid thigh. Lorcan's amused rumble irritated her even more, because it had been a half-hearted kick from one who was warrior-trained.

"You lie." He grinned, challenging her honesty before an expert spin took him out of her reach while she readied for another attack. Springing to his feet, he chided, "Admit it. Your body tells me."

Incensed by the truth, Nara glared, a hot flush blistering her cheeks when he plucked her hands from the sword hilt she yanked up.

"Why should I leave you be? Did I not save you from the boar's tusks?"

As he disposed of the sword Nara fought against frustration and confusion. "I am beholden to you for that, maybe, but that is all. Would you force me, Brigante?"

"You think I need to force you? Or any woman? As in your tribe, the women of mine mate when they like what they see."

Arrogance dripped from him, confidence filling his gaze, though a glint of some humour twinkled there too.

"You have a high opinion of your prowess, but your fame as a fabled lover has not reached the Selgovae, yet."

Her words had the opposite effect from she intended since her bold scorn stimulated the warrior even more. "Maybe you are the one who needs to inform your worthy bard of my skills. Time my prowess is tested?"

The sudden ripping startled her when his one tug burst open the leather strap around her waist, tumbling her pouches to the ground. Raising her tunic, the Brigante's questing fingers tunnelled. The tightening and tingling at her chest drove her gaze skywards in confusion. A deep groan escaped while he whispered kisses at her neck, one hand reaching inside the gathered waist of her *braccae*.

"*Dé thu a déanamh*?" Her gasp shared the warrior's breath. Her head swam from a lack of breath and something else. "By the Lady Rhianna? What are you doing?" Sagging against him her legs could no longer support her weight. "I cannot..." she mumbled, unable to think coherently. Like a runt puppy, she lapped up the scraps of his handling. Seeking. Something. Yet, she did not know what she sought.

"I feel..."

"Aye. Let go. Let the feelings take you, Nara," Lorcan muffled more encouragement into her ear. He changed her position against the tree his questing lips, tongue and hands continuing to roam. His fingers explored through the soft wool of her tunic before he pulled it clear of her head, the cloth unbearable when it scratched past her sensitised skin, the coarseness of the tree bark against her bare spine not mattering a whit. His lips continued their torment while he loosened his sword belt and let it thud to the ground. Releasing the thong of his forest-green *braccae*, he allowed them to glide to his knees. She felt the urgency in his movements.

"I'm a...aahhh!" The words of explanation died in her throat as the warrior's twisting search found spots Nara had not known existed. Supporting her body against the tree, Lorcan wrapped her legs around his waist.

"What is wrong? Has it been such an age since your man took you?"

Wriggling away from him, she yelped. "Rhianna's wrath be upon you! I have never coupled with any man."

"What did you say?"

He held himself immobile before the breath rushed back into him; noisy inhalations through his nose. His eyes displayed great confusion when he stared at her, glazed with some enormous emotion Nara had no name for before they screwed tight shut for a few heartbeats. With a frightful force Lorcan yanked himself free and dropped his grip of her body as though scorched. She slumped to the ground, her hands flattening to bear her weight while she gawped up at him. His disbelieving eyes raked her, the veins in his neck pulsating, his breathing laboured.

"You cannot possibly still be an unmated woman?" Bewilderment shrouded Lorcan's expression, but his fury was even more dominant. "You must be more than twenty summers?"

She refused to answer the man whose resentment could not possibly be greater than her own. Her gaze slid sideward, since she could not face the warrior who now despised her.

Chapter Two

"You tell me you are not promised to the goddess? How can you still be unmated at your age and not be a priestess?"

Lorcan of the Brigantes could not credit it. The woman was beautiful. How could the Selgovae males of her hillfort have left such a woman untouched? He scanned her furious expression.

"Tell me!"

Tight lipped and defiant, she divulged nothing. There had to be an exceptional reason she remained untaken. Her being out of the realms of normality had shocked him, halted his ardour. He did not doubt her claim, backed up by the power of the goddess, because he had found her reactions to his touches and kisses inexperienced and startled. He still trembled with the need to take her, but he would not. Not till the riddle of her unbroken state was unravelled.

Clamping her shoulders, he worked his way through the gamut of possibilities whilst watching the play of emotions in her expression.

What he saw was conflict. She was, in truth, irate. Her teeth clenched so tight her jaws were locked, her neck muscles straining with tension. Her loathing blistered him, but behind that he could see hurt – a deep abiding hurt of some kind, which she valiantly attempted to mask.

"How can this be? Tell me, Nara, because I do not understand."

Refusing to answer, the Selgovae woman glared, a fierce burn in the strong blue eyes that challenged him. His opened palms set her away. He tugged up his *braccae*, tied them roughly and trod back a pace.

"Who are you?" Again he got no response bar an angry glower.

14

Lorcan was shaken by his handling of her. Her beauty had captivated him from the moment he had spied her up in the tree. Even after realising she was Selgovae, and an enemy of his own tribe, he had still wanted her with an unaccustomed ferocity. That first unconscious reaction to him, the first linking of their eyes had told him just how much she desired him since she was a mirror to his own craving. Still thrumming with arousal he paced around, momentarily at a loss over how to deal with the aftermath of this shocking revelation.

"Tell me all, Nara."

Something fascinated her on the forest floor. That she refused to answer was no surprise, her disgust a blistering scald, yet he persisted.

"Where are you from?"

His plan to enjoy a happy coupling with this beauty, before freeing her, had spectacularly failed. She was his enemy, an effective capture, but to now take this woman for her first mating in lust, or in anger, seemed wrong. Some unknown reason had made her bypass the mating ritual.

"All you need to know is that the goddess makes men pay for their misdeeds."

The woman was bent on revenge; Lorcan could see it in every flicker of her aggrieved blue eyes and in her rigid body stance while her tongue whipped him. Apart from being given to the goddess, few other reasons made a woman unavailable. Un-matured girls who failed to experience the natural bleeding courses were so rare Lorcan had never met one, though he had heard tell of them. Unable to breed, they were deemed untouchable and spent their lives as hearth slaves. Superstitious, in the way of the Celts, the thought of his treatment of such a forbidden one revolted him.

He vented his anger on the woman before him. "Then the goddess truly mocks me by bringing me to you this day."

"You should indeed be a feared, Brigante."

He sensed the woman's confidence increase, her waspish tongue matching her abrasive expression. Lorcan faced her again. Standing legs braced apart his arms unfolded. Knuckles bracketing his hips, he raked her features, eliciting the truth of the matter. On this he would not back down. He had had time to think further on her condition. An un-matured female hearth slave of her age would be submissive and would never have made warrior rank. No. She was no failed female, her body too mature. His loins tightened again.

"Whatever makes you remain unmated I will find out, but regardless of that your tongue does you no justice. I did not violate you. Our passion was mutual, and if I have offended the goddess, I stand judged by her alone."

He dragged his gaze away from her nakedness, from the splendour that had held him in thrall. His hand raked errant strands of hair from his forehead and lingered there. He needed to think more clearly. Mostly think about what to do with her, now.

Taking advantage of his distraction, the woman rushed for her spear, but he was upon her in a heartbeat, his strides outdistancing her easily. Wrenching the weapon from her grasping hands, he rebuked, "Nay. That will not harm me."

Her face reddened with temper. When he swivelled to pitch the spear well away from her reach, he glimpsed her scuttle for her knife. The woman was still determined to do him harm?

"Leave go of it. Now!"

Undaunted by his warning, Nara whipped the knife from its sheath. Before his fist could grasp the blade properly she lunged, the knife-tip slicing through the cloth of his tunic near his shoulder and into his flesh, while he faced her blood-wrath. Again she scowled, looking as enflamed as he felt. Her pressure on the blade deepened, quivering only when his command whiffed at her face, so close to his own. "Desist, Nara."

The blade trembled in her grip, distress flashing. A great pain lingered in her eyes – he was sure more than he was feeling – even though her sharp blade nicked straight into his muscle. Her breath hitched in her throat while her hand continued to shudder. As their gazes held for an endless time, his probing fingers covered her fist before he pulled her knife free of his body and fumbled it into his own leather sheath. The tingling sensations he felt had nothing to do with his wound. This woman blazed something deep inside him. Yet, it was hatred that now glittered her bright blue eyes. She was furious; enraged he had foiled her death attack.

"Do not attempt that again. Your weapons will do me no harm."

The very words grated in his throat when he hauled her against him, one strong arm pinning her in place, his lips a hairsbreadth from hers. He could not prevent his next move when he squeezed her tight to the length of him, since the feel of her naked skin still relentlessly tantalised him, even though it should not as the woman had just stabbed him. The emotional struggle he felt was an agony when he released her, his fingers threading into her braids, this time to push her away.

Nevertheless, he still sought answers.

"Though you are a branded warrior-woman, I will not kill you, as I should do, but you will come with me."

His intention resolute, he detached his fingers, his gaze an involuntary lowering to her body when he stepped away. Her breasts heaved, her breathing remaining ragged. He could not help staring. She may be furious with him, but she was, as yet, just as aroused as he was. Forcing his head up, his word snarled. "Move!"

"Move? This is Selgovae territory. Your tribe will pay for my mistreatment."

Nara stood her ground, defiance in every utterance and in her haughty appearance. His laugh scathed while he gathered up both spears and her long knife and set them down by the carcass of the boar. "A woman of no consequence in your tribe, and you say you will make me pay?"

Collecting her tunic, he threw it well to the side, away from the weapon hoard. Though a woman, he should have killed her. She was a branded warrior who had harmed him, yet he could not bring himself to do it. Hurtful words went some way towards ameliorating that flaw in him, easier to heap scorn upon her than to own up to his limitations.

"Your standing in your clan can be no better than the field mice scouring around the chief's roundhouse. I doubt anyone will miss you."

Lorcan found it disturbing when a flash of utter hurt whipped across her expression before her jaw locked with insubordination. There was something badly amiss between this beautiful woman and her tribe. He did not know what, but he made up his mind to find out ere long. Brandishing the long knife from his scabbard, he slashed it down on the boar's pelt, venting some self-disgust. Issuing orders made him feel even better.

"Get dressed. It seems you are a creature even the goddess has spurned."

His thoughts were vicious; his slashing at the boar's tail matched his flaying words, his temper a slow abatement. Yet an engulfing disillusionment lingered which he could not dispel. Not assuaging his lust on the woman was only part of his disappointment; he could not yet decide what the rest was.

While he hewed at the boar his wound smarted. For certain, her small blade was sharp. The pain of sliced muscle he ignored, just as he ignored the ooze of blood flowing from his shoulder down to his wrist. She would not have killed him, he was too powerful for that, yet why did she stop before the blade did more damage? The slightest of turns would have been sufficient. What he had seen in her eyes – a rapid blinking she tried so hard to mask – was a profound hurt, and in spite of her having wounded him, he wondered what caused it.

He thwacked the boar's tail free discarding it wide to the forest, but no matter how much he contemplated it he knew he could not dispose of the woman so readily.

***

What could Nara say to this seething warrior? The truthful answer was she was not promised to the goddess any more. It was an affront to the goddess to lie, yet this Brigante had started something momentous, leaving her in a place where

18

the tantalising end had been within a blink. An end she had only glimpsed, and now she was curious to experience the whole process of making love. A sense of deprivation, and of another failure, gnawed at her. His rejection injured her still trembling body as well as her pride. Why should she humour him by giving answer?

"Make haste." He urged her onwards, his face thunderous while he hacked at the boar's head.

Nara's thoughts were mutinous. What did she care for this man who mocked her so cruelly? Why should she concern herself if he thought her to be a woman of no consequence, unable to do her duty? She had never had the luxury of feeling herself a normal woman of her people, since from early years, she had been promised to the goddess. As an acolyte, it had been necessary for her to suppress all mating contact during the years since reaching her maturity.

Though, those truly were not her circumstances now, had not been for these last two moons. It was a relief the Brigante had stopped for he should not be the one to take her maidenhead, even if he had stirred her passions. She would never allow him to get close enough again.

"Where are you from?"

The warrior's demand came again, though he avoided her gaze. Her mind worked quickly. This warrior would not be in Selgovae territory alone. He must be with a raiding band, but where were they? Could the man have been bluffing? Maybe Cearnach was still alive? Still at the ford where the horses were? Wriggling into her tunic, she watched him bend over the boar.

The thwacking of his sharp sword, then the well-honed knife slicing through bone and flesh was a powerful reminder of how strong this man was – that brawny body, which had cradled her just moments before. Another shudder wracked her which had nothing to do with cold, or vulnerability, when the warrior tracked her movements.

Between glances, he hacked off the head and legs of the kill, discarding them, one by one, wide to the forest floor for other animals to scavenge.

When he tossed a boar leg to the side, she sped off in the opposite direction aiming for the best bush cover. Two steps into her flight a whup, whup, flipping over of the sharpest of small blades flashed past her shoulder and embedded itself into the tree trunk just ahead. Fighting down both alarm and nausea, she willed her feet to fly faster.

"Next time it will be deep into your flesh." The warrior's growl blasted in her ear as he halted her escape, the force of his lunge propelling her forwards onto the debris of the forest floor. Barely down on her hands, Nara felt herself soar up again, and then he dragged her on towards the bark grabbing one of her unfurling braids in an excruciating grip. A quick flick, his blade was free and back into his waist pouch.

The knife was free, but she was not.

Nara cursed her long hair as he hauled her back to the animal carcass and released her well away from any weapons, his fingers a lingering slide through her waterfall of tangles.

"Make haste and ready yourself, Nara. Attempt no more escapes. My knife skills are unsurpassed, yet I would have you live."

Her scalp a burning tingle, Nara braided her mess of waves, fumbling around for the tie that had dropped to the ground when she had pulled her tunic over her head. While she tied her hastily repaired waist belt, she watched the Brigante unfurl a strip of strong cord which had been slung cross-wise over his chest. His whipcord movements were precise, his upper arm muscles rippling. Those same strong muscles which had just grasped her body and had effortlessly held her aloft, so close she had felt every single part of him.

Lorcan of Garrigill had the cord around the carcass as a dragging harness in a blink, ready for towing along the forest floor. Bound to him – like she had been.

"Move or you will feel this." His spear tip thrust towards her as he rose to his feet, the tip close enough to show he meant it, yet not close enough to penetrate her skin. He tucked her long knife and small blade into his waist scabbards with his own, grasping her spear in the hand that was enwrapped with the twine.

20

"Move!"

How could she outwit this incensed man? Nara walked. Why did he not kill her? She had given him ample justification, trying to flee and throwing him a challenge in reaching for her weapons – even though she had been a measly coward about properly drawing blood. Humiliation flooded through her. Another failure.

It had not been blood-rage she had felt when her blade had been poised to drive deeper; it had been an inexplicable anguish over harming him. She had been doomed, unable to wound further, though he had disregarded the small cut she had made, and even now he ignored it when she glanced back. A thin trickle of blood from the wound still seeped, but it did not trouble him sufficiently to even wipe it from his skin.

His knife would have ripped her flesh asunder, though, had he aimed truly for her shoulder. She had no doubt about that, but she was still his prisoner. Dragging the burden of the carcass over uneven ground, the warrior was at least five paces behind her. The track ahead was bordered by low scrubby ferns and gorse bushes already thick with yellowing foliage. Picking the most successful space ahead of her, she surged.

Twwww…aaa…nnng!

The humming of the reverberating spear blocking her passage was deafening, having missed her by a hair's breadth. The clattering noise of a weapon dropping was surpassed by the roar of the warrior when he leapt upon her, easily subduing her struggles and cries. Her knees ground into the forest floor before he whirled her face-up, his fingers encircling her throat poised to throttle. The speed of his attack, and the dead-weight of him fully atop her, should have brought forth the blood-rage of battle, but…it did not.

From neither her, nor him.

Yet again their gazes locked and lingered. Nara panted, but not because he was stifling the breath out of her. He looked dismayed; maybe even guilty. She was not convinced which emotion he felt most, but though his hands remained in place, the tension in his fingers relaxed. His thumbs gentled the skin

21

they had just pressed upon while he, too, fought hard for his breath, his glowing brown eyes sliding down to stare at her neck.

"*A ghlaoic!*"

She stared at him, her answer almost impossible to mouth. "Aye, I may be a fool, but I would be free of you!"

His voice grit against her ear, "You are not going to escape from me, Nara."

"Your spear did not hit its mark…" Nara gasped, struggling under him to no avail, the hilts of his weapon hoard digging deep into her stomach.

"My spear hit exactly where I wanted it to. If I had wanted to fell you, I would be walking past your lifeless body right now." Lorcan moaned into her face while she squirmed.

She watched his eyes shut tight in anger before he rolled off her, the leap to his feet agile as a gambolling lamb as he dragged her upwards. Her hands were clamped in front of her before she took another breath, a long cord from his belt lashed securely around them before she managed any real struggle. The other end of the leash he entwined with the harness for dragging the carcass of the boar, fisting both of them in a firm clench. Forcing her chin up with his free hand, his words whiffed through the whiskers bordering his upper lip.

"No further escape attempts. Now walk."

Nara felt him push her into motion none too gently. The leash was only long enough for her to be a few steps away from him, yet was secure enough for her to know trying to break free was futile. He seemed reluctant to kill her, though why? The local Celtic tribes did not generally take slaves. Sometimes captured women were absorbed into the tribe as concubines, bringing new bloodlines to the families. If that was his intention, why had he not taken her maidenhead?

Lorcan of Garrigill's conduct made no sense.

Yet, how dare he treat her so? She raged at the situation, her feet stamping the ground mercilessly, but jerking the leash only hurt her wrists for the warrior yanked it back with double her strength. She was a warrior-princess, though how was he to know? Unless she told him, and she vowed she would not do that. Apart from the warrior's mark on her arm, she wore no other sign of her status; no rings, no torque and no arm bands of precious metal. This enraged man knew nothing of her purpose, or who she was. Ceasing her stomp found not his spear but his splayed fingers at the small of her back.

"Do not touch me!"

She hoped her defiance betrayed none of her actual feelings, since it was absurd she felt a craving for his touch. His presence behind her she could not ignore for the heat emanating from his powerful body scorched her. It galled that any contact from this warrior so easily stirred her.

"Keep moving."

Braving a glance behind her eyes connected with his. Though he held a potent fascination, he was actually not the best-looking man she had ever encountered. The tight, shuttered expression on Lorcan's face annoyed her now. It seemed he no longer found anything about her tempting, if the grim set of his lips was anything to go by. She stalked ahead which only yanked on the leash, drawing her back to him, yet it made no impression on her captor. His grip remained as tight as it had started out. Nara blocked him from her mind. Any attraction would fade if she willed it so. During the last two moons, she could have taken a warrior of Tarras as her lover. Some of the men of her home hillfort had been handsome enough, but she had not done so. No warrior had stirred her passion with just a look like Lorcan had done.

Nobody at Tarras had even gained a single kiss from her...

The disappointment of not finding a mate at Tarras hurt badly, but the most discomforting thing was none of the men of her hillfort had made any determined attempts to woo her.

Her lack of desirability to them was a bitter taste to swallow since feeling unattractive was not pleasant.

Neither did being a prisoner.

"Must you push me so fast? You make me stumble and fall."

Her grumbling continued when they left the forest fringe and headed for the flat river bed spread out in front of them.

Nara watched a thunderous expression flit across Lorcan's face, then as swiftly as a cloud would sometimes roll away to reveal the sun his mouth curved up in a mockery of a smile.

"My princess wishes to go at the pace of a snail? We will never get anywhere if you move like that." He pushed her on again with a rough prod, the sarcastic twinkle gone just as quickly as it had come.

Could the man have guessed her true rank? While Nara wondered how it could be possible, her filly, Eachna, whinnied a welcome from the far bank. Rowan, the chestnut stallion, was tethered alongside, but of Cearnach there was no sign. Not on this bank nor, as far as Nara could see, on the other. No body. There was nothing to display the truth of Lorcan's statement. Was Cearnach really dead?

"That horse is a bold strong one," he commented as he viewed the large stallion.

Nara read the new scowl crossing his features; suspicion and distrust lurked there. His gaze narrowed first on the horse, and then on her. When he forced her around to face him his fingers tightened around her upper arm. Under his intense scrutiny she felt her cheeks heat again, and it was a struggle to maintain her defiant expression.

What vexed the man?

Chapter Three

Lorcan, son of Tully of Garrigill and a prince of the Brigantes, wondered how someone who professed to be Selgovae owned a Roman horse. He was in no doubt the massive stallion was exactly that.

No Brigante would have anything to do with the murderous Roman Army, and he doubted any Celtic Selgovae would either. As his father's second son, he had been trained as an emissary of his people, and over the last years he had met with many southern tribes. They had not all been Brigantes but were equally in accord in detesting the advance of the Roman forces.

Recently he had journeyed to southern Brigante clan holds, had heard tell of marauding Roman scouts moving northwards, but this woman did not fit the criteria even if she did have a Roman horse. Her Celtic dialect was slightly different from his; hers of a softer lilt to his strong burr.

He determined to draw her out, having learned a smattering of the Latin tongue of the Romans. Grasping her arm, he rattled out a few questions, unsurprised she did not respond.

Her auburn eyebrows furrowed at his change of language. Her reply eventually came, her teeth tight with irritation.

"I do not understand you. If you wish to insult me, offend me in the language of the Celts so that I may ignore you, or return your affront." Her heated words spent the woman shrugged out of his grip and stomped ahead.

Lorcan wrenched the leash, dragging her back. Her eyes snapped, darting cold shards while she resisted the tether, her mouth grimly defiant.

The words used meant he would give her gold for the horse, yet they had not registered a flicker of interest. Either she was very good at masking her reactions, or she had no notion of what he said. He veered towards the latter.

Maybe not working for the Romans, though it did not explain how she was in possession of such a fine animal. He would find out, though; patience was a trait he was known for. A frown rutted his forehead for this woman was already trying that patience very badly.

"I ask again, where are you from, Nara?"

No longer able to withstand her odium-filled malice, Lorcan shoved her forward. A few paces staggered, she then stopped dead at the banking. Even more annoyed by her resistance his fingers pressed into her backbone, hurrying her along, heading for the flat stones dotted across the narrow stretch of water.

By the ford of Sequanna, the water level was low, no more than the knee height of a man. Its tinkling tumble over the stepping stones set in honour of the river goddess Sequanna was a pleasant hum. Travellers left offerings which drifted downstream to a little pool, the most precious of the gifts eventually wending their way to the nearby druid *nemeton* since the local tribespeople would never dare touch the goddess's gifts, would never court her wrath even if they were known to be less than honest.

Beltane, the beginning of summer festival, was soon to come – less than half of the cycle of a moon. Barren women would seek Sequanna's help to bear strong sons and beget useful daughters, though somehow Lorcan did not believe that was why this particular female was in the vicinity. An untouched woman would have no way of knowing how fertile she was. He flicked the leash.

"Cross!"

When the Selgovae woman picked her way to the centre, he watched the awkward raising of her bound hands, her lips moving in silent invocation. Her prayers seemed automatic, though he could not tell who she favoured.

His derisory laugh startled the birds nearby sending them upwards in a flurry of beating wings. His taunt was hurtful, yet he could not quell his nastiness.

"You do well to pray to Sequanna, though has the goddess not rejected you too long, since you remain un-seeded by a man?"

The woman's piercing glitter chastised him. Raw resentment, and another impossible-to-suppress current, flared across to him before she lowered her head. There had been the tiniest flicker of satisfaction in her gaze which disconcerted him, as did the twitch of enjoyment now curving her lips. Lorcan's brows knotted, unwilling to believe she was stealing a march on him in some unfathomable way as though her knowledge of the future was infinitely greater than his. This striking woman had secrets he could not wait to reveal.

He had thought her attractive before, now she was even more so. He wanted to smother that seductive smile with his lips because she was a temptress, a harebell-blue eyed enticement swathed in deep bronze hair.

What thought made those lips curve in satisfaction? Treading over the stones, he grasped the leash and drew her around.

"Do you mock me, woman?" She slowly shook her head, her smirk diminishing, the sparkle of her eyes like a light rain on a patch of borage flowers. "Why do you laugh in such fashion?"

"*An cù!*" Her mutter was breathy and low.

His grip tightened. "Say again!"

"You would not wish to know. My thoughts would not likely please you." Her challenge was insolent.

"Tell me or—"

"You will what, because you are a pig? There is no need for more violence, Brigante." Her head shook a slow tempting pout.

"Brigante! I am Lorcan, son of Tully, the Chief of Garrigill." He echoed her accusatory tone, exhaling deeply, whispering over her trembling mouth. For seconds neither moved. Lorcan felt a strumming tension reverberating between them, his huffs of breath mingling with hers. Then, unable to bear her so near he thrust her aside, turning instead to the meat he needed to gut.

27

Tumbling off the stone she was perched upon, the woman griped when her foot twisted. Her leg jarred against a jagged rock embedded in the water before she landed bottom first on the pebbled riverbed with a yelping splash, the action wrenching the leash from his wrist. Her wheeze of fury suggested many grievances. Scrambling up, she dripped towards him her bound hands held outstretched.

"Release me, Brigante, so that I can see what damage you have inflicted."

Lorcan's knife flashed, releasing her in an instant. The water beneath her was a livid pink – and none of it boar blood. He muttered oaths while hacking the pelt from the beast before slashing at the remains. Whipping out the entrails, he wiped pieces he wished to keep with furious fervour since he had not intended the woman harm, but knew he was culpable. Fighting against his conscience, he was unable to mete out the retribution the warrior-woman clearly deserved for wounding him. An unaccustomed restless, frustrated irritation overwhelmed him.

Out of the water at the far side of the ford, his Selgovae captive nursed her bloodied and ripped skin, for the foot bindings she wore were not high enough to offer her protection from this kind of injury.

His sword whacked through the carcass of the boar, quartering it, while he watched her rub the wound lightly with ferns from the banking, then she turned on hands and knees and tore out some moss. Closing his eyes, he breathed deep and willed his body not to respond, but he could not prevent his eyes straying again. A small pad made, she applied it to the gash, using a leg binding to secure it tight. All the while she muttered low oaths, whether to him, or Sequanna, he could not tell. It mattered not; she remained the most alluring woman he had ever met.

The goddess Sequanna did not play fair with him either. His thoughts were an over-bubbling cauldron, his hands an unconscious butcher of the boar meat. What must he do with this female who continuously provoked and aroused him? And who now swamped him with guilt? He should have killed her earlier. Much more goading, though, and he would be sure to wring that delicious neck, but first he would take her, whoever she was, and whatever her state.

With increased vigour he tossed the unwanted pelt and boar's entrails to the banking, leaving the water to clear it naturally. Then, with deliberate movements, he wiped his arms and hands clear of all blood traces from his own wound and those from the boar.

"Make haste!" His bellow validated the impatience engulfing him.

Loping across the ford with the butchered meat, he dumped the sections by the bank, and then released the rein binding the brown filly to the small willow near the water's edge. Briefly, he leaned his head against her mane to gather his wits. Drawing deep breaths, he suppressed the all-consuming surges of emotion which did not abate, and then he raised his head to look back at the woman still sitting on the banking.

Why this woman? Was a questionable, very-old-to-be-unmated woman of the Selgovae the only female who was ever going to give him this rush of anticipation? A feeling that was well beyond normal lustful desire? Was he condemned always to a half-life of sensations with other women? Or worse still, the numbness after a coupling that meant nothing beyond an emptying of his seed.

Banishing his frustrations, he investigated the bulging skin pouches attached to the filly. Satisfied there were no weapons secreted in any of the bags tied around her flanks, he pulled forth pieces of cloth to enwrap the sections of meat, securely tying them with thongs drawn from another pouch. The chestnut stallion next had his attention, his gaze admiring its strong flanks while he strapped on the meat packs. It was a fine horse, indeed.

Having secured their spears and other weapons to the chestnut, he renewed his questioning. He had to find out how this woman had such a good beast in her possession; though this time he used their own tongue.

"This is a fine horse. Big for our chariots, but fit for me to ride."

"Fit for a better man than you!"

Lorcan admired the woman: even in her obvious pain she had the spirit to answer back. That very courage brought a genuine smile to his lips. "You do not know that yet, woman of the sharp tongue. It runs away with you." His laugh cruelly taunted.

***

Nara refused to answer him. Lorcan – meaning the fierce one – suited him for the name seemed accurate. By Rhianna! Furious at her response to him, she berated herself. This Brigante warrior brought out the worst of her wayward temper.

Eachna whinnied in delight when Nara approached, restless and straining as Lorcan held her rein. Seemingly back in reasonable humour, Lorcan ran his free hand over the stallion's rump to calm it, too.

The true smile she had just seen caused flutters to her stomach; flutters she wanted to chase straight back out. She hated her inability to control her emotional response to this warrior.

"This is a Roman horse from the south?"

"It is a Selgovae horse and no matter of yours," she snapped, annoyed at his change of mood.

Questions rattled at her.

"This horse is too valuable for someone like you to be riding. How did you come by it? Did you steal it and run off? Are you a runaway being hounded?"

The unjust accusations stung at Nara's disintegrating pride, anger winning over control.

"The only one hounding me is you, and I did not steal the horse. What do you take me for, Brigante?"

His words were slow and deliberate when he reached for her. "I do not take you, yet!"

The long pause on his last word said even more than his intimidation, the sound escaping his lips more of an exasperated hiss than a breath. The veiled promise in it Nara

30

could not deny thrilled her, for, though his look was severe, he also appeared in the grip of emotions as deep as hers.

"Leave me be, Brigante. By Rhianna, unhand me!" Her order had the effect she requested, though did not expect. Crashing to the ground, her swollen leg jarred a further time on the rough banking.

"You got what you wanted, did you not?" he gibed nastily, her attempt to hide the mutter of pain having been unsuccessful.

Unwilling to guard her tongue, she railed, "How would you know that? Revenge is all you care for."

"Revenge? Aye, I want revenge, but I desire much more."

His tone controlled, Lorcan loomed, his questioning relentless with barely time for a breath in between. Nara's refusal to answer remained firm, yet her silence fanned the flames for he insisted.

"Who was the warrior riding this fine horse, having such a prized animal? I know now he cannot have been your hearth husband!"

His gaze strayed to her chest. Nara felt a flare of gratification when he appeared exasperated with himself. Ignoring his hurtful probing, she rolled to her feet and hobbled to the other side of the filly, favouring her weight on her good leg.

"Give answer. Was he your husband?"

"Nay, not my husband." She confronted him, her words beseeching. "What did you do with Cearnach? I see no sign of him."

Ignoring her plea, Lorcan tugged the horses away, keeping both reins when he agilely sprang up onto the stallion.

"Mount!"

He pulled her filly forwards, kicking his heels into Rowan's flesh. Turning their direction south-eastwards, he headed for the flat river's edge leading to the deep forests far to their left.

If she escaped, she would be done with the infuriating man. Whirling around, she darted off for the edge of the woods.

Twww…aaa…nnng!

31

Again, a humming spear blocked her path.

"I have warned you. You will not escape, Nara of the Selgovae." Lorcan's words came whilst he swivelled the horses around her, casually plucking his spear from the ground.

She considered launching herself on the mounted warrior but knew there was no point, her leg was weak, and in a heartbeat she would be dead, probably by her own spear.

"Mount!"

His spear made a mute demand.

Limping after the horses, Nara sprang onto Eachna. It required balance, speed and agility, usually easy enough, yet it took all her strength and determination hampered as she was by her injury. She would never beg him to stop, though.

The chirruping bird song around them was accompanied by the thuds of their horses on the soft earth as they cantered alongside the meandering river, where it twinkled on the flat valley floor. A short while later his voice startled her.

"So, no warrior has found you pleasing enough to bed?"

The question ripped Nara to shreds. Her eyebrows twitched before she controlled her temper for this warrior gouged at those vulnerable feelings that had attempted a recovery. Again, refusing to answer, her eyes dropped to search the ground.

"He was your brother?"

It was pointless to ignore this irritating man. He would clearly revel in that. It appeared his questions would come at her unendingly for he was the most tenacious man she had ever encountered. What if she gave him the answers he sought? What difference would it make to her captive status? Nara imagined no answer was likely to alter that.

"Neither husband, nor brother."

The Brigante's curiosity was unquenchable. "He was a warrior of your own tribe?"

"Aye."

"Why would a proud warrior have been riding with one such as you?"

"One such as me?"

32

Nara was affronted. People of her clan had looked to her for judgment and guidance, but they did not poke at her like a piece of meat roasting over a spit. Biting her lip to quell her tongue, she worked out how to escape. No signs of human life were around, the tree cover sparse, the bushes low. There were no Selgovae warriors to assist her, but no other Brigantes either – though tracks of many horses had made recent passage on the path they trod. Only small animal movements dotted the marshy ground along the twisting banking, a soft wind soughing through the reeds and willows, marsh birds dipping back and forth.

"Ah! I have it."

He sounded buoyant as though he had worked through a great riddle, his words a hurtful taunt.

"You were being taken to another clanhold? Shackled off like a discarded piece of cloth. Were you found an ancient man's fireside to tend, an old one too worn to bed a young girl on the brink of womanhood, which you are clearly not?"

The sheer injustice of his remark was demeaning. Her wild temper surged – and she forgot her resolution to ignore his jibing.

"I was not being taken to an impotent old man's hearth." She hauled on Eachna's rein to free it, flight uppermost when she urged her filly into a gallop to escape her tormentor.

The warrior jerked the rein and set the poor horse tussling around. Nara flew off Eachna's back and landed with a thump on her rear. While her breath returned, she lay prostrate, thankful she knew how to relax when she fell off a horse, or chariot. Her bottom ached, but she was otherwise only winded.

The Brigante brought the two horses back, slowing their pace down to a steady walk, and then calmly dismounted. Drawing her up the look on his face was indescribable; seething with disturbingly quiet rage...and something else she found forbiddingly stimulating. His husky tones slid under her skin, his eyes mere black slits, his hand shaking at her throat.

"One more attempt, and you will suffer the direst consequences."

Though her body was trapped, Nara's tongue would not be stilled. "Why not just strangle me and be done? What good am I to you?"

***

What good indeed, Lorcan wondered. The sight of her bristling pride meant there was much more to learn, but torture of women was not his way. He had been in a torment witnessing her fly off the horse. Her neck could easily have been broken, though why he particularly wanted this woman to live he could not exactly say.

He could see why her warrior's mark had been attained for she was courageous. Good at concealing information, she was no simple tribeswoman in the way she conducted herself; this warrior – as yet a maiden – who burrowed under his skin. Her responses were instinctive. He would swear by Taranis that she had been ready for him to take earlier; she must have passed twenty summers at least, so why still a maid? His answer to her bold challenge was long in coming, his face pressed so close their chins touched.

"Why, indeed, do I not throttle you?" He cradled her chin in a light grasp to remind her how easy it would be, his lips a whisker away. "It does not suit me to kill you."

Her eyes shot white sparks on blue, quivering in his hands. A deep shudder ran through her, transferring into his light clasp before he released her.

"Mount!"

After the briefest of hesitations she squelched a moan of pain when her rear hit the horse's back. While she shuffled around to find a comfortable position, he whipped free a cord from his waist band and had it tied round her foot before she could properly kick out at him. The other end of the tether thrown under the belly of the horse, he dodged her flaying fists as he nipped behind the filly. Her second foot was secured before her kicks could do him any damage. Her pummelling knuckles, and dire threats, he warded off with amusement while he tightened the cord enough to keep her on

34

the horse. Since he would have the rein, he left her hands free to clutch the filly's mane for he intended to ride hard.

His captive harangued him, but the measure satisfied him for he wished to prevent further damage to her. Back astride, he loosened the rein, easing the distance between them. The puzzle she was became an even greater challenge.

"You were headed for the hillfort at Raeden?"

"Aye." She was irritated, her eyes ablaze.

Digesting her reluctant reply, he gazed into the distance. Down the plain, where the river meandered, hills lay high on the left and deep forests lay to the right, and the track in front of him split into two. When he urged the horses to take the right-hand one, Nara arrogantly challenged his decision.

"That way leads to the Sacred Groves. You cannot mean to go there?"

Lorcan observed her, heedful of her expression. That she should know the way to the Sacred Groves was not unusual. All tribes within a day's ride would know where the groves were, but they would not venture there without escort, or without good reason. The Sacred Oak Groves were feared by all...yet her horse strained to head that way. In his recent visit, only a little more than a se'nnight ago, he had trodden this pathway with his druid guide, Maran, when he had been unexpectedly summoned to the Sacred Groves. Loathing shot through him; the memories and dire consequences resulting from that visit he wanted to banish forever.

"I will not go to the Sacred Groves."

His captive's eyes were defiant, unlike the reaction of most tribespeople. Hatred was unusual: terror was common.

Lorcan ignored her ranting. He, too, had hated every single pace it had taken to reach the malevolent depths of the dreaded grove. Once there, the sacred stones and notched sticks of ancient oak-wood had been thrown for him, the interpretation done by the chief diviner, Irala. An eerily-chanted animal sacrifice had been made by Maran at the revered stone altar; the still pulsating bloody innards read in tandem with the diviner. The signs had portended two things. The first being his impending rise to power as a principal negotiator. The second was that he would pass those negotiating skills to his firstborn son who would be an even greater leader of the Celts.

He had felt great relief over such a positive divination; had departed the groves exhilarated by the notion his arbitration skills would lead him to become the chief envoy of all northern Celtic tribes. The second part, the passing-on of his skills to a son, he did not think much on. As far as he knew, he had not yet fathered a male child. No woman had made that claim on him, though he had had a daughter.

Lorcan's eyes softened when he thought on the babe who had survived less than a day. Like his frail young wife, his too-early-born daughter had slipped into the beyond, the dark blood-red cloths around them a mismatch to their white and lifeless bodies. But that had been many seasons ago.

As befit a son of a Brigante chief, his marriage had been arranged to a woman unknown before the ceremony. He had been adamant about his father not finding a replacement wife after the deaths – even though Tully had niggled at him to take a new wife and beget heirs. He would not take another unloved wife, as that was how it had been. He had liked the woman, had used her body, but he had not loved her.

Instead he had focused on being the best envoy the settlement had ever had, happy to be more often away to other Brigante strongholds than at Garrigill. To become the most proficient peace maker of all the northern Celtic peoples had much merit. Talking had its place, aye, undoubtedly, yet Lorcan was no coward. A bloody battle was the usual Celtic way to solve border disputes, or for showing supremacy, and if that was the way of it, he would do that too.

But the Celtic fight with the Roman Empire was something entirely different. Parleying was needed to maintain a longer-lasting peace, to create stability throughout the land of the Celts. Ideally, his island that the Roman aggressors had named Britannia needed to be free of Roman influence.

Wending his way home from his visit to the Sacred Groves, he had been inspired about his future. It had never occurred to him his older brother's fate had been sealed too

36

and that, within days, senseless murder would take Arian from the tribe. Death at the hands of marauding Selgovae, for no justifiable` reasons. Selgovae. His mind refocused on the woman beside him who challenged his direction.

"What do you know about the groves?"

She remained steadfast in ignoring him, controlling the urgent fidgets of the brown filly while she clung to its mane. Why did the horse strain to go to the groves? Halting at the fork, he scrutinised his beautiful captive.

Impatience misted her gaze, since she clearly hated waiting for his decision.

"What could be amiss in going to the Sacred Groves?" His smile was a calculated gleam intended to provoke her.

"Perhaps you should tell me, Brigante!" The challenge was bold, her consideration of him calculating as she parried his question. She piqued his interest even more.

Lorcan sifted over the information already gleaned. Comfortable on the filly, though few in a tribe had their own horse, she knew the way to the Sacred Groves. A Selgovae chief might go there, but less likely a female of no consequence. If she was a tribal leader, why would she journey with only one man? An acolyte of the goddess, or a priestess, would journey to the groves – but she denied being a priestess, and she had far surpassed the age of an acolyte, many sun's calendars ago. Nothing about the woman made sense.

"Are you a priestess? I demand your answer."

Cold eyes swivelled to him, challenging his tone.

"I am not given to the goddess. I told you so already." Her jaw firmed up, a loud snort of frustration and disgust bursting forth as she rounded on him, pulling at the rein he still gripped as tight as a clam. "Will you make up your mind?"

Her eyes sparked enough to rival the fire god, Belenos. He did not even want to squelch his grin. "You should control that temper you have in abundance."

Undaunted, Nara maintained her impertinent confront before his head swivelled south-eastwards, towards the high hills, back to his own settlement.

"Not the Sacred Groves. We will take the other track. Home."

"Your home, Brigante, but not mine."

Lorcan's lips parodied a smile. "You mistake the situation. You have no home, displaced woman of the Selgovae."

He caught the wounded flare, a single tear hovering against her long brown eyelashes before her eyes shut tight. Moments later, they twitched open, temper flashing before her head whipped in the opposite direction. Witnessing that momentary wounding meant yet another time his sarcasm reaped no satisfaction.

When he dragged her unwilling horse away from the groves, Lorcan watched her survey the ground. She was no novice at reading the signs the earth held, studying like one who made her own way in the forest tracks and byways.

"You came from the clanhold of Tarras?" His abrupt speculation startled her into responding.

"Aye. From Tarras."

As though annoyed at giving even that bit of information, she clamped up. It did not matter, though, because he knew the chief of Tarras was not a woman. No chief then, but who was she? And what was he going to do with her? He would not kill her, yet he was unwilling to free her.

Some instinct, deep in his gut, told him the woman was important to hold onto for some momentous reason: perhaps even more than that.

They still had a long trek to his settlement, too far to reach that day for already the pinkish hue heralded dusk, so they would shelter for the night in the cavern above the river. His band would be encamped there awaiting his arrival.

His cheek twitched. He knew exactly what his warriors would think of his captive. By the time he reached the cave, he had to have some reasoning for her presence...something which would keep the woman unharmed.

Five warriors had accompanied him to avenge the cruel deaths of Arian and five other Brigantes. He and his band had killed six men from Raeden, except it now seemed they had also felled one from Tarras. The injustice of the seventh warrior's death bothered Lorcan, since he had no direct quarrel with Tarras.

The woman's voice startled him from reflective thoughts. "If you will not kill me, why not let me go? I am of no use to you."

"Who says you are of no use? You will come with me. Do you understand?"

"Oh, it is very clear, Lorcan of Garrigill, son of Tully. You do not want to kill me. You tether me down and no longer want to touch me, but you do not want to let me go either."

His captive goaded, using his name properly for the first time, incapable of biting back her sarcasm, but she was accurate in her deductions. He did not want to want her. He did want to touch her though; wanted much more but could not have it.

He convinced himself her use of his name mattered not a whit…but that was an untruth.

***

Hillfort of Raeden – Selgovae Territory

While dusk closed in, Cearnach's barely conscious body was supported into the settlement of Raeden. Since being pierced by the spear, his injury had bled severely, yet he had struggled through the forest and uphill to reach the Selgovae hillfort. Deep shame and regret flooded him as he related the surprise attack by Brigante warriors. He had been forced to draw his assailants into the woods on the opposite bank from Nara.

Catching his breath, fighting against the searing pain of his injury, Cearnach whispered, "The warrior…who went in search of Princess Nara…was high ranking. His torque and arm bands glistened in the sunlight when he sprinted into the woods, following my tracks." His voice faded. "I am not sure if he found her. I let her down. And they have the stallion…"

"Do not spend your energies on the horse. You did well to reach here, Cearnach." Rigg, the Chief of Raeden, patted the young warrior's good shoulder, for he understood only too well the humiliation Cearnach was feeling. "At first light, men

39

will check the woods, and then someone will go to Tarras with the updated news."

"My thanks…"

Cearnach was drifting off again while Rigg explained. "My own sons started this killing raid without my authorization, so if there is any blame to be attached much of it falls at Raeden's feet. Those Brigante warriors would not have been at the ford had they not been avenging the deaths of their own."

Cearnach was slipping into sleep.

***

On the way to Garrigill

Sundown dipped as Lorcan and his captive wound their way into higher ground, the exposed landscape for the last long stretch having offered little protection against the elements. A pre-dark chill had descended; a searing wind whipping up a bone-chilling cold which goose-pimpled his bare arms.

Stopping at a small spring to water the horses, he noted Nara's strength seemed depleted as she lay hunched over the mane of her horse. Her tugs at the leash to escape his clutches had ceased, seemingly resigned that he would not relinquish his tight hold of her, and she had stopped muttering her dire low-warnings over what she would do to him, for capturing her.

He was not sure about that lack for he was becoming used to her whinges, her voice lowly seductive. There was little resistance from her when he untied her leg restraint.

"Nara of Tarras, dismount and drink! There are bannocks in a pouch. Eat them now."

Her shrug of disrespect emphasised his captive did not like being given commands, though she said nothing when she slid down from the horse.

After a reviving drink from the cold spring, he sat down on a flat stone bedded in the heather-clothed hillside to contemplate his problems. The previous two days had been taxing. The need to avenge his brother's death had been necessary, the revenge killing not a procedure he reaped pleasure from, but it was the way of the tribes.

He rested his eyes to think on a solution to the problem of his Selgovae captive who stirred something in him, no matter what she did, or how she regarded him. As a hostage, she would garner him poor reward: a woman of no status was worth little trade.

Without opening his eyes, he recalled her in vivid detail; the proud flash of her magnificent rich blue eyes, the tempting fall of fiery deep auburn hair, in lowering sunlight more bronze than brown...and the charms of her body. Why forbidden? She was too womanly... A groan rumbled deep inside him.

A sudden awareness pricked him from his thoughts for the noises were not expected. The foolish woman pounced on her horse, alarm on her face when he jerked to his feet in pursuit of her. In haste, her palm stuffed the remains of a dry bannock into her mouth before she wrenched the reins of both horses from the large stone that lay alongside him, where he had tethered them, but her movements were too jerky as she mounted.

The little filly protested the command, wildly bucking to be free of her. The woman was flung hither and thither while the horse resisted, the stallion sidling around in confusion.

Reaching for the flicking tethers, his cry of rage cut off short when he watched the blood seep from the woman's face. The fiery red of her anger transformed almost immediately into a death-mask grey. Her eyes were agog, her fingers clutching at her throat.

The filly still threatened to unseat her while she clung on with strong thighs. She gagged, but by the great god Taranis, what else ailed the woman?

Lorcan wrestled the horse to a halt, his hands settling the frightened beast. He murmured soothing words until the horse calmed and eventually stood steady. Only when he had the horse controlled did he look up at the woman whose gurgles had ceased. Her eyes were closed, and her head flopped down on her chin, her arms hanging limp at her sides.

When he reached forward her lifeless body slumped boneless off the horse.

He grasped her before she hit the stony ground, his hands jerking under her ribcage. A plug of half chewed food shot from her mouth, followed by a spectacular gush as her stomach emptied. The blockage gone, the woman coughed and spluttered and heaved some more, till there was nothing left to bring forth.

Holding her loosely in his grip, Lorcan supported her kneeling body until her breathing had steadied. Lifting her to her feet, he pressed her face into his chest. He stroked her hair till she stopped shuddering – though many of the shudders of relief he acknowledged were not hers. Once again, he felt challenged by his own emotions. Somehow, it was of grave importance to him this woman should not come to harm.

Eventually, the quivering ceased. Her breathing almost normal his captive's head rose to look up at him. Her stare softened – no more than a blink – but it was filled with some reasoning he could not quite interpret. Exactly what she thought he did not know, but found he liked that new regard, liked it much better than spitting ire at him as an angry cat. A wry amusement sang out to him, drew him in and held him tight.

He had never felt soul-deep closer to any other human being in his life, but it did not last for she wrenched herself out of his light clasp and turned away. The mystery of the woman deepened further. His gut told him taking this woman's maidenhead could not be done without much consideration. Whatever made her pure at her age was too important to sever by mere lust.

Chapter Four

On the way to Garrigill

This man earned her gratitude like no other. Nara had given herself up for lost when the world around her had blackened, her breath gone. She should be giving him her trust, but he was the enemy. The battered croak of reluctant thanks coming from her bitter-tasting mouth was nothing like she intended.

Lorcan suppressed a grin, his eyes twinkling as though he found her pathetic gesture amusing. Leading her to the spring water, he cupped some to her lips to ease the ugliness in her throat, gently clearing away the traces of vomit. She pushed out of his arms, embarrassed by his ministrations, but had to admit she liked his tenderness.

"I am not a child. I can wipe myself."

"I know for sure you are not a child, Nara. You are not an untouchable either. Will you tell me your story, now I have saved you from ignominious death yet again?"

"Ignominious?"

She could not remain impervious to his wit, was not prepared to divulge who she was just yet, though it had been a sure sign from the goddess Rhianna – bringer of plenty – that she had been selfish. He was her adversary. That remained true; however she was shamed by her shabby behaviour. She tottered over to collect the remaining bannock and held it at arms length to her captor.

"The goddess, Rhianna, has shown me I should have shared this with you…and not gobbled the other…while attempting a feeble escape…with both horses."

The warrior took it from her. In his expression, she detected some measure of respect as he answered. "I believe the goddess mocks me, too, this day."

Unable to face his teasing any longer, she walked to Eachna and drew out her woollen bratt. Pulling it around her still shuddering body, she retrieved Cearnach's bratt from Rowan. She would not offend the goddess a further time by being unworthy. In silence, Lorcan accepted the cloak from her thrusting hand, though he still looked suspicious of her gesture.

"You are ready to continue?"

For the first time it seemed he gave her a choice, yet Nara was not prepared to trust him. "Aye."

"Ride then." He fisted both reins and gave her shoulder a gentle prod, to remind her of what he could do if she put up any resistance.

As they re-mounted, she expected him to reattach the leg shackles, but he made no move to do so. It was most likely the open landscape all around them that made him confident she would not make another attempt to flee. He was correct in that since there was nowhere for her to hide.

Their trek continued in silence for the most part, the river coursing below them when they moved up the bush and fern laden gully, the varied greens of the leaves shadowing to greys and blacks. Dusk eased into the dark blue of the early night, the silvering moonlight just enough to see by.

The strange feelings the warrior engendered continued, but they were not so overpowering for it now appeared only she felt the attraction. It peeved her he seemed to have lost interest in her so quickly. Though he glanced her way at frequent intervals, he did not meet her gaze.

Lorcan gradually drew out more answers from her, but she would not divulge the reason for her retained maidenhead. Their exchanges became a challenge; she withheld, he probed even more. Nonetheless, in the process of his questioning she became aware he divulged information about his own settlement. His reasoning she did not understand, but the particulars he imparted she had not known before. Against her better judgment she enjoyed learning more.

During quiet moments, though, she imagined herself around the fire-side at Raeden, being accorded a guest's welcome. She shivered, the night chill numbing her toes. The injustice of her capture stirred her resentment again, she should be warm, but where was she instead? She was being dragged along by this strange Brigante warrior who was too craven to kill her. Eventually, misery was not to be borne.

"If you will not strangle me, Brigante, dispatch me with your sword, and be done."

"I will not kill you. I have a much better fate for you, Nara of the Selgovae, so keep moving."

"Are you too gutless?"

She was heedless of how foolish it was to provoke him. A growing heat returned to his moonlit eyes, exasperation and something sensuously dangerous animating them.

"Do you ever think before you snarl? Has it occurred to you any one of my five warriors may violate, and then kill you, without me having to taint my hands? Warriors who await our arrival in a cavern just ahead of us."

Nara had never considered he could plan a fate so dreadful. Visions of being thrown to his antagonistic warrior-band terrified her, since being in the company of a group of men was not something she was used to. Her breath clogged in her dry as dust throat.

She knew a man to mate with was inevitable in her new life, but not five, or six including the warrior beside her. Her next thoughts were fervent pleas to Rhianna to save her from such a fate.

"Go in front, woman. Take the upper track."

Lorcan indicated the higher of the two paths winding their way steeply up the broad rock face as he manoeuvred Rowan behind her filly. The lower track looked much more passable as it snaked along the line of the river, lined with ferns and scrubby bushes clinging to the banking. The higher track was etched into bare rock; a narrow pathway.

"Up there?" Her answer was a squeak.

"Have I not just said so? Here, take your rein."

He gave her free rein, yet only when flight was impossible. He now blocked the way behind, and to rush forward was too foolish to contemplate. Swallowing the huge lump blocking her throat she suppressed her dread…and put her life in the hands of her goddess.

Alert to the dangers underfoot, she urged Eachna to move up the snaking trail that hugged the cliff side, her thoughts gloomy. Five fearsome warriors awaited her at the end of the trek; warriors bent on retribution and revenge against her tribe. They hated the Selgovae, so why would they tolerate her? Though, whatever happened, she would not allow them to abuse her without a struggle.

Despondency enwrapped her much like her cold bratt while her numb fingers drew the chilled wool tight around, but the damp cloak could not warm her soul. Forcing herself to cling to a brighter future kept her inching forward along the increasingly narrowing ledge.

"Stop! Go no further."

Lorcan's abrupt warning came at her out of the dimness. Cautiously dismounting, he edged past Rowan to regain charge of both reins, looping them over his wrist. Grasping her arm, he pulled her off Eachna, growling low in her ear, antagonism at full blast.

"Do you know what is likely to happen to you in the hands of five warriors who lack the company of a woman?"

Nara willed her eyes to look unperturbed. A frustrated grunt escaped when his gaze slid to her lips, his sudden exasperation replaced by a startling flame in his night-darkened eyes which burned her. She scarcely had the opportunity to blink before he took her mouth in a harsh kiss, scattering her senses and sending her body into turmoil. She should have protested, should have struggled…yet did neither.

This warrior was like a second skin, his natural warmth enwrapping her securely. And she wanted more…of it?

Surely not!

All too soon his lips ripped away, and he exhaled against her before rasping at her cheek, "That is not what they will do to you." He pushed her away, holding her at arms length as though he could bear to touch her no longer. "You will do best for yourself if you follow my directions. Stay close by me this night."

What directions should she follow? His ultimatum made no sense, but it might keep her alive. Was he saying his warriors would ravish her body without any tenderness at all?

Lorcan pulled her closer again, though she guessed he did it unwillingly since the muscles in his powerful arms trembled.

"Take heed, Nara. Some of my warriors are very persuasive."

Whatever Lorcan would propose had to be better than the fate which could await her. In the dark, five lusty warriors would not withdraw like he had earlier on finding her still a maid, but she protested his tight clasp, breaking free of him, though no words were uttered.

"My men are around the bend up ahead. One wrong move from you, and I cannot be responsible." His last words were fierce, his fists shaking her shoulders, his expression somewhere between enragement and anguish. Shoving her aside, he hollered into the distance, his voice echoing over the noise of rushing water tumbling down the hillside.

"Brennus? Who guards?"

Urging her to walk beyond to the rounding of the rock face, Lorcan followed in her wake. Without warning a torch brand thrust out flaring yellowish in the moonlight. She reared back when the dark shape of an immense warrior came into view from behind the flames.

"Lorcan, my brother! What kept you so long? So…this is what delayed you?" A gusty roar broke free, bouncing off the echoing walls as the young warrior took his fill of her.

The man's teasing tone made Nara shrink back against Lorcan. She felt his supporting hand at her back, her mouth suddenly parched. Soon there would be four more of them around her. The prospect filled her with horror.

"This is who delayed me, Brennus." Lorcan's tone was firm and decisive while he pushed her reluctant body forward.

A huge cavern was set back from a wide bend in the cliff-face, the front of it a natural open shelf jutting out for five or six paces beyond an overhang which ceilinged high above them. The shelter stretched back so deep Nara could only see a hint of the far wall in the dim light shed by the flickering fire. A clutch of horses were tethered over on the far side of the wide opening, snorting and whinnying gently.

One warrior sat guard near them, ensuring no animal strayed too near the edge. A heap of brushwood had been dumped just inside the opening, in far enough to be away from the elements, but the fire was a few paces back and centrally situated.

Nara sensed Brennus' interest as Lorcan passed over their horses' reins, his silent scrutiny embarrassing. She was puzzled. Did this warrior find her desirable? This was only the second Brigante she had ever met, yet he too was blatant in his sexual appraisal.

Brennus, though younger than his brother, was at least half a head taller than Lorcan with much wider shoulders. A powerful warrior, his shock of blond hair attractive, more handsome than Lorcan, but he made no blood-rush in her veins.

Her gaze trailed Lorcan while he crossed over to one of the horses on the far side rubbing it reassuringly when it whinnied a welcome – evidently his own – while Brennus stroked the flanks of Rowan as he moved the stallion, and Eachna, over to the herd.

"This is a mighty stallion, Lorcan. If you do not claim him I would be happy to. Too bad his former master is not in good shape, not like this powerful beast."

Brennus' chuckle rang out across the cavern while Lorcan reached forward and detached the packs of meat from Rowan's flanks, to dump them on the ground nearby.

Nara swallowed awkwardly. Brennus spoke of Cearnach. Ignored by them both, she headed for the warmth of the fire where lingering food smells revitalised her appetite, her empty stomach growling in anticipation of being filled. The warmth of the burning logs licked out to her cold body, their instant heat searing her freezing cheeks; the smell of the smouldering wood reassuring. Throwing her bratt back from her shoulders her bare arms welcomed the fire's radiance when she stretched her hands out to its blue-tinged orange glow.

The three warriors surrounding the crackling fire had been chatting quietly around its dancing light, smoky sparks billowing around the walls and upwards into the darkness hovering around the natural ceiling, creating strange shadowy shapes around the edges of the cavern – but on her approach, all conversation stopped while they stared.

Loud guffaws were followed by vulgar comments and gestures of intent.

"Now we know why you tarried." One young warrior gestured lewdly at Lorcan, his laugh a ribald hoot. "Took your time, did you, Lorcan? Not a boy? Instead it is a woman well grown."

She went on full alert when the warrior's speech faded, his gaze blatantly feasting on her.

Yet another reached out to snake a hand around her calf, dragging her close to him. Kicking out wildly she barked, "Keep your hands and comments to yourself!"

"Ah, hah! A woman with spirit. Is that why you kept her, Lorcan? And with the sign of the spear on her arm? Come closer, Selgovae captive."

The man laughed, ignoring the fact her kicks had connected hard on his thigh, the impact much more effective than her feeble attack on Lorcan of Garrigill. The warrior's hands continued to snake around her legs as he scrambled to his knees not put off by her censure, or lunges, at all. His words cajoled, a feral gleam lighting his eyes in the sparkling firelight. His tongue snaked over his upper lip hair, his slashing scars stretching his cheeks.

The third man joined in the amusement, his hands tugging at her bratt.

"Leave me alone!"

Nara batted his head while she struggled, but the warrior snared her, his brawny arms imprisoning. Then she was free…but only to be trapped in the arms of the first one. Too late to remember Lorcan's warning about staying close by him. Was she now to be left to these ravening beasts to slake their lust on? Was Lorcan going to let his marauding band do as they would and then dispatch her?

49

The thought was horrifying, but by Rhianna she would not go down without a screeching fight!

The three warriors tussled her protesting body back and forth, their wicked mirth of what they would do to her echoing around the cavern, till she stumbled and fell to her knees. One of them forced her to the ground and had her flat and squirming under him before she could retaliate. His lips slammed down making her want to retch while she bit and struggled free. His hands were all over her breasts, squeezing to the point of pain, his lower body grinding hard against her as she shrieked and scratched any part of him she could reach. Her strength was all but gone when the hands were lifted away from her body, and her legs were no longer compressed into the cavern floor.

Relief!

She truly was free.

Strong arms had hauled the warrior off her, and only then did she hear the crack of Lorcan's fists connecting brutally with the warrior's jaw – a double blow which smacked the smaller man across the cavern floor. Lorcan followed with his body as he hauled the warrior upright and renewed the attack of his fists to the man's chin. Another two blows followed, the warrior's retaliation halted by Lorcan twisting the man's arm behind his back and holding him in an excruciating arm lock.

"You will leave the woman alone, Fergal!" Lorcan's command was ferocious as he dropped the grip and thrust Fergal to the ground, his glares even more severe as the warrior lay prostrate nursing his already swelling jaw.

Nara looked at Lorcan, a flush of relief at being free of the warriors' clutches making her legs tremble and her breath hitch in her throat, glad she was not on the receiving end of his powerful fists. Yet, though he defended her he did not look towards her; not yet finished with his men. When he strode to confront the other two, his decree was severe.

"None of you will touch her. Do you hear me?"

"I hear you," Fergal slurred while he noisily clicked his jaw back in place. He did not seem pleased with the situation but did as Lorcan bid as he slunk out of the cavern, no longer amused. The other two sat down, looking equally displeased. Neither ashamed, nor apologetic…riled they had been thwarted in their pursuit.

Nara sidled closer to Lorcan. For protection. To feel less threatened, if that were possible, for the hostility in the cavern was palpable, their insolent stares continuing.

It lay heavy on her conscience that she sidled closer to the man she had been trying to escape from earlier.

"Then what is she doing here?"

It mattered not who blurted the question; Nara was sure it was in all of their minds.

"Enough!" Lorcan snarled into the tense silence. "It was not the horse of a boy, as we had expected, but the Selgovae woman is my captive."

The men looked away from her and stared into the flickering fire, frustrated tension knotting their neck and arm muscles. Nara felt they were only a short breath away from defying Lorcan while she stood close to him. Though the situation remained volatile, Lorcan's order permitted no opposition, his rage visible in every taut muscle when he hunched over the fire warming his hands. He rubbed his bruised knuckles where he had contacted with Fergal's jaw, then he removed Cearnach's bratt and spread it down.

Scowling like black fury, he nodded that she should sit down, but she held back: the notion of sitting close to his warriors repulsed her. The same warriors who had been pawing her body only moments before.

Though Lorcan still glowered, he did not force her; he ignored her while his gaze searched around the fire's edges.

"Is there any food left?" His clipped inquiry fell into the uncomfortable silence.

One warrior responded. "Not much, but enough to stave off hunger. It was already darkening when we reached the river track. We killed and guddled sufficient, not expecting more than you."

Reaching towards the fire's edge the warrior extracted a long stick with the roasted meat of a small animal still clinging to it and indicated baked fish wrapped in leaves.

"Nay, you would not have expected more than me, but this cooked food is better than what we had earlier." Thanking him, Lorcan rose to approach the horses.

A small glow suffused Nara, since she could only interpret his words as also meaning her.

Removing a chunk of meat from its wrapping, Lorcan passed it over. "Here. Fresh kill, but it should fill us a bit more."

"Boar meat?"

"Aye, but I could not lug the whole beast. That is all we will reap from the kill this night."

Without a word, the warrior flashed around his sharp blade, sectioning the ribs into smaller portions. In moments, they sizzled on the fire, the smell tantalizing Nara's hungry stomach.

Another shiver of apprehension beset her. They had not expected him to bring a live captive, and certainly not a woman. The silence was like a thick bratt all around – heavy, and threatening. She held back from the fire when Lorcan settled again, unsure about going closer. Sensing her still paces away, he confronted her.

"Sit here, woman." His order was gruff and detached. "By the warmth."

The warriors edged away, leaving a good space, still dissatisfied she was not there for their amusement, distinct resentment abounding. Disturbing shivers overwhelmed her slender frame. Her captor, Lorcan, had to be her protective buffer against their threatening proximity. Close to him, her leg deliberately touched his for reassurance. When he slid his body away, she shivered. He wanted no contact with her. Feeling deeply vulnerable, she faced the intimidating scowls around her.

A complete hush descended before the men restarted their previous conversation. Lorcan passed her a share of the already cooked meat, as he had still not relinquished her knife. No meat had tasted finer as she nibbled, the overcooked drying fish coming a close second. The lightly sizzled boar ribs were soon shared out amongst everyone when they had

52

cooked sufficiently, murmurs of appreciation breaking the high-strung silence.

One by one the men rose from the fire and wandered outside, chatting coarsely together, breaking the inharmonious lull.

Nara's head bent to dispel humiliation. A light touch at her elbow raised her face as Lorcan's eyes sought hers in the flickering darkness. A hint of warmth, a softening maybe, lurked there? She was not sure...

"It is to be expected." His whisper was for her ears alone.

She knew Lorcan's men were circumspect; their ribaldry could have been much coarser; their actions harder to control. It seemed Lorcan had saved her virginity, and maybe even her life, yet again.

Lorcan turned to Brennus when he sat down beside them. "Well, little brother? Did you have success in the chase?"

Little? Nara smiled at the cavern floor. A misnomer indeed, for Brennus was a very large warrior.

"Nay. I did not follow his trail of blood." Brennus' answer was gruff.

"If the gods wish him to live it will be well; if not, there will be a reckoning."

"Should you have brought the woman here, Lorcan?" Brennus' voice was hesitant.

Nara winced and lifted her eyes to Lorcan, wondering what he would say.

"Discussion of her will come on the morrow." Lorcan's tone was unyielding.

Though he spoke to his brother he held her gaze, his unfathomable. A question hovered; she knew the answer to it, for she still had not told him all. When she gave no response, he stood up with an offhand grunt, scowled and strode off.

Nara trembled, not from cold, but from trepidation. He abandoned her. Her throat hoarse, she watched him approach his horse where he withdrew his own cloak from a dangling pouch. Returning, he spread it behind her. Relieved, her breathing restarted.

"Sleep there. Your own bratt will cover you."

She scrambled to her feet, looking to the cavern entrance. "I must…"

Lorcan nodded, his hand grasping her shoulder. Her initial shrug to detach him died an instant death since he was her only protection against the other men present. Though he seemed to dislike her intensely now, he still publicly laid claim.

Leading the way, he bypassed the warriors now congregated near the cave mouth who spoke together in hushed murmurs. The men raked her slender body, setting her teeth on edge. She had hated their hands on her, but Lorcan's touch she could not dislike: quite the opposite, she relished its security.

The path on the other side of the cavern was wider, but it was in the night-black, shielded from the moon's light. The darkness was so deep Nara could not make out any of his features.

"Go no further than this, the risks are too high. The waterfall you hear runs down the rock a few steps along, but after there the path narrows to a dangerous degree. It requires daylight to traverse. I will await you here."

Backing up against the rocks, Lorcan allowed her to bypass him, her body brushing against him. Immediate warmth rushed to her face, and that unbidden tingle coursed through her again. It seemed her instinctive reaction to this particular warrior remained constant, even though she did not wish it to be so.

Making a hasty toilet, and using the nipping-cold water, Nara knew she should try to escape, but the other warriors would also be in pursuit if she made a bid for freedom. Though Lorcan had not killed her, she did not think the result would be the same if his band chased her. And the darkness was too great a deterrent.

"Do you tarry much longer?" Lorcan's irritation reached her.

Ignoring him, she bathed her leg and walked back after securing the binding. Impulsively reaching for his arm, she found he was freezing to her touch. He had waited for her without his bratt, no wonder he sounded cantankerous – he had sought to protect her from his own men.

Something warmed around her heart that he should do so since it appeared he now found her an unwanted burden. Laying both of her hands on his cold arms, but keeping her body at a distance, she dared the question that had been eating at her conscience.

"Could Cearnach still be alive?"

His clipped answer reached her in the darkness. "Does the man mean so much to you?"

Nara no longer had any wish to taunt; she now had to trust him to look after her wellbeing, for she had no other.

"Aye, but as my loyal bodyguard."

Chapter Five

On the way to Garrigill

A bodyguard? She must have some standing in her tribe if she
merited a bodyguard. Lorcan needed answers, but at that very
moment he needed to be free of the icy wind.

Feeling his tremors, Nara tugged her bratt open, drawing it
as a protective shield around both of them, her body heat
instant warmth radiating towards him. Though it seemed a
reluctant gesture – she held herself so awkwardly – Lorcan
acknowledged what it cost her to make it while he snuggled
in. She started back, instinctively, before she relaxed. A
strange contentment washed through his body, as though her
embrace was a long-awaited haven. His breath fanned her lips
while he reassured her.

"Your man hesitated before running off, giving a taunting
challenge. His deliberation meant he was caught by one of our
spears."

His arms broke free from under her, reversing their
position and holding her forearms. Gripping her firmly, his
voice held unconcealed annoyance. "I regret that the spear was
thrown. We had no direct quarrel with your clanhold, but one
of my men was too quick to complete our work at Raeden."

He pulled her closer, his arms encircling her tense middle,
his eyes seeking an understanding, though the gloom
prevented clear sight. "It caught him in the chest, though he
could have avoided the spear. He could not get back across to
protect you, but instead attempted to lure us into the woods on
the far bank. Brennus order was to leave him to fend for
himself if he yet lived."

He felt her tremble, her relieved sigh a whiff of breath at
his chin.

"My thanks, Lorcan of Garrigill. It gives me hope. I have one more question."

"Ask, Nara, and then comes my turn."

"What would you have done if you had found a boy?"

"A fair question." His hands tightened, his legs widening to cradle her better – more room since he could not prevent his response. Though she tensed even more, her struggle was minimal, as though a protest was necessary, yet not desired.

"A boy would have lived to tell the tale since six men had already been put to the sword. I would have disarmed him and sent him home." His voice was low in the ensuing silence. "But I came upon you…"

Lorcan could maintain his resistance to this woman no longer. The initial taste turned quickly to a desperate need to learn everything: all of her, and definitely her secrets. His hands roamed inciting moans from her; cries neither of alarm nor anger. He was sure it was reluctant pleasure before she squirmed and struggled against him.

"You know I am Lorcan, second-born son of Tully, Chief of Garrigill, but I would know your full story. Please?"

Nara tensed even more in his arms. The sigh that eventually rippled across his skin was one of resignation, as though a vital decision had been made. It came as a mere whisper.

"My name is Nara, eldest child of Callan, Chief of Tarras."

"Nara of Tarras."

Lorcan breathed her name experimentally while his mind flurried over the revelation. He did not question that she was telling him the truth; he knew it. The bond he felt for this Selgovae captive grew stronger, a sense of inevitability falling upon him. "Thank you, Nara of Tarras."

No menial member of her tribe, though her situation remained unusual. The child of a chief, princess to his prince. Her rank changed matters drastically, her unbedded status having been kept for some momentous reason. She could become no inferior concubine at his hearth, for the lands of her tribe lay too close to his own. He had to think long and hard now about what he would do with her come the morrow.

"I had surmised you must be an important member of your clanhold."

His arms tightened around her in a clutch of tender harbouring, his body remaining stirred for he wanted to do more, much more. Still, for some strange reason – perhaps the cold of the night, or maybe because her rank matched his own – whatever, he found the discipline to resist.

As she pushed away, her movements made an abrupt halt when one hand reached the wound she had made earlier, for the cloth of his tunic was stuck fast to it. Her gasp of dismay muffled against his neck.

"Oh. I…regret my actions earlier. It was…"

Lorcan appreciated how much effort it took for her to attempt an apology. "It matters little. Your blade was well-honed. The wound is clean and will heal. There is much more I would learn of you, Princess Nara of Tarras, but not now. It is time to sleep, but…remain close by me."

Slipping from the confines of her cloak, he groped forwards to the cave mouth expecting her to follow. Striding to the fireside, he pointed to his spread cloak.

"Sleep, Princess Nara, daughter of Callan, Chief of Tarras, of the Selgovae."

His words were purposeful, loud for all to hear her rank and status, the implication being she was beyond the aspirations of most warriors present in the cave. That had to be entirely clear to his warrior-band.

He sat down by the fire, whispering quietly to Brennus, and ignored Nara. Divulging her status now caused him even more problems. She had settled down on the cloak, yet he sensed sleep eluded her. Her body looked far too tense, stiffening when the sounds of sleeping warriors huffed and snored in the gloom of the cave, a light whistling here and a tiny shuffle elsewhere.

"Goodnight, my brother," Lorcan said as he clapped Brennus' shoulder. "Sleep well."

Brennus' gaze strayed towards the huddled figure of Nara. "Sleep? I am a man, Lorcan. I do not think I will sleep much this night."

***

A laden scabbard and other pouches softly thudded on the cavern floor. A large body snuggled in, rumpling the material beneath Nara, instant heat transferring to her through the bratt she had wrapped firm and tight around herself. Exhaled breath gusted on her hair, and soft grunts flit past her ear when the person angled even closer and drew a cloak over both of them.

Lorcan. It had to be him and none other, she was already attuned to his body scent. His fidget continued till he found the most comfortable position on the hard bedrock of the cavern. One arm crept across her middle, and gradually his breathing slowed to a steady rhythm. Her breathing did the opposite.

Was the goddess giving her a taste of what sleeping with a man was like? Would she find another man like Lorcan? A Selgovae warrior? Thinking about it made her blood heat while she focused on the firelight dancing on the walls sending eerie shapes around the chamber and tried to ignore the virile body at her back. Her skin shivered when his breath suddenly gusted on her neck, small trembles besetting her that she could not stop.

During the last two moons, much of her time had been spent thinking about the first man she must give her body to. Forced into her new situation, she had looked critically upon the men of her tribe, but not one warrior had made her want to choose him come the fires of Beltane. Their reaction to her was demoralising; she was all too aware the men of Tarras wanted nothing to do with her.

"Foolish men!"

Her low muttering she hoped was disguised by her wriggles, when she freed herself of Lorcan's clasp and lay flat on her back.

Though mistrustful of the warrior-band here in the cavern, as they had scrutinised her, Nara had also studied them. None of them made any impression on her senses. Not even the handsome giant, Brennus.

59

Why was Lorcan different? Her senses really did sing when he was close, yet, she could not forget he had taken her captive. The goddess surely must mock her, for nothing altered the fact that he was a Brigante.

It really was not just. Beltane loomed, only half of the cycle of the moon was left to pass, and by then she needed to have chosen a lover. Her sigh went deep.

The Brigante's arm tunnelled under her cloak, and curved her into his now glowing body, the intimacy making her gasp. She struggled – a token protest – but was too aware that a show of rebuff on her part could lead to even more dire consequences. If the warrior-band found out that Lorcan rejected her, they would be upon her in a blink.

She felt his fingers tenderly cup her breast without urgency, though she could not miss the hard ridge pressing into her buttocks. His voice whispered into her hair, his lips a butterfly kiss. "Do not fear me, Nara, I will keep you safe. For now you must sleep. Difficult decisions will come on the morrow."

His large hand slipped down to gently settle on her stomach. She was sure he must feel the turmoil that was going on there, but if he did he did well to ignore it, for his fingers remained hot, and widespread, but at rest.

As tiredness crept upon her, she reflected on what he had just said, reassured to find his protection would continue…and he had called her Nara. No formality…just Nara. Though his hand still rested at her waist she edged away from full body contact, for she did not think she would be able to sleep at all if she stayed close.

Drifting into a light doze, she revisited earlier that day when she had found herself responding to his kisses. Her first ever embraces. In all honesty, she had liked them. As though her very thoughts seeped into Lorcan, his fingers caressed her waist before he burrowed closer again…

She woke many times through the night, but always Lorcan was nestled protectively around her. In spite of insecurity over her captivity, which pervaded her light dreams, the protection of his arms was reassuring.

Rustling sounds woke her as pre-dawn broke, faint light filtering into the cavern. A hard ridge pressed against her bottom, and Lorcan's large palm gently brushed her breast, eliciting her thrilled gasp before she remembered where she was, and what was happening. His face nuzzled into her hair, his voice a frustrated and heated rasp.

"Believe that I wish to make love to you, Nara, but this is neither the place nor the time."

Nara tensed up, her whole being in a state of confusion. It was definitely not the place to have anyone make love to her, not the time either, since it was not yet Beltane...but did she want it to be Lorcan? She feared she wanted exactly that. But it must not be.

After some noisy moans, Lorcan rolled to his feet and strode to the cave entrance.

"Did you gag her to keep it quiet, Lorcan?" Fergal's words incited further grinning and ribald banter among the warrior group, but all it took was Lorcan's low menacing growl to halt their amusement. His cool anger and biting words rebuked the band, reminding them of her rank in her tribe.

Nara was not convinced, though, that her status as a Selgovae princess meant as much to his warriors as it seemed to do to Lorcan, for they appeared unimpressed.

"No one will touch Nara, Princess of Tarras!" Lorcan barked before he strode out of the cavern.

Low mumbles rumbled around the area as the warriors gathered up their things, and made their horses ready. To Nara, it was an endless wait since she did not dare move, her attention focused on the cave entrance, awaiting Lorcan coming back.

When he returned, Lorcan disregarded the glowers.

"Must the woman come with us, Lorcan? She causes trouble already."

Lorcan rounded on his warrior, verbally lashing him. "She is not the one making trouble. Look to what you are doing!!"

Lorcan's physical control, Nara thought, looked strained to the very limit, his fists bunching. She matched the tension rippling from him since she felt in some way his rage was her own when he growled again at his warrior.

"I will repeat for those who are not listening well enough. Nara of Tarras will come with us to Garrigill, and will remain untouched the whole journey."

No-one answered.

"Get up, Nara. We leave now." Lorcan's order was impatient.

She waited a moment longer wondering where the empathy of the night had gone; the sympathetic intimate tone of the dark had fled with the dawn. Finding herself a spot out of everyone's sight, she prepared herself for what was to come, for her prisoner status was not much changed now Lorcan knew who she was. She considered running, but one look at the precarious track made the decision for her.

Lorcan was correct; it would take all skill to traverse with, or without, the horses and, it was not one to flee on.

As the warrior-band moved off, with their skittish horses in tow, last of their line was Brennus, leaving Nara and Lorcan at the very rear. Reaching back, she clutched Lorcan's arm, angered by his antipathy, for now he was a different man from the one who had held her tenderly.

"Let me make my way back to my tribe? Keep both horses, but let me go. You see already how I make trouble between you and your warriors."

"I cannot let you go, Nara."

Frustrated anger emanated from him in waves, so intense Nara backed away.

"Why can you not? You will regret this decision."

"You are most likely correct, but by the great god Taranis, I find the decision has already been made for me. Move on, Nara!" His tone was just as hostile as hers.

She was glad to find the path was narrow only in a small section, and the anxiety of traversing soon over.

Later, when they rode, her ownership of the rein was a surprise to her as she had expected to be tethered again. Brennus turned back often to look upon her, his gaze a calculating one though not, in any way, threatening. She was flattered by his attentions, but he created no inside fluttering. So far, only Lorcan managed that.

The track snaked across the ridges of the highest hills, the going more difficult above the tree line where the barren terrain lay open to the sky god, Taranis. Random lumps of greywacke littered the surface making it too risky for the small Celtic horses to carry their human burdens.

After dismounting, they climbed higher. A last difficult scramble, the horses in tow, took them over haphazardly-strewn boulders and slippery scree, where they rested for a brief time near the summit.

Nara sat away from the warrior-band, deliberately turning her back, and railed at what had been dealt her. She had not attempted another pointless escape. Six warriors heightened the odds too much. Breathing deeply of the clear air, she quelled her resentment.

Looking around was a welcome distraction, the view breathtaking. Selgovae territory to the north-west lay stretched in all its beauty and magnificence, the varying greens of the endless trees broken up by an occasional patch of blue waters, and less so by the brown of tilled earth.

At Tarras, they would not realise anything untoward had happened to her, since she had been expected to stay at Raeden for more than a day.

Turning to the east, Nara viewed the land stretching out for many days walking towards the sea. The day had dawned so clear and crisp a blue haze was just visible, twinkling far in the distance.

Lorcan sat down beside her, his voice having lost the hard edge of earlier. "You have never seen the glory of this land all around you?"

Nara was annoyed for his interruption had overridden her pleasure. "I personally have never gone to make war on Brigantes, so there has been no reason for me to cross over these hills."

"Nara, these hills should also be climbed for peaceful reasons, to enjoy the beauty the earth goddess has gifted to us. Sadly, you speak true, we cross these peaks to make war, though soon it will not be so, for the Celts who dwell around here must make peace with each other."

Nara did not even attempt to prevent her scoff. "You really believe there will be a time when we do not make war on our neighbours?"

Instead of answering, he stood up and took in the view full-circle. Pulling on her hands, he dragged her upwards, and against her will that tingling anticipation began anew. All it took was a simple touch of his fingers and...that soft brown eye heat. Passion flared again in his fervent gaze, but she was not so naïve to believe she was the one stirring his present passion.

"Look all around, Nara. You have looked to the lands of your childhood, and you have looked north, and east towards the rising light of Lugh. I watched you, but you have yet to look south."

"Why should I look south? That leads to your home." She sidled away.

Taking hold of her shoulders, Lorcan propelled her slowly round, forcing her to view the landscape towards the south, his body sliding in behind her while he pointed. Shivers beset her as he snuggled closer. She pulled herself forward, but it was so difficult to disobey the commands of her craving skin when he pulled her back to him again. His lips whispered at her ear, the fervent words a caress of their own as she felt the thrill of his whiskers tickle her skin.

"Our future danger lies to the south. In years to come, I wish to stand here and see this glorious land with my own free eyes. Free from petty tribal warfare. But more crucially for us, at present, is to be free from Roman domination. We must work to make that be true, and if that means no warring on our neighbours, so be it!"

"Free. You talk of free eyes? You hold me prisoner." Bewildered once again by the passion in his voice, her emotions were unbridled. Yanking her elbows back into his ribs she forced her way around to challenge his zealous talk. "Tell me how my eyes will come to be free? In fact, maybe you could tell me how my eyes were ever free?"

She noted how her challenge dismayed Lorcan. Her bitterness caused his grip to slacken, not understanding her anger stemmed not only from her present captive state, but from her reflection on her whole life. Thrusting him away, she avowed, "I look forward to the time when I am free of you, Lorcan of the Brigantes!"

Their gazes locked for long moments, neither relenting till Lorcan strode off, calling for the warriors to make ready, looking as though he loathed her once more.

Chapter Six

Crannogs of Gyptus.–Brigante Federation Territory

Lorcan of the Brigantes appeared to have been having a vision, some strange resolution for the future. To the south lay his home, not hers. In truth, she did not have a place she could call home, had not really had one for two long moons. The view southwards was breathtaking, Nara had to admit reluctantly. There was a whole land down there she knew nothing about, but it seemed – according to Lorcan – in the near future she was going to sample it.

Though she remained unfettered, and had control of her filly, escape was nigh impossible. The scree top provided no cover. When the orb of Lugh was no longer overhead, their traverse of the ridge was over, and they had made their way down to the tree level.

"Go by the crannogs of Gyptus," Lorcan announced.

Jolted from her resentful daydreaming, Nara paid more attention to her surroundings. Through the thinly populated trees at the edge of the denser wood they had just cleared, she caught glimpses of a lake basin, stretching a good distance, long and narrow in shape. The going underfoot became increasingly hazardous when they made trail across boggy ground densely colonised by tall rushes and marsh grasses; the pathway used very narrow, the edges sloping into trenches full of rank-smelling water. She could no longer see the lake water ahead of her, but smoke billowed up into the air, swaying up in the wind.

"Who comes by my dwelling? Name yourselves!"

The startling inquiry rang out long before they reached the waters edge. At the end of the file, Nara could not see the person when the warrior-band dismounted, but from behind her, Lorcan's returning bellow deafened.

"Grond? Lorcan of Garrigill asks for your crannog hospitality before continuing our journey."

"Lorcan? Show yourself that I can be sure it is you visiting."

Lorcan thrust the rein for his own horse at her, before picking his way past his men. Though she could not see their meeting, dense reed cover obscuring it, the friendly backslapping and banter indicated Lorcan was a welcome guest.

Grond's cheery voice was ear-splitting. "I deduced it might be you when we spied you up at the tree line. Welcome!"

Nara wondered whether the hospitality Grond offered extended to a Selgovae captive. Exactly how welcome would she be? If it were a crannog near Tarras, there would little welcome for a Brigante captive. The treatment she was likely to receive held no appeal.

Last in line now, still mounted, she darted a furtive look behind her. Whirling Eachna around, a quick surge took her past Lorcan's horse.

"The boggy ground is treacherous for the untutored. Come back now, and walk in front of me!"

Brennus' peremptory demand whipped her head round. He was now in pursuit. Though she knew it to be dangerous, desperate not to miss a chance at escape, Nara urged Eachna into a canter. Obedient to the command, her horse launched forward, but clearly unhappy with the terrain under her hooves, Eachna halted her flight. Eachna, it seemed, had more sense of impending doom than Nara, though the little horse could not stop herself from an inevitable skitter towards the edge of the pathway.

Struggling to gain control, Nara found their progress to disaster averted as Brennus slipped behind the horse's rump and shoved with his powerful shoulders. Eachna protested the mistreatment, her frantic neighing wild and loud, but Brennus' superior strength held her hooves back from the edge. Once the filly was stabilised, Brennus dragged Nara from Eachna's back. Even before her feet touched the ground, she broke free of his grip and pelted back down the path she had come on, her heart pounding like the beat of war spears upon the soil before battle.

"We have you in our sight, woman of the Selgovae. Follow the warriors of Garrigill!"

Nara skidded to an abrupt stop. Her breath heaving, she frantically searched for an escape route. She had nowhere to go except into the ditches, and they were not an option she would choose willingly.

The command had not come from Brennus. Four unknown Brigantes had sprung through the reed cover as though from nowhere, bursting onto the pathway and blocked her way, using their spears as a barrier. Sentries of Grond, they had been guarding the rear of Lorcan's band. It was a bitter truth for Nara to swallow. Escape would have been impossible, even if she had managed to elude Brennus – Brennus, who now clutched her elbow and marched her back to their horses.

She tugged and hauled to free her arm, but to no avail; Brennus' grip was far too strong. Furious at her failure, she vented her wrath on her captor, her blood stirred to a frenzy. With her free hand she lashed out at him, caution having fled into the reeds alongside. "Unhand me! I am well outnumbered and can see no escape. Let me walk alone." Her slaps and entreaties did no good at all. Brennus continued to drag her protesting and cursing body along the path.

She fumed at all Brigantes, her jaw aching with rage as she continued to berate them for her capture. Equally as vehemently, she railed at these new warriors of Grond, her glares fit to scald. The goddess Rhianna did not escape her livid muttering either…but mostly she was deeply infuriated with herself. Nothing worked out as she had envisaged when she had set out on her journey to Raeden.

The ribald comments from the warriors behind her made her teeth gnash even more. They shamed her, but the shame of her failures was worse. Lorcan would be displeased to hear of yet another foiled escape attempt. Her heart tripped a beat, the momentary closing of her lids stemming the flow of moisture that threatened to well up. Her trembling legs would have caused her to stumble had Brennus not been maintaining such a tight grip. The thought of Lorcan's wrath made her even more miserable as Brennus continued to draw her along the pathway, till it narrowed down to a comfortable width for one person. He freed her elbow and prodded her ahead of him.

Above the noises of the marsh creatures, and the flapping of birds rising out of the boggy waters, Nara heard sounds of people at their daily work as Brennus padded behind her, keeping her moving at a steady lope. A child cried somewhere, but the direction was impossible to tell. The marshes deadened the sounds, muffling them, baffling inexpert ears like her own, and tall marsh plants set up an odd sort of disorientation. The sounds of iron on an anvil hummed close by; a voice sang a merry accompaniment. The acrid reek of the forge mingled with the smells of the waterside, and the nauseating stench of tanning leather.

Brennus forced her into a large clearing close to the lake's edge, Lorcan's warrior-band having spread around the perimeter, where they sought somewhere sound enough to tether their horses. Nara had no need to do so as Brennus kept a tight grip on Eachna's rein.

"Lorcan!" Brennus' laughing tale was imparted deliberately across the clearing, loud enough for all around to hear. "You will be glad to hear your Selgovae captive did not succeed in her futile escape attempt."

A glower, wild as a thunderstorm, raked her for long moments before Lorcan spoke to the warrior beside him, the torque and armbands adorning the young man proclaiming his rank at the crannog settlement.

Nara felt the back of her throat thicken as she tried to ignore the umbrage in Lorcan's gaze, his saying nothing making failure feel even more acute. Anger she could rally against; ignoring her was more hurtful to her frayed emotions.

The ground Brennus then forced her over was solid underfoot, constructed of hard packed earth reinforced with binding materials to keep it firm. A timber walkway, some twenty paces long, led out across the lake water to platforms accommodating two crannog roundhouses with adequate space all around them. One dwelling was of the usual size; the other a smaller one for storage. Two horses were tethered alongside the smaller in a covered but wall-less enclosure. A forge just outside the larger roundhouse spewed out dense black smoke while a smith plied his craft, hammering a rhythmic ring-ting as he fashioned a metal tool.

Grond called out to the sweating smith Nara could see hunched over the anvil.

"Look after these horses for Lorcan. I will send a boy to help you. We go to see my father."

Grond took another pathway leading out of the clearing, Lorcan following him. Just before they disappeared out of sight, Nara felt Lorcan's gaze fleetingly alight on her, as though making sure she was still there. Though he was across the opened space, his eyes held hers in silent censure before he trudged on, the downturn of his lips marking his displeasure.

Willing herself not to be upset by it, Nara pretended indifference…but it hurt to see condemnation in Lorcan's eyes. And that was foolish. He was her enemy as much as every other Brigante around her.

Head down, she trawled behind as the warrior-band followed Lorcan, making their way along another reinforced pathway and across a log causeway bordered by wattled walls. Brennus followed in her wake, taking his guarding seriously. Once into the open at the lake's edge, she could see the roundhouse they approached more clearly, no longer obscured by the tall reed and fronded light-green willow cover.

The crannog dwelling sat tall and proud, this one a little larger than a typical roundhouse. Built out over the water, its circular wooden platform sat on stilted foundations, the walkway access edged with a waist-high woven wall of willow, with an infill of thinner twigs. The wattle and clay daubed wall of the dwelling was low, no higher than Nara's head, the thatched roof beams protruding over the top of it, creating a shady overhang. On the outer circular platform edge two children played a game on a wooden board with marked coloured stones. Close by, a young woman stood weaving at a tall upright loom under the overhang near the children. A little further round, Nara could just glimpse a skin-covered coracle and a dugout boat floating at a protruding landing stage, accessible from the platform edging.

"Mother," Grond called ahead, "Lorcan is here to visit Father. Where is he?"

On their approach, the children scurried away, a woman appearing almost immediately. Then, more slowly, a man of similar age emerged one whose smile was a beam of sunshine.

"Lorcan. Welcome!" The older man clapped Lorcan on the shoulders, greeting him warmly while he gave an invocation of hospitality to all. "It is long since we talked."

"My thanks, Gyptus. It is good to be here again."

Lorcan's confident smile as he and Gyptus walked round to the landing-stage made Nara feel neglected. She wished the smile was for her, now her own situation was back to threatening. A lone Selgovae, she was surrounded by even more Brigantes; from the hostile look on their faces none happy with her presence.

The older woman begged the warrior-band enter her dwelling. "Come, please, all of you. My hearth is yours. Rest while I gather sustenance."

Bringing up the rear with Brennus, Nara could see how extensive the settlement was as more than a few curious families clustered around their crannogs, looking eagerly across the head of the lake waters, towards the newcomers. She followed the line of men, but at the low entrance tunnel Brennus pushed her to the side and stood guard. Wiping her hands on her tunic, feeling dirty and unkempt, she seethed alongside him.

A huddle of local men sped across the causeway, glancing at her briefly, before they stooped to noisily enter the roundhouse, hauling Brennus along in tow.

No Brennus to guard?

It made no difference as two brawny warriors remained on sentry duty at the shore end of the causeway. It was not possible for her to contemplate anything other than wait where Brennus placed her. Around the platform edge she could hear

Lorcan and Gyptus discoursing heatedly together, and it seemed she was the topic of their conversation.

She waited, her breath coming harder, nerves jangling. And waited some more. An upsurge of noise came from inside the roundhouse, drowning out Gyptus' angry tones outside. She turned away from the door, two steps only onto the walkway. At the far end, one of the burly guards took two steps towards her, gesturing with his spear, indicating she return to her previous place.

Nara's heart seized, there was no escaping them, either. Swimming was something she was strong at, having lived on the *nemeton*, the island home of the priestesses. But she would not outreach the spears of the guards, for any attempt to dive in would easily be thwarted. And if, by some chance, she managed to reach the water she could only maintain a breath hold for a short time. By then a hail of weapons would pin her to the lake bed.

The concept of another failure made her huddle in bitter silence, tucked in to the overhang of the roof, as she rocked on her haunches, still angry with herself. Though, no-one heard her dire mutterings. Not one Brigante came anywhere near her.

Eventually, Lorcan and Gyptus had circled the crannog. It was evident Lorcan had been having difficulty in persuading Gyptus about something. When he stopped at the doorway, Nara felt the old chief's wintry, calculating stare, loathing oozing from it.

Lorcan's unwavering gaze was formidable, no hint of softness there either...or of the desire she now knew him capable of. His eyes imparted a strong message commanding her to wait at the doorway. Unwilling to display any insecurity, she pretended indifference. Lorcan followed Gyptus inside without uttering a word.

Nara cringed. The full dread of her captive position now hit her – a bolt from Taranis would not have hit its mark better. Any affinity lately created with Lorcan she had ruined by her futile attempt to escape. A terrible loneliness engulfed her as her eyes drifted to the wattled fencing, absorbing nothing. Her lower back slid down the wall, till she sat with knees drawn up to her chin. Her arms enfolded her shins, protectively, yet so tense her shoulders soon ached with the effort of maintaining the position.

She had often been alone at the *nemeton*, left to her own devices, and had learned to enjoy her own company, but she had never experienced such feelings of isolation, and vulnerability, as she now felt. This abandonment was of a totally different nature from any she had ever encountered before. She waited and waited. Her fingers picked at the planking of the crannog decking.

The noises inside the roundhouse increased, disturbing her gloomy thoughts, the tone she was hearing not a happy one. Angry cries vied with others that sounded more of a plea for understanding. She closed her eyes against the sounds of anger, her chin dropping to her chest

The voice at her side startled her. "*Ciamar a tha thu?*"

"I…I am well, thank you."

It was the young woman who had been working at the loom. "Come with me, stranger."

"You do not realise just how much of a stranger I am. Perhaps you should check before you share your hearth with me." Nara appreciated the woman's welcome, glad to find someone talking to her, yet her reply was more abrupt than intended. The woman disappeared inside the crannog, returning immediately.

Peering at Nara's Selgovae marking, the woman sounded puzzled. "My father, Gyptus, bids you enter."

Nara felt uneasy…and contrarily curious. Enter the chief's hearth? Befitting a princess, but not a captive. Lorcan knew her name, and status, yet knew nothing else about her.

She followed the woman through the wattled entrance tunnel into the dim interior, natural light almost non-existent since there were no wall openings. Reed torches burned in sconces at both sides of the entranceway, and a tall freestanding flame sat in an iron post at the far end of the central fire, the light given from them a sputtering pale-yellow glow.

73

Gyptus beckoned to her, his voice distrustful, not at all welcoming. "Sit here, Princess Nara of the Selgovae." He made a space available close to him, the situation a princess would be afforded, yet Nara felt Gyptus appeared disgruntled to have her there.

She sat feeling even more threatened than the previous evening in the cavern. Lorcan, seated on Gyptus' other side, still ignored her.

Warriors encircled the fire, its smoke and sparks funnelling up to the top of the high conical roof where it drifted in a smoky pall. Food appeared and was handed out to the hungry band – flat breads and oat rounds, dried berries, and smoked fish. A young girl carried a wooden pitcher of barley beer to fill wooden cups and bone horns.

Gyptus formally, and Nara felt with rancour, introduced his son Grond to her. Nara guessed him to have lived about the same winters as she had.

Grond's interest was blatant throughout the meal. Passing her bread and fish, he unnecessarily stroked her fingers during the transfer. Nara found his attention baffling. Gyptus demonstrated great hatred of her, yet his son…appeared to do the opposite. Though whatever made Grond interested in her mattered not, for he did not stir her senses in any positive way. Yet another man she would not choose to mate with at Beltane, but seated beside her, he could not be ignored.

"You are very bonny, Selgovae Princess Nara."

Grond's tone was so low; it was barely discernible when he edged closer, his tickling reddish whiskers whiffing her ear. The brown specks in his tawny eyes twinkled at her in the firelight, a bold invitation in them Nara had difficulty ignoring when thanking him for the offerings.

Heat warmed her when his attention continued; heat which had nothing to do with the flames from the fire. It was not the same warmth that suffused her when Lorcan had sent gazes the previous day. Her embarrassment was merely due to Grond's perseverance…and some measure of bewilderment that almost all the Brigante men she had recently met appeared to find her beddable. The new ones around the fireside notwithstanding, for their stares also appeared interested when she dared raise her eyes to them.

Grond had called her bonny. Not one man at Tarras had ever called her pretty, or comely. The thought she might actually be attractive deepened the heat in her cheeks. Now she believed the men of Tarras had not shunned her because she was undesirable – it rather seemed in their superstitious minds she was still an acolyte of the goddess, and untouchable.

Nara could not prevent a small smile, when the notion of her attraction to the Brigante warriors became clear, but she was careful not to encourage Grond. She looked beyond him to Gyptus, and then to Lorcan.

Lorcan's stare was baleful. Why frown in such a manner? He had ignored her, since she entered the crannog. She had darted glances at him often enough to know, and on the few occasions when their gazes had collided, he had pointedly looked askance.

Reacting to his frown, the smile she bestowed on Grond was not received well by Lorcan, not well at all. Out of the corner of her eye he glowered even more.

"Greetings, Lorcan. It is too long since your father visited us. Is he in good health?" An attractive young woman asked Lorcan as she bent forward to offer him salted fish from a wooden platter, her flirtatious smile for him alone.

A previous lover? Angry it mattered that Lorcan might choose to take up the woman's current invitation, Nara turned more of her attention to Grond...but could not block out Lorcan's reply.

"Good day, Eilidh. My father no longer travels; journeys weary him."

Nara could not stop watching when the woman's hand curled around Lorcan's shoulder and squeezed, the invitation unconcealed in her eyes while she leant down to whisper in his ear. Lorcan laughed and shook his head. Nara was heartened to see the woman melt away when Gyptus claimed Lorcan's attention.

"You have been successful in your revenge?"

"Aye, we have avenged Arian's death." Lorcan's gaze swivelled towards her, his stony gaze discomfiting. "The deed is done, and we go home."

Nara looked away from his penetrating stare. He might be going to his home, but not her if she could prevent it.

"Tully will have great need of your help now," Gyptus replied, his words sober. "It will take all your talents to replace the brother you have lost and continue your own position as negotiator, but I have faith in you, my foster-son. We face death and destruction at the hands of a greater enemy than has been seen before."

Nara felt Gyptus' sour gaze linger on her while she listened to their talk of dire times ahead. When they spoke of the direct threat of Romans marching through Brigante lands, horror made her fists clench against her knees. Her stunned gaze whipped back to stare at Gyptus, willing him to divulge more. The Roman invaders had conquered much more territory than she had realised, and that the treaties between Queen Cartimandua's Southern Brigantes and the Roman Governor had been abandoned lately was distressing news indeed. Her thoughts whirled, her glance rarely straying from Lorcan's features while she absorbed every nuance of his moods. He mesmerised her yet again, skilled in imparting knowledge.

"Roman scouts have passed into our northern domain," Grond told the Garrigill Brigantes. A cry of dismay echoed around the room. "There have been perhaps no more than eight or ten of them, but more than sufficient to glean details about the landscape hereabouts. The Romans value information about the territory before they make offensive surges."

"When did this infiltration occur, Grond?" Lorcan snapped.

Nara thought Lorcan looked ready to hare away immediately. Already attuned, in some way, she felt tension grip his fingers while he drummed them on his thighs.

Grond gestured to a warrior at the far end of the room. "Struan spotted their trail."

"This very morning," Struan informed them, "I was on the high pass, two ridges from where you crossed today, since we

76

have patrolled all the heights for moons now. Movements down near the ford of Cumrue, well to the south-west of our crannogs, caught our attention."

Another warrior spoke up. "Their horses leave tracks much deeper than ours as they have larger, heavier beasts."

Nara felt the gaze of more than one Garrigill warrior swing towards her, not just Lorcan, their regard deeply suspicious. She realised it was the reason Lorcan had been distrustful the previous day. Rowan was a Roman horse. Her heart jolted, and trepidation like she had never before experienced crept over her.

Was that why Lorcan kept her alive? Did he believe her to be a Roman messenger? Her brows crinkled in anger though, mercifully, Struan's update pulled back their attention.

"In the main, they kept themselves hidden from view, but not when they crossed the ford. It is open country there, and we spied them from the peaks. The sun was bright, the sky clear. The glinting metal of their armour and shields flashed way below us."

Apprehension rocked Nara. She had never been so close to Roman presence before. It was dreadful. Insecurity rose even more. If the present company considered her a Roman spy, what would they do? Her gaze dropped to her feet once more.

Chapter Seven

Lorcan noted how the attention of his warriors had shifted to Nara. Though he was convinced she had nothing to do with the Romans, it was not the occasion to discuss how the stallion had been acquired. Her attendance around the fireside was tenuous, and it had been difficult to persuade Gyptus to accord her the status of a princess.

Gyptus remained unconvinced that keeping Nara captive was wise. When told about the future plans he had for Nara, the old chief was even less enamoured. In truth, they were plans that Lorcan was rapidly adapting, on hearing about recent Roman infiltration from Gyptus. It was now imperative that he get his father's agreement, to implement his proposal without delay.

Nara avoided him, continuing to stare at the floor in a sullen manner. He presumed she felt threatened in the company of so many Brigantes, but soon her captivity would be at an end. She must be made to believe his plan would be best for all – not just for her own future.

Lorcan knew a Roman cohort, numbering close to five hundred men, often followed their handful of scouts, when advised of the straightest pathway to forge. Even worse, a whole legion might follow, those numbers easily amassing five thousand men. He was deeply disturbed by either prospect.

"They could still be within our lands. Do they travel northwards?" he asked.

Struan's head shake denied the route. "They journeyed north-west of the Cumrue ford. We sent word to Shea of Ivegill since his settlement is within their sightline."

Lorcan knew Shea, Ivegill being located near the western coastline. Ivegill was not as extensive as Garrigill, but it was an impressive settlement, built well back from substantial coastal defences. Lorcan had no personal liking for the man, but Shea was a sharply astute chief, difficult to drive a bargain with.

Nara's head was bent in a brooding study of the floor, yet he was certain she listened attentively. He turned to Gyptus.

"Disturbing news, Gyptus. They must have approached your lands from the south-west, I deem, for the outposts of Garrigill would surely have spotted them crossing our terrain."

Struan answered. "They may be circling around, information-gathering about our western shores, to the north and south of Ivegill, investigating all the firth openings."

Lorcan glanced again at Nara to gauge her response for they referred to the estuary close to Tarras, which sat on the opposite bank of the firth from Ivegill. Though she must know whom they spoke about, she continued to avert her eyes as soon as he made contact with her, but not before her fingers clenched in tight little fists at her sides.

His annoyance was great, too.

This beautiful woman continued to thwart him, made attempts to run from him at every opportunity. But he would not allow her to flee. Nara's compliance was now crucial to his new plan being successful.

***

Nara observed Gyptus surreptitiously as the warriors speculated about Roman ships making landfall on the western coastline. Gyptus' old eyes were melancholic as the incursion of a scouting party of Romans could only be a foretaste of the evil soon to come. She knew now the hills she had just crossed would be no barrier at all to the Romans if they were set on conquering all in their path. By land and by sea, it did not bear thinking about.

She wondered if her father, Callan, had any idea the Roman scourge could be close to Tarras. As a warrior she would fight to the death to preserve her culture, as indeed would her whole tribe, but they had to know about the menace first. Callan had never included her in his decision-making; she had no idea of how effective his acquisition of information might be. Yet, regardless of her feelings towards her father, it was her tribal duty to bear this new information to them. A new escape attempt must not fail.

When her gaze drifted to Lorcan she realised he had been staring at her. Could he know what she was thinking? Just by regarding her? His expression discerning, he listened to Gyptus, but held her gaze.

That flush started again, but she had to fight it, and escape…had to flee this man's capture and help her own people. Breaking eye contact, she looked to the other Garrigill Brigantes. She would have to outwit them, too.

A soft tap on her shoulder jolted her. It was the young woman who had bid her enter the roundhouse.

"Come," she whispered in Nara's ear.

Unwilling to miss anything important, she hesitated.

The woman assured her. "Their warrior-talk will soon be over, and Lorcan will set off for Garrigill. Water is prepared to refresh you."

Nara followed to an enclosure at the back, separated from the main room by a head-high partition wall of wattled young willow twigs interwoven with reeds.

"I am Lleia." The young woman's declaration was gracious, curiosity in her regard.

Nara was wary, though mindful of manners, when she pointed to the ablutions. "*Tapadh leat*, Lleia."

"No thanks are needed; you are a visitor." Lleia sat on the low cot while Nara washed her face and hands.

"Why do the Garrigill Brigantes look keenly at you, yet do not include you in the conversation? Lorcan insisted you should be seated with us, even though my father is displeased."

Nara used the drying cloth then took the bone comb Lleia held out. Untying her long braids, it was a pleasure to pull the comb through her snagged hair.

Lleia carried on, her grass-green eyes clouded with confusion, even though Nara had not answered. "My father

80

does not normally ignore a high-ranking guest, therefore you must not think ill of him."

"Do not trouble yourself."

Leila's next words were disconcertingly blunt. "What are you to Lorcan?"

Nara had seen Lleia avidly watching him, guessed the woman held him in high regard. "Do you and Lorcan have an understanding, perhaps come Beltane?"

Lleia twiddled the cord at her waist. "I want to pick Lorcan come the Beltane fires, but he shows no interest in me. I am not the woman he seeks."

Curiosity prompted Nara to ask, "Who does he seek?"

Lleia's stare was uncomprehending. "Why do you accompany him?"

Nara drew a long breath. "He took me captive near the ford of Sequanna, after his band had killed men of Raeden to avenge his brother's death."

Lleia looked horrified. "My father invited you to sit with him? Though he must know your prisoner status from Lorcan?"

"I have no answer for you." Nara looked away. "I have no way of knowing what the Brigante plans for me."

"He does not regard you as a prisoner." Jealousy tinged Lleia's words. "Lorcan cannot stop his gaze from devouring you."

"You mistake the situation, Lleia." Inside a tiny glow warmed.

"He watches you with great hunger, Selgovae woman." Lleia looked close to tears.

"What do you mean?"

"Lorcan fostered here when I was very young, but he has never bestowed his favours on me since I came to maturity, yet I long for him to notice me."

Though saddened by the young woman's anguish, Nara revelled in the fact that she had stirred Lorcan's desire the previous day.

Lleia seemed desperate to share information. "Lorcan's first hearth wife died many moons ago, but he has taken no second. My father claims it is because as emissary of his tribe he is rarely at Garrigill and would spend no time with a wife and family. Yet, I know that is only part of the answer."

Lleia looked so disconsolate, her eyes straying to the doorway.

"Only part?"

Lleia attempted a weak smile. "When I was younger – some six summers ago and just after the death of his wife in childbed – Lorcan declared to me that he would only take a new wife to hearth when he found the one woman he truly wanted to mate with for the rest of his life."

"Then Lorcan of Garrigill has waited long for this woman."

"Nay! I hear he is a lusty lover, he does not deny himself the company of a woman, but he has not chosen a wife…till maybe you!"

"Me?" Nara was confused.

"Lorcan lusts after you. I watched from the door. The warriors all look on you favourably, and Lorcan hates it. His glance strayed to you many times though you kept your head down. Do you not like him at all?"

"Lleia, he is my captor." Nara hoped her voice betrayed none of her inner feelings for she could not show a liking for the man who took her prisoner.

"Then he must wish to secure a large ransom from your father."

The hopeful tone in Lleia's voice made Nara wince. Carefully unwinding the binding around her leg, she bathed her wound. Lleia seemed to take the hint; did not press for an answer but bustled around, hanging the drying cloth over the wattle divider.

"Lleia, our destinies lie in the hands of the great goddess."

A strident call from beyond alerted them that Lleia's assistance was urgently needed. Emerging from the stall, Lleia dragged Nara away, clutching her elbow, the conversation of the men briefly interrupted by their departure. Lleia tugged her from the crannog and across the causeway in search of a missing child. Living around water, accidents happened; children tumbled into the depths of the lake, or got into difficulties in the reeds around the settlement. In moments they were into dense plant cover, Lleia hollering for the child, while she parted the tall foliage bordering the pathways.

Nara scanned around. No warriors were nearby. They were still inside the crannog, and she had already bypassed the two sentries at the end of the log causeway. Slowing her steps, pretending to inspect the plant undergrowth for the missing child, she allowed Lleia to get ahead of her. Lleia was soon lost to the undergrowth.

Conscience pricked. Nara knew her actions would get the woman into trouble, but it was imperative to warn the Selgovae at Tarras about the Roman presence. She knew where she had come from, but not where the other paths led to. She retraced her steps. On approach to the smithy roundhouse she cautiously crept forward, needing Eachna to make her escape.

The smith still fashioned metal, the loud ring-ting only barely heard over his booming voice. Creeping around the corner her heart dipped. Two striplings now attended the herd tethered by the horse enclosure – she was not going to easily get past them and flee with Eachna. She backed up to replan. Into a very solid body.

Lorcan's angry rasp at her ear brought her up short. "Nara? You did not intend to leave without me?" His fingers pinched her shoulders while he prized her away from his body. A shiver of apprehension ran through her when he turned her round. Ripping censure assailed her, his condemnation scalding. "Not for one moment did I envisage Lleia would lose track of you. She must be no fit companion for you, or you are too discourteous a guest."

"Do not blame Lleia. She cared well for me." Nara defended the woman as she shrugged out of his grip. "More than you have cared for her needs."

"What do you mean?"

"Lleia was sympathetic to my captive state, Lorcan of the Brigantes; curious also about your future intentions towards me. It appears you have chosen to ignore it, but she has been pining for your attentions and been denied them."

Nara flinched when his fingers trapped her shoulders yet again. His grip tightened, almost shaking her, his eyes clouding with an annoyance bordered on resignation. "I have told Lleia many times she will never be the woman of my heart, but that she will always be a sister to me."

Confrontational glares were exchanged for long moments before Lorcan turned from her to give terse orders to his band now approaching the horses.

Nara was incensed. Yet again a chance to escape had been foiled. Antipathy burned. She was worthless and disgusted with herself for it seemed she could not escape this Brigante. And deep in her heart she was torn. She was still so drawn to this man who was all wrong for her...this warrior who held her future in his grasp. And maybe now the future of her tribe as well.

"Mount!"

The order blasted in her ear when Lorcan jostled her towards Eachna. Surrounded by Brigantes, Nara again had no option but to do as commanded, even less sure of her situation after talking to Lleia. Lorcan had barely mouthed a word to her since early morning. Now, it was exasperation that drove him when he grasped her legs and tied her down once again, handling her as little as possible, his gaze daring her to challenge him further. Resistance was a token gesture as a vehement protest would lead to more ridicule, and she had had quite enough of that from the bystanders around them.

Grond was a surprise, his smile inviting. "I will think fondly of you, till we meet again, Princess Nara, maybe even before Beltane, as by then we will know just how close our association will be." His intent regard gave the impression he was party to information she was not aware of, his hand lightly grasping hers, his long fingers lingering. "I would have you think well of me at the Beltane fires soon to come."

Nara snatched her hand away, confused by his overt declaration.

In silence the band set off for Garrigill, as before with Nara and Lorcan at the rear, Nara humiliated by the leg tether since many more people were seeing it.

Some time later, they stopped by a ford to water the horses, all the warriors having tried riding Rowan. The last one to ride the stallion called over to Lorcan when they sat on large stones by the riverside and drank of the pure clear water.

"Though Roman, this is a fine animal. A worthwhile capture, Lorcan, he will breed some powerful stock. It is a pity you do not have a fine mare of the same breed to mate with him." Nara felt his eyes straying towards her, his mouth twisted with sarcasm, a husky and grating laugh accompanying it. "But then, you have acquired another female…"

Her embarrassment was acute as she sat tied in place.

"Come!" Lorcan's mouth was as a thin cord, when he loosened her leg restraint. Meeting resistance, his tone moderated, but only marginally. "Do not fear, no harm will come to you, but we must talk." He pulled her down to her feet and gathered the reins of their horses before turning to his men. "Continue to Garrigill, and take the extra horse with you."

Nara heard ribald comments so low they were almost not discernible, and lewd chortles accompanied the band's departure.

Lorcan dragged her with him when he strode along the riverside, the vegetation low and easy to walk on till he stopped at an old willow blocking the way, so gnarled and twisted it provided a natural seat. Tapping the wood, his tone was brusque.

"Be seated, Nara!"

Belligerence rippled through her till an exasperated sigh passed his lips. Smoothing back a straying lock of black hair his dark eyes requested rather than commanded.

"Nara, sit. You have my word I will not hurt you." The black centre of his eyes darkened even more and widened while he paced around. "I do not wish anyone's words, or deeds, to wound you, but it will happen unless matters are made clear. My warrior has difficulty riding alongside you. He is a healthy man with healthy appetites." Lorcan sought her compliance, his candour disturbing her. "He cannot understand my motives. As a captive, he believes you should be available to any man to slake their lust on, and is annoyed I deny him. He is even more confused by recent events."

Nara watched him stare off into the distance, his pacing halted.

"Recent events? What do you want of me, Brigante? What are your intentions?" Her forthright questions seemed to startle him as he turned, taken aback, his brows raised.

"You are a chief's daughter. That is a good bargaining tool." Lorcan strode back and reached for her hands. Ignoring her protests and slaps to evade him, he held them tight.

***

Lorcan had been thinking long and hard about what to do with her once they reached Garrigill. Since knowing her princess status he had planned a positive method of using her abduction, the recent conversation with Gyptus' warriors making him decide to speed up the process. Now, he needed Nara to believe in his plan.

"Nay, Brigante." Slapping at his arms, Nara of Tarras' manner was unyielding. "You are mistaken. Callan will not negotiate."

"Why continue this pretence? You hold high status in your tribe."

"Callan of Tarras will not bargain."

Her jaw was so set, her voice almost to shouting level. The vehemence could not be faked, but Lorcan was not ready to take her at her word just yet. He maintained his level tone. "Then I will know the truth. There is much you have not told me."

"In that you are correct."

Nara jumped up and stomped off, gaining little ground before he snaked his arm around her shoulders. Pushing him away, her chide was as brutal as the sharp blades flashing from her eyes, her mouth whipcord lean.

"You declared you would not touch me. You are just like your warriors."

"Aye, but I am the one who prevents them from accosting you."

Nara's furious face held his attention for a moment before he continued. "Perhaps I am wrong? It may be you would not deem their advances unasked for?"

Lorcan loathed that she misunderstood his motives. Restraining his anger, he sought to explain his reasoning.

"You are a temptation, Nara. They must believe they cannot have you because I deem it so. That gives you a measure of safety."

His fingers tightened around her shoulders when her resistance to his grasp intensified. She looked bewildered; fighting against passions which seemed as strong as his. He felt her trembles against his fingers, Her eyes beseeched...though, exactly what she sought from him he was not sure. However, he was certain that her intuitive response matched his, a tide of something inexplicable flowing from him to her, and back again. "Soon I will bargain with your father. He may not like the negotiations, but I will make him accept them."

Nara's expression scathed when she broke away from him. A cynical laugh rang out, biting in its severity. "Your own father, Tully, will like your bargain even less. You are indeed deluded if you believe your father will deal with the Selgovae."

"Tully may not like it, but I will make him accept it too." He challenged her to refute.

"What makes you so confident, Brigante? I will have some choice over my future." Defiance sparked from every part of her as she tossed back her braids, squirming from his renewed grip, but he held firm.

"A woman of choice? You are not, and you have none." His eyes traced every one of her features. "You must accept the bargain I will make with your father."

"So certain, Brigante? Show me proof that the gods have willed your plan." She stared open-mouthed at him when he bent his head to kiss her. Still resistant, Nara jerked her chin away from him.

"You may deem it so, but I demand to have some say in the future you talk so lightly of." Rebellion continued, scathing disdain colouring her tone. "Not everyone appears to have the same plan as you do. Grond spared no time in telling me he would like me to choose him at Beltane, so why do you insist my future lies in your hands?"

"Ahh! Now we have it." Lorcan stepped back, relaxing the tight grip on her shoulders. "You have as good as admitted that you will seek a mate at Beltane, but I will know why the lover will be your first. Tell me, Nara, for I wish you to reveal your secrets." Disdain marred her pretty features, but he ignored it. "You want proof of my plan, Nara? That I alone will seal your fate?"

"Give me proof, then, of this ridiculous plan of yours."

His lips dropped to hers, gently seeking a response that Nara refused to give. She remained stiff in his embrace, keeping her lips firmly closed, her eyes screwed shut, though he knew too well she was infuriated by his presumptions. Secrets had to be unlocked, and he would do what was necessary to make that happen. It was imperative he gain her compliance. To befuddle he used his tongue to break her resistance. She could not resist him for long; he could feel the change creep upon her. Need roared, a sensation he had never before experienced with any other woman. He travelled his lips up to her ear, whispering against her skin.

"Why do you imagine I must be last in line, Nara? Leader of the band at the back? Have you not thought that strange?"

He was not entirely sure why, but she no longer kicked out at him, or scratched, or bit…and she had just as much trouble breathing as he did.

"My warriors must be in front of you, not behind. You are too much of an enticement for them to constantly view."

Chapter Eight

Nara was in turmoil. Presumptions about her future made her exasperated. Lorcan seeming so convinced he was correct angered her even more. She had made a firm decision that a joining with a warrior must only happen at Beltane, with the correct lover for her future to be assured.

"I do not wish this…Brigante!" Her denial seeped into his mouth.

Lorcan's answer was uncompromising. He tightened his grip. "Aye, woman, you do! You are as drawn to me as I am to you."

It was not yet Beltane. Could she learn some ways of lovemaking from Lorcan before she made her Beltane choice? She was curious to find out what had been denied her for years. Maybe she would only ever find satisfaction from Lorcan's touch and no other? If so, she must snatch at that happiness now as he could not be her lifelong mate, yet something stopped her and made her think beyond the moment. "Nay…Lorcan!" Her feeble protest was muffled in her squirming. "I…cannot…"

Still clutching her, Lorcan's voice was a determined oath. "You are right. This is not yet the time for us. But I vow, Nara of Tarras, your father must like the bargain I make with him."

Her heart thundered guiltily as she spoke words she knew to be false. "That was a grave mistake you have just made. It must never happen again."

"It will be better between us when we are truly joined."

"By Rhianna, you are deluded. That will never happen."

Clearly, he had no idea why the notion annoyed her so greatly. Somehow she had to dissuade Lorcan from his intentions. "I will not be your bargaining tool with my father. My future will be different." She stalked away from him back

89

toward the horses, well aware Lorcan was angry at her change of attitude.

"Nara, stop!" His imperative voice halted her. "If you go back now, and catch up with my warriors, any one of them will take you – maybe even all – because I will remain here."

Nara was horrified but could not let him know how his words affected her.

"Could it be another of my warriors you would choose? I do not think so. I have watched you. You have looked at no other man with intent. You deftly ignore all the signals my brother sends you, and you shrink back when Soveran leers at you."

Nara held her breath. Soveran, the warrior with many scars, did alarm her. The anxiety she had felt had not a thing to do with how well he displayed his battle wounds but all to do with the unkind gleam shining in his regard. She sensed Soveran was not a man who dealt well with women.

"Mark my words, if they believe I no longer want you they will be upon you in a blink. If they believe you are mine they will ignore you. It is also the only answer when we attain Garrigill."

The truth of it Nara knew already but was not prepared to meekly submit.

"I hear you, Brigante, but I am no bargain. You will get not a thing for me." She allowed the bleakness she felt to be visible to Lorcan. "It seems my fate is sealed according to you, but I have a better notion of my destiny than you have. This captivity is but a temporary lull."

To her surprise Lorcan looked almost impressed by her frankness, her words appearing to please him. This she did not understand for she had rejected him. Yet though resigned to her immediate situation, her sarcasm spilled forth.

"May we go? It seems I must follow where you lead. I must show eagerness to see the future you order for me."

Before he had a chance to humiliate her with the leg binding, she held her hands outstretched, crossed at the wrists and ready for tying, her expression challenging him to do otherwise.

Lorcan's booming laugh was unexpected, tinged as it was with appreciation, as well as humour. "Then mount first, my accommodating Selgovae captive. That will save me the effort of loading you onto the horse."

Glare for glare Nara was on the filly and tied in a blink, and then, both reins fisted securely, Lorcan set the horses into motion.

"I will make a good bargain with Callan of Tarras, whether, or not, you believe it can happen. But for now, there are things you must know about Tully."

His tone was impassioned, while they crossed the ford. Spurring on the horses, he picked up the pace as they cantered across flat ground. "My father is distressed by my brother's death. He is old and weak from a wasting disease, no longer fit to guide our tribe and needs replaced soon, but though he knows it to be a fact, as yet he refuses to accede."

The sadness in his voice touched her, but Nara refused to mark its relevance. "Your father is nothing to me."

"He will be. Listen and heed." His command sought her co-operation. "My brother Arian was two winters older than me. Our clan held him in high esteem, and he was likely to replace my father at the coming Beltane rites. Certainly well before the Brigante High Council, at Samhain, when the weather turns cold and frost sets in."

Empathising with his genuine sadness, Nara's response was careful. "I had nothing to do with Arian's death. I commiserate, but I did not know him."

"That you listen is all I ask." Riveting looks relayed his strength of purpose. "Now is a time when all tribes of the north, who speak a common Celtic tongue, must work together. The Brigantes confederation is large in numbers, and we are spread over a huge area, but it is vital we join forces with other tribes to repel the Roman threat. That means we must make peace with our neighbours, even though it seems contrary to our usual habits."

"You seek the impossible, Lorcan." Her answer was derisive, but she needed him to appreciate she was not fooled into believing him. "How do you expect to achieve peace? We have been enemies for time immemorial, yet you expect accord at your command."

"It must not be impossible, Nara. We must join forces. It is the only solution for our whole way of life to be safeguarded. We must be in accord, standing together, when we confront the Romans."

Lorcan's voice rose dangerously, passion flaring with every utterance. Firm fortitude set his features in a grim mask, yet Nara found she was not cowed by it; rather she was impressed by his stubborn persistence. The man was indeed a worthy enemy. Lorcan slowed their horses to a walk when they skirted the edge of a forest.

"We have no time to waste, Nara. They march on us even now."

"Though you ignored me, I listened well to your talk with Gyptus. Your warriors brace themselves for conflict with the Romans, but I heard no mention of your plans for allying yourself with tribes such as the Selgovae." She shook her head remembering her failed attempt to pass on the information to her father. "There was no talk of making peace with my tribe, but now you tell me these ambitious plans of yours." Her voice rose, agitation mounting. "I am your enemy, yet I seem to be told more of your plans than your faithful warriors. Why me, and why now?"

Lorcan looked as exasperated as she felt. "What you say is not true. I discussed this with Gyptus and the other warriors when you were with Lleia. Nara, do you not see we are the answer?"

"The answer to what? Now you have lost me, Lorcan. Explain!"

"Explain?" The strain again building up between them was broken by his sudden laughter. His voice mimicked her terse tones. "Now you speak like a true Selgovae princess. I will explain, but first make me understand why your father holds you worthless."

Nara stared ahead feeling her jaw lock, unwilling to answer him. Yet, when Lorcan's tone softened, it was difficult to maintain resistance.

"You protest this fervently, Nara. Make me understand."

If he had commanded she would not have, but the appeal in his voice broke down her reserve. Still, she procrastinated.

"Say what you will first, Lorcan."

They rode out of the forest onto a flat plain. His silent scrutiny confused her; so much she felt heated all over, and eventually she was the one to break contact. Ahead of them she could see the warrior-band approaching a small hamlet, on the foothills of higher ground. He followed her eyes when she surveyed the land.

"The main settlement of Garrigill is over that hill. A short while only to ride; we must come to an understanding before we reach my father's house."

"An understanding?" Suspicious, but that was how she felt.

"You and I must make peace, then all else will follow, you must see that is our only course."

Nara's lips pursed in annoyance. "I do not see it is the only course at all, Brigante. Perhaps Tully of Garrigill will not be of your judgment. It may be he will not wish to be so closely associated with his enemies of old. Maybe he will think his son's wits have become addled. Have you considered that? You do not speak for all of your tribe."

"I do not know how my father will take my proposals, but we need action to benefit our whole Celtic race of peoples."

Looking at his solemn countenance Nara knew without doubt he was serious about his ideas. What harm would it do to tell him of recent weeks? There was little chance of escape from this powerful man riding beside her. Her father could not easily broach Brigante territory to release her – not that he would do so anyway.

She glanced over at the man riding alongside, this time surveying him critically, much to his amusement. Lorcan was a fine warrior, even though he was her captor, and the man who had saved her from life-threatening hazards.

Telling him her tale of woe would make little difference to her situation, and she had to make him understand why he was deluded about her worth. She felt the need to be fair about that.

"Are you ready to listen? You want to know why I am worthless in your bargaining scheme. Are you prepared to have your mind changed for you?"

"I do not think I will be changing my mind, Nara, but I will hear what you have to say."

***

"I am Callan's first born child."

Lorcan could not miss the bitter tone that accompanied Nara's tale, the recall seeming to pain her.

"My father was disenchanted for he desperately wanted a son."

"A man always wants a son, but your father must have loved you?"

"You could not be more wrong."

He wondered who could not love this woman. She must have been a comely child to be so striking now. A strident laugh prefaced the rest of her story…and the bitterness continued.

"My father's first wife, Brynna, was barren, but since he loved her, he kept her as his only wife for seven turns of the sun's calendar. He married my mother as a second wife, though he had no love for her. She was very young, and he already five and twenty summers. I came to the world the winter after their marriage."

Lorcan felt Nara's pain as she related her tale. Drawing a deep sigh, determination sharpened her voice, her eyes reflecting something he could not really understand.

"Obsessed with the need for sons, he ignored me from birth. My mother blamed me for his manner and also neglected me. If Brynna had not been still at my father's hearth, I would have died of neglect, regardless of my princess status. She removed me to her sister's roundhouse and looked after me there."

A well-loved son of Tully, as all his siblings were, Lorcan could not comprehend how it could be that a father did not love his child.

94

"As I grew older the very sight of me irked Callan, though Brynna made sure that happened seldom. I remember the feeling of rejection, not something I could ever forget."

He interrupted, aware that the stress of sharing her upbringing caused deep frown lines at her brow. "You dredge up unhappy memories, you need not continue."

"Listen, Brigante! So there is no misunderstanding over my worth to Callan. When I was five winters my brother was born."

She attempted a weak smile, a harsh laugh ringing out.

"Callan at last had a son, and for a long time I never ever saw him. Brynna kept me well away, but she died when I was seven winters."

"What happened then?"

"Barely one moon after Brynna's death, Swatrega – our High Priestess – came to my father. She had seen in the entrails that my future lay as a priestess. I was whisked off, forthwith, to live with the priestesses on the sacred island *nemeton*."

Nara's laugh was triumphant, yet to Lorcan the desperation in her beautiful blue eyes was too revealing. His heart lurched at her revelations, making him pause before he could continue for the implications were dire.

"Then, you are an acolyte?"

"My story is not yet done."

Lorcan was desperate to confirm this woman truly was not promised to the goddess.

"My father and mother rejoiced to see me go."

Nara pulled up her horse and silently beseeched the skies as he reined his own. When she bowed her head she barely kept tears at bay. Their glints hovered on her shiny brown lashes. He wanted to kiss away every unhappy tear and give her joyful memories for the future. Dismounting, he pulled her down, enfolded her, and for long moments held her close stroking her hair, aware her story was not yet done, though she stood tensed in his grip.

Gradually, Nara slid free of him, her lips trembling when she tried to jest. "My last comforter was fairer of face than you. I have not cried since I was a young child: warrior-maidens learn not cry."

His finger under her chin raised her face so that he could see her better, while he sought to chase off her misery. "Who was fairer of face than me?"

"Brynna was beautiful, in features and heart."

He watched her draw in a huge breath to compose herself, squaring her chin firmly, her eyes self-deriding.

"You would not believe it of me, but two moons ago I never would have lost control, or done the things you have seen me do."

The sardonic tone crept back into her voice, and he was glad; the warrior-woman he was gaining respect for returned. Resignation flashed when she grinned at him and drew her chin aside.

"I am well now."

"I see that." He remained close, though she no longer needed his support.

"Now hear the end, Brigante." Harebell-blue eyes glistened with humour as she continued. "I grew up believing I was destined for the priesthood."

"What prevented it?"

Since Nara's hands were still tied he flipped her up onto her horse before he remounted.

"By the time my seventeenth winter passed I was ready for the priestess rites, but for another four winters Swatrega delayed my initiation ceremony, always finding a credible reason. Then she called me to her two moons ago."

The harshness of her words surprised him, her expression a rueful one as she settled on the horse's back. "You were no longer to be a priestess?"

Her nod confirmed his guess. "A new premonition denied the priesthood."

"She informed Callan?"

"Aye, with undue haste. I was banished from the *nemeton*; denied access to that sacred island that had been my home for nigh on ten and four winters." Nara's voice hardened, her gaze glittering with hurt tears while she huffed her disgust.

"My mother died of a wasting sickness some time past, so I was once again my father's responsibility."

Lorcan looked at the set of her mouth and her deeply repressed rage.

"Before the expulsion, my father had begun to have some toleration of me. Not respect – never that – or any softening of feelings, but I was an apt pupil for the priesresshood, so eager to learn. My clan deemed me useful. As a healer I treated their ailments and counselled them in other matters."

Her eyes gazed reflectively into the distance though he guessed she saw none of the surroundings.

"And as a princess I was given warrior's training. You may laugh now, Brigante, but in this I excelled."

Her triumphant crowing hid inner despair.

"I took my place among the warriors when we trained. I learned well to defend our priestess *nemeton*, and the larger territory of the Tarras settlement, but that did not stop you from capturing me." She mocked further, her eyes a glittering blue. "My life is littered with failures."

"Nara, you demean yourself." His authoritative tone brought her up sharp. "You could not have prevented me from taking you captive."

"Do I believe that, Brigante?" Her eyes searched his, he guessed seeking his assent. "I would not have been taken two moons ago. I would have killed you, or died in the attempt."

Knowing her sense of worth was broken, he pressed her to move on from her gloomy declarations. "Continue."

"My father deems me a failure. Of course you will wonder why that should trouble me, since he has a son to train for the future."

At his nod she carried on. Having a younger brother should have made her rank and position less of a burden, but it did not appear so.

"The goddess does not always look favourably on everyone. A breathing disease has always wracked my brother. I am a healthy encumbrance Callan does not want, and he has a sickly son he does not want either." Lorcan heard resignation oozing from her. "Since my expulsion I am only allowed menial tasks. My skills as a healer are no longer required. My father never invites me to his hearth, to sit at council, or to any gatherings. He banished me from the training field."

"That may explain your rusty skills?" He now understood better why the boar had defeated her. Nara's shrug was an acceptance of truth when she continued.

"Do you understand now why my father will be glad to know I am gone? He will not bargain one grain of emmer for me."

They bypassed a small hamlet, the inhabitants out working the fields. Greetings were exchanged, but Lorcan did not stop to talk. Nara's story tied up many ends. It explained her reaction to events, her maidenhead, it clarified why – though a strong woman – hesitation had caused her distress and confusion. Guilt settled over him for it seemed he had compounded her problems by capturing her.

"Explain the reason for you being where I found you?" His question was abrupt, but he wanted everything made clear.

"Callan reluctantly agreed with our Council of Nobles that I needed a bodyguard, even though I begged not to have one. The elders safeguarded my princess status, reminding my father of his duties to me." Derisive laughter pealed out before she carried on. "For years I roamed the land freely, responsible only to myself and the priestesses. Can you imagine what it feels like to have that curtailed? Can you imagine what I feel like as your prisoner?" Her gaze dropped to her bound hands.

Lorcan understood the new lifestyle forced upon her must have been grim to accept and regretted he had removed her decision making even further. "The bodyguard…"

"Cearnach's wife is my only friend. My life has taken different turns, but it has also been so for my clan. They have had to regard me in a different way, and the new situation has been equally hard for them."

"After all this you can be magnanimous, Nara?"

Her feelings were obvious while she sought to exonerate her tribe. He found even more to admire in his captive.

"You know an acolyte is not perceived in the normal way. Now, the women cannot talk to me. They have no wish to offend, but they may no longer rely on me to help them with their personal problems. As an acolyte I listened; I helped them pray; suggested ideas for a solution."

A blush flooded her cheeks. He smiled, remembering how eager she had been to learn the ways of making love.

"Because you do not have practical experience does not mean you do not have some knowledge, Brigante."

"I must agree." The whole idea amused him. "Continue."

"I now understand the attitude of the women since I have been taken captive. Your men look at me with sexual intent; see me as a woman they want to mate with."

Lorcan knew his expression would appear wry, for he intended it to be so. "It is because you are beautiful. They do not view every woman in the same way."

"I understand now that the women of my tribe regard me a potential rival. I am in a position to choose one of their husbands to bed me, and they do not like it…or me. I am despised and avoided by all, with the exception of Cearnach's wife who has remained true."

No rejoinder came to his lips which would soothe her ruffled feelings. Listening to her story had made him want to bring back the competent warrior-maiden he was sure she must have been, but he held back from touching her. She needed to regain self-respect, but could he give her that? Considering he had captured her and taken her prisoner?

Hatred of all those culpable for her mistreatment nurtured in his breast, along with a fierce protection, unable as he was to quell the growing feelings of rage he felt for the weaknesses her father showed.

"Why were you near Raeden?" The last part of her tale needed to be pieced together.

"I needed freedom." Nara's satirical chuckle was a delicious tinkle when her humour surfaced, though he suspected she chose her words very carefully. "I had to be away from the stifling confinement of the tribe, and I was as curious as everyone else about the Roman advances."

He frowned. "Why would you visit Raeden for news of the Romans?"

"A druid from the south was expected there a se'nnight ago. My clan was heavily involved in battle rehearsals, to sharpen their skills, so I volunteered." The derisive tinge to her laugh did not escape his notice. "My father acquiesced."

A deep sigh of disgust escaped, and her lips pursed. "I was not intended to hear, but he told one of the elders if I chanced upon a Roman legion, then it would make no difference to him…I was expendable."

"Your father actually voiced those words?" Lorcan had never been so angry. How could a father treat his offspring so badly?

"Aye, I heard the words, Brigante, but he also insisted I take Cearnach with me. His reasoning, of course, was two-fold. Cearnach accompanying me would appease the elders, and Callan had decided to send the stallion to Rigg. He had heard that Rigg might have a mare of similar breed to mate with. "A huge sigh slipped free. "Now I wish it had been otherwise."

"Do not despair." He found himself hating to view her despondency.

"There is a rare healing herb I had collected on one of my previous visits to the Sacred Groves. I knew it to grow somewhere around where you found me, but I had trouble locating it. I insisted I be left to search while Cearnach watered the horses. I disturbed the slumbering boar…and you know what happened after that…" A rosy blush flooded her cheeks.

Their gazes locked and held. Lorcan felt the breath rush from him as quickly as the blood coursed to his groin. He remembered all too well the feeling of almost being inside this now very intriguing woman. And wanted it again.

"That explains why I found you alone." His voice was a croaked whisper. Knowing her background made him sure he was about to make the correct decisions for the future. "I am glad you have told me your story, Nara of Tarras; it makes more sense now."

Nara's voice was sarcastic. "I am pleased for you, Brigante! I do not think anything happening to me makes sense at all."

"Come, Nara, look to the future. Not the past."

Lorcan made his tone resolute, but the conversation was over. He needed to think on all she had told him.

They continued over the high spur where riding alongside each other was impossible. The rain started; low cloud a menacing blanket around them. At first it was lightly dripping but gained in strength till soon they were saturated. A boost to the spirits was needed, for both of them. Loud clearing of his throat gained her attention.

"Not long now. We will soon be home."

Nara's regard was one he could not interpret. She looked dismal, not a surprise given the drenching rain, but he regretted that she was unhappy on account of him.

Chapter Nine

Garrigill - Brigantes Territory

"Garrigill lies ahead."

Lorcan appeared eager about reaching Garrigill, but Nara was not feeling anything like he did. He returned home.

She was a woman of no choice.

Emerging from the tree line, they were still high enough to survey the land around. Casting her eyes across the landscape, she appreciated the earth mother's creation. It truly was a magnificent sight.

In the distance, lay the largest hillfort she had ever seen. The valley floor and hillside fringes were well cleared of trees, the lower slopes heavily cultivated, tilled ready for planting. Many people would need to work in the fields below to sustain the huge community. The defensive position of Garrigill was perfect – for the Brigantes who lived there.

Not for an enemy.

Looking to rescue a captive.

A large adversary force would have great difficulty sneaking in undetected anywhere around the valley. Hills surrounded the huge basin, densely forested to the tree line, above which were heather clad peaks – excellent vantage points for protective scrutiny. She had no doubt Lorcan's band had already been spied by sentries.

A wide meandering river snaked along the valley floor providing a source of water and no doubt plentiful fish. The sun, now breaking through the clouds, made the recent downpour sparkle on the verdant green below, the heathers above the tree line a contrasting vibrant purple. The varying browns of the roundhouse wattles, and thatched roofs

102

contrasted with the grey-white smoke gently drifting upwards, coming through the tightly woven plant materials.

"Do you see peace and productivity below, Nara?"

A serene haven, aye, but it was not hers. The thought of no home was wearying; of a sudden she was physically and spiritually in need.

The closest hamlet of roundhouses, minimally fortified with a single palisade of upright timbers, were the homes of nearby field workers. Repetitions of such hamlets dotted themselves around the fringes of the valley, but the main settlement of Garrigill lay centrally, built on a low hillock.

"Garrigill's triple ditches and mounds are well constructed, do you not think?"

Nara deemed them virtually impenetrable. A sturdy timber palisade completely encircled and protected the inner living areas. Roundhouses of differing sizes, perhaps hundreds of them, lay behind the timber walls. Each one would house a large family. Garrigill was three times as large as Tarras, and much more difficult to breach with a raiding party.

Her harsh laugh made Lorcan look at her uncertainly. "Very few of Tully's enemies would be so foolhardy to attack such defences. I am of a mind to think, if combat goes on here, then it must only be between the champions of the tribes involved?"

"That does not happen often." Pride in Garrigill shone like a high sun on a hot summer's day.

At this point Nara accepted her lot. Yet, to despair was futile: a waste of her valuable energy. No Selgovae would rescue her easily, if they ever chose to come at all, and the likelihood of her making a successful escape attempt, very bleak indeed.

Still, she could not forget a few Selgovae warriors had recently breached one of Garrigill's outposts, had breached and killed Arian, who had been riding the outskirts ensuring all was well with the outlying Garrigill Brigantes.

The high ditches of the main hillfort slowed their access progress when they aimed for the entry tunnel where Lorcan held Eachna still. She bristled, thinking he meant to humiliate her by leading her horse in. Those sensuous deep brown eyes of his looked so serious. Why did the man have to confuse her so much?

"No. That is not why I hold you still. I go in with a Selgovae princess. Show them your worth. I may take in a captive, but do not forget your rank, since it is indeed your future."

He looked confident of her compliance when he flipped her rein towards her. His sober regard gave her nothing but respect, very persuasive, as she guessed he intended it to be. It soothed the rough edges of her captivity – a little.

"I alone know your story. Do you understand? No one else should know the extent of it yet. Heed my words, you must be accorded the rank you richly deserve and have been denied."

She was doubtful, suspecting motives he did not reveal to her at present, though she felt she knew him sufficiently to know she would find out ere long.

"I will do as you bid. There is little hope of escape, but my destiny does not lead to the otherworld yet."

"Nay, it does not. Of that I am certain. Now we must speak of other matters." He dug his heels into his own mount setting it in motion while she followed alongside.

"In my father's roundhouse there has been no woman since the passing over of my mother two Samhain's ago. Women tend daily to his needs. Tully's body is pain-ridden though he does not admit it, the smallest task giving him untold misery."

Lorcan's deep brown eyes displayed the sorrow she had seen before when he had talked of the death of his brother, his chin firm.

"Only Brennus and I live in Tully's roundhouse. Gabrond, born after me, lives with his wife and family at the eastern end of the settlement. My youngest brothers Calmach and Rhyss are fostered at distant clanholds. My two sisters are likewise fostered elsewhere since my mother passed over."

"Why do you tell me this?"

Lorcan's expression was taut, his words clipped. "I cannot expect you to join me at my father's hearth immediately. I do not know what Tully might plan for you, but I will make sure your rank is accounted for. You may perhaps be forlorn, at first, but do not try to escape."

His flecked gaze was fierce. Nara could see he was in the grip of some strong emotion again. "I am not so foolish, Brigante. I see the position and strength of your clanhold. And besides, you still have my weapons. Otherwise, my escape attempts might have been more successful."

His talk angered her, made her feel an encumbrance he now did not want since her bargaining power was non-existent.

"The only reason?" His chortles startled her. Her lips were soon twitching in answer since he was not inclined to believe her boast for one moment, but she would not allow herself to laugh along with him.

"No, you are not foolish, and by the god Taranis, I make you a promise. Your situation will improve."

She watched the warmth in his eyes increase, his assurance bringing that instinctual awareness.

Though encouraged by the thoughts he provoked, Nara was not willing he should believe she acquiesced too easily to his demands. Yet, he had given her a very needy gift – restored conviction could be worth something. Her chin shrugged up, her eyes challenging. "You do assume much for my future."

Lorcan's regard did not falter. Confidence sparkled and remained while they wended through the twisting entrances designed to make it difficult for raiders to enter the settlement, but he said nothing in answer. Instead he greeted many people, returning their shouts and welcomes.

She rode silently alongside, a spectacle to be stared at. Some of the observations were merely curious; others directly malevolent. Although Lorcan did not hold her rein she felt a captive.

Again resentment against her treatment stirred furious feelings, an almost permanent frown across her brows.

Inside the innermost gates, a large crowd had gathered near the horse enclosure. Rowan was being much admired, men clapping the warriors heartily, congratulating them on their prize. No riches had been expected from the raid on Raeden, the acquisition consequently a welcome surprise. When Lorcan drew up near the enclosure, two young striplings rushed forward to tend to their horses.

"Come, Princess Nara of the Selgovae!" The command was for all to hear, as he tugged her down and made swift work of removing her wrist bindings. "Tully awaits us."

Striding ahead, he left her no choice but to follow in his wake. Ignoring the stares of the crowds eagerly watching their progress, Nara concentrated on her surroundings. The biggest roundhouse she had ever seen stood before her, far more impressive than her own father's.

"My father ails, but you can see that he rises to welcome me home. He will come to welcome you, though do not look for a courtesy at present since he grieves for my brother and blames all Selgovae."

Lorcan strode forward to greet Tully, who was bowed and stooped over a wooden cromach.

"*Athair! Ciamar a tha thu?*"

"Well enough, my son."

Tully's body displayed the ravages of protracted illness, nevertheless, though the chief's frame was frail, she perceived piercing blue eyes encased in a face of strong character. His regard for her was mistrustful, Nara guessing Brennus had forewarned him of her coming. The old chief granted her a brief, intense stare.

"Come, Lorcan, sustenance awaits us." Ignoring her, Tully beckoned his son inside.

Hesitating at the low tunnel entrance, for the second time that day she felt adrift like a bobbing coracle.

Would Lorcan have his wishes taken into consideration? He was not chief here, and Nara had a deep mistrust of fathers. She wondered if Tully would even listen to his son, far less accept the scheme he intended to put forward.

Tully's greeting was unconventional when his bark reached her though he had moved through the entrance tunnel.

"Woman, do not dawdle. My son does not haul you shackled to Garrigill. That tells me he regards you as no commonplace prisoner. You will enter now."

As she went through the entryway, Nara thought of the tethering Lorcan had subjected her to the day before; and of the band around her hands he had just removed. A small smile was repressed, but, in truth, she was not leashed now. Except maybe by something still misunderstood that bound her emotions to him.

Tully's voice was forbidding when he recovered sufficient breath to continue, the awkward angle of his head menacing as his old eyes raked her from hair to feet. "I am not so sure as my son you should be welcomed, but he is normally of sound judgment, and I trust him. We will eat, and afterwards you and I will talk, but for now you will say nothing."

Nara moved towards Lorcan who seated himself by the fire set in the roundhouse centre where a gently bubbling cauldron sent a faint steam trail up into the roof beams. A smith of veritable worth had painstakingly created the carved iron tripod from which the cauldron hung. Tully pointed to a low wooden stool set next to the most ornately carved one around the fireside. The carved one clearly belonged to the chief for it was raised a little higher than the others and was heaped with a pile furs for better comfort.

"Sit there!"

Tully's tone was menacing as his old gnarled finger pointed. When she hesitated a moment his voice demanded even more. "I will tolerate no refusal. You will sit alongside me, or I will order you lashed to that pole."

She knew which pole he referred to, though the old man did not even look towards it, as she slipped down into place between the chief and Lorcan. Brennus placed himself at Tully's other side.

"Carn!" Tully's bellow was particularly strident, and Nara wondered if that was the only tone of voice he ever used.

A young woman entered the roundhouse. Lifting wooden bowls from the fireside, she ladled thick broth from the cauldron into them, before uncovering recently baked flat bread. Tearing chunks from it she served Tully first, Lorcan and then Brennus.

Turning towards Nara she hesitated.

"Give the woman food, Carn. She has come a long way since yestre'en. Feed her."

Nara returned the young woman's smile, hoping it revealed some empathy with Carn's plight. Captives would not normally be brought to the hearth of the chief in this fashion. Dipping her bread to the thick vegetable and barley broth, she savoured the food.

"Thank you, Carn. Go." Tully's bark was to be obeyed. After Carn exited he turned to Lorcan.

"Brennus gave me the latest updates on the Roman scouts. Grave news indeed that they infringe on our territory. Border watches of our stronghold have been increased, just in case you ask, my son. I am not so weary I am unable to see to our defences."

Nara looked to Lorcan to see how he took Tully's brusque rebuke. Lorcan's face was impassive, listening only, adding nothing.

Tully fired on regardless, in spite of his laboured breathing. "Other plans we make tonight with the Council of Nobles."

She felt his pointed stare before the old chief continued. It was not hatred, but neither was it friendly.

"Now tell me of yestreen's deeds. I would know it all."

Between mouthfuls of the nourishing food, Lorcan related his band's attack at Raeden. The food she had eaten lay heavily in her stomach. Lorcan had not spoken of Cearnach. Sat in between them as she listened she was aware of Tully rubbing his lower back; aware of his valiant attempt to mask the grimace of pain torturing him. She had seen such ache before and knew of healing herbs which might alleviate some of the discomfort. From his posture and winces she believed Tully was being given no soothing remedy. It was not her place to impart such knowledge, yet it gave her satisfaction to know she could help the man.

Tully's head nodding and crackled tones betrayed his grief as he continued. "My son, Arian, is avenged."

An awkward silence descended before Tully continued. Nara glanced at Lorcan who had been staring all the while into the fire, as though remembering his dead brother. A measure

108

of strength regained by the pause, Tully restarted his questions.

"Now, to the Selgovae woman, I would know her part in this and why you drag her here. I do not judge you yet, Lorcan, but I do require good reason for her presence in such unfettered fashion."

Lorcan looked into the crackling fire then caught her gaze for short moments before answering his father. Those warm brown eyes seemed less confident than before, making her wonder if he was seeking a diplomatic way to tell Tully he brought a worthless hostage.

"There is a failure in this part of my dealings." Lorcan sounded sombre.

Nara felt her breath leave her body. If not already seated she was sure she might have fallen down for her leg muscles were trembling. Was Lorcan going to turn her over to his father? To be ordered to death by Tully since he himself appeared unable to do it? Her head dipped down to her bowl.

"A failure," Tully roared, surprisingly loudly considering his feeble old body. When she dared to glance at the old chief his expression was one of disbelief, as though Lorcan never failed at anything. She shivered and not from cold. "I will hear this, my son."

Sheer relief flooded, then a rush of embarrassment as Lorcan related their coming upon Cearnach, and the rash attack on him by one of the band. The embarrassment was because she had been thinking about her own plight. Chagrin crept in as he finished speaking of Cearnach.

Tully looked gravely upon Brennus. "Now your part in the chase of the warrior of Tarras."

Nara listened keenly as Brennus told of Cearnach's wounding and of his subsequent escape.

"So he may yet live?" Tully stroked the long white facial hair around his mouth, nodding and tutting all the while. He rose unsteadily and hobbled slowly around them as though it pained him more to sit than to walk. "Not good, my sons. We had no quarrel with this man although he was of the Selgovae." He tottered around, grimacing all the while.

109

"Woman, where were you when your husband was attacked?"

Nara was taken aback. Tully's heated words were the first he had directed at her since ordering her to sit. "Cearnach was not my husband. He was my bodyguard," she answered, bristling at his imperious tone though she tried to keep her answer emotionless. "I remained across the ford seeking a healing herb."

Tully looked to Lorcan, summing up the facts he knew so far. "There were two horses, so you assumed another warrior?"

"Aye, but the filly is short. I suspected a young lad. I ordered the band to go forward to the cavern while I searched the woods."

"And you found this woman," Tully declared.

"Aye...up a tree." Lorcan smiled at the memory.

Nara's gasp was audible, unable to believe he had revealed her pitiful humiliation to his father. A resentful simmer began, for how could he shame her so in front of the Chief of Garrigill.

Glaring at Lorcan made no difference, his grin deepened.

The mirth in Lorcan's answer brought Tully to a standstill, his reply acerbic. "Your humour does you no credit, my son."

Then, stopping in front of her, Tully's glower was even more scathing. "Up a tree? You wear a warrior's mark, but you cowered up a tree like a helpless bird? I would have you de-branded, woman."

Nara was incensed by his mocking and forgetting caution rounded on him. "I did not cower from your son, Tully of the Brigantes! A mighty boar was beneath. My sword and spear were lost having already pierced it but, unfortunately, they did not kill it."

Tully seemed amazed at her audacity. "Guard your tongue, woman of the Selgovae! You will do well to remember who you speak to."

Nara was contrite; she would never have dared to speak so to her father, or to any of her elders. Squaring her chin she faced Tully. "I spoke out of turn. Forgive my outburst."

"Hmm…" Tully's acknowledgement was caustic, his eyes like little blue gemstones, cold, hazy and razed. "Lorcan. Tell me more of this woman who does not know how to behave in the company of her elders, and I will have none of your inappropriate humour either."

Lorcan related how he had helped her kill the boar – to her relief he left out private details. She felt inner trembles begin anew, and looked at the fire, hoping it could be blamed for her discomfort.

Tully shuffled around, scratching his hairless chin. "I ask again, my son. Why did you not turn this sharp-tongued woman loose? You had no quarrel with her. Why, instead, did you bring the imprudent Selgovae woman, and plead she be admitted to my roundhouse, though more of her tongue lash may give me just reason to whip it out?"

Nara refused to flinch before the irascible old man who could easily do what he just said…and worse, but prudence kept her silent.

Lorcan's answer was slow to come. "Father, she is Nara, daughter of Callan of Tarras, a Chief of the Selgovae."

"Brennus has already informed me of that. Callan is not the Selgovae High Chief, though I have heard tell of him, and none of what I have heard is good."

"Nara is his eldest child."

"Hmm…" Tully moved around in an agitated lurch, rubbing his back frequently. "Do you realise the harms which may incur from bringing her here?"

"I asked about that," Brennus interrupted.

Brennus received Tully's frown and censure. "Yet you did not prevent him from bringing her here?"

"Father?" Lorcan gained Tully's attention again. "I believe it will be the opposite from harm. Princess Nara will be the answer to the current perilous situation."

Nara's gaze fastened on Lorcan for he sounded so determined. Tully was not in the least convinced, though, as he stopped in front of Lorcan.

"How so? You speak strangely. There will be retribution for her abduction."

"I have a solution, Father, which I would share with you, but Princess Nara requires rest. Where should I quarter her?"

Lorcan's question reminded her of his earlier conversation.

Tully hovered behind her, making her squirm, though she prayed her disquiet did not show. His old frame made its way beyond Lorcan to see her better.

Nodding his white head and observing her keenly, he took his time. "Princess? Mmm... Can there be any doubt of that, Lorcan?"

"No doubt, Father." She found Lorcan's gaze assuring, a bolstering message for her alone, as though he had never doubted her rank. "She is indeed a princess."

She remembered his urging to not forget her status while she faced the old chief who still scrutinised her from top to toe. Tully continued his perambulations, all the while clicking his cheeks at the exchange of looks between her and Lorcan.

"We need to quarter her well if she is the daughter of Callan of the Selgovae."

Tully stared for a long time, his bent body looking painfully rigid. Nara faced him, neither deferential nor cowed, stoically awaiting his judgment.

"Quartered here, I can guarantee comfort as befits a princess, though nowhere else. Aye. Here it must be." He lurched around, before facing Lorcan again, his old eyes shrewd. "You mean her to be hostage?"

"Not exactly." Lorcan's reply was unexplained, his smile betraying nothing.

Nara tried to gain Lorcan's attention, her hand reaching out towards him to find out exactly what he meant by his words, but he was focused only on Tully.

Tully teetered to the door as quickly as his disability would allow. "Carn! By Taranis, where are you?" His domineering tones rang out over the room as Carn scurried in. He gestured impatiently. "Make a stall ready for this princess of the Selgovae. Have her needs seen to."

Nara smothered a smile for Carn's look was sceptical. "In here?"

"Aye, woman, she needs a stall in here." His tone was bitingly sarcastic as he awkwardly staggered to the back of the roundhouse. "This one here will do. Have bedding arranged and water fetched immediately. Make haste."

Chapter Ten

Lorcan regarded his father, amusement twisting into a full-blown grin, for Tully was a wily old man.

Nara could not escape easily, having been placed right at the back. Tully would also hear any approach to her stall. Carn bustled in as his father manoeuvred his aching body back down, his breath a painful scratch when he faced Nara. "Go rest, woman. Questions will come later, Nara of Tarras."

He was thankful to see Nara did not rebuff Tully's command when she made her way to the back of the roundhouse. Her bearing was regal, showing none of the insecurity he knew she must feel. He had told her to remember her rank, and it pleased him to see her pride was not forgotten.

A commotion at the entryway halted any further study of Nara, Lorcan groaning as the newcomer backslapped him in welcome. His brother, Gabrond, matched his height but had the facial features and hair colour of Brennus.

"Lorcan, what do I hear about a fetching Selgovae captive? The whole settlement buzzes of it like a beehive making honey and is full of you being awestruck. I have waited long for this day. Where is this woman? I wish to see for myself who has ensnared you."

Gabrond's head rose as he followed Tully's gaze to the back of the room. Lorcan knew his brother was startled she should be entering a stall in his father's house, but the chortle of amusement was typical of Gabrond.

"You are indeed beautiful!" Gabrond's strong-toothed grin spread wide, his gusty laugh reverberating inside the roundhouse.

"Take your insulting self from my hearth, Gabrond. Return when you remember good conduct." Tully's voice was authoritative, yet Lorcan knew his father to be amused by the

114

interruption. Tully chided but always appreciated Gabrond's brand of humour.

Wandering to the back of the room, he was pleased to see she seemed cheered by Gabrond's words. "You will have deduced this disreputable warrior is Gabrond."

"How can you declare that of me, my dear brother? You know how well you love me." Gabrond chuckled as he playfully cuffed him on the shoulder before turning to Nara.

"My apologies, Princess Nara. It seems I did not wait long enough to be informed of your rank before I dashed in."

Lorcan took note of the appreciative flashes Gabrond sent towards Nara. A burst of jealousy ate at him, even though he knew his brother teased almost every woman.

Tully intervened. "Nicely said, Gabrond. Ingratiate yourself later, but for now this Selgovae princess will remove herself from my sight. Carn?"

Lorcan frowned at Gabrond who still ogled Nara; a Nara who bore Gabrond's barefaced scrutiny with an assessment of her own. Stepping between the two of them, he deliberately shielded Nara from Gabrond's sight. Though he had admiration for his brother's levity there also lurked a fiercely protective urge in him, an urge to spare her from any kind of hurt. It was an urge he could not seem to prevent.

"All is ready, Tully."

"Then go, Carn. Await my call." Tully's command was brusque.

Lorcan watched his father turn to Nara. Tully's expression was severe, his words berating. "Rest, woman, but remain in the stall. You will be informed of when you may exit."

He wished his father to be more accommodating to Nara, but knew it was far too soon. Eyes meeting hers, he silently gave her reassurance, wanting to touch her, but could not and neither could he detain her any longer as Tully had to be apprised of his plan.

Noting her indecision, he heard Tully's tone become even more ill-tempered. "Fear not, Selgovae woman, you will not be murdered as you sleep. I deem that is not what Lorcan has in mind for you, after dragging you here. I have much to discuss with my son. Take your rest, but make no attempt to leave. Do you heed? Otherwise, you are as safe as you would be in your own father's home."

***

Nara knew Tully had no idea what made her smile, for how was he to know just how unsafe she had felt at Tarras, and how little confidence she had in Callan demonstrating concern over her safety. Tully would learn, in due course, though. His attitude was callous, but Lorcan had already proved he could protect her, and she must trust he would continue to do so. She had to believe that for who else was there to turn to?

Though, in fairness, Tully had not ordered her shackled, and, apart from his tongue flaying her, he had not threatened her. It was unusual in a hostage situation, but she was reassured it should be so. She had been ordered from the hearthside, yet stretching out comfortably appealed very well, and, in truth, she was glad to leave the bold admiration of Tully's three sons. It did seem very strange that she did not feel endangered, but that truly was how she felt. There was animosity there, there was distrust…yet Tully did not appear a direct threat to her survival.

The space between leather door screen and bed was wide enough to take two small steps; sufficient room to wash and change in. A large copper bowl full of warm water lay at her feet. Stripping off her tunic and *braccae*, Nara revelled in the luxury of properly cleansing herself.

Carn had provided a dress of very fine wool for her to change into. The weave was expertly done, the colour still a bold deep blue even though the garment had been worn many times, and though looking a little tight it would fit well enough. She crawled onto the straw-filled pad just wide enough for two people. Covered with a fine cloth, the bed was topped with light skins cleverly sewn together, and Nara was happy to snuggle in naked below them. After the hard bedrock of the previous night it was sheer indulgence and especially good to properly rest her still weak leg. She caught the buzz of

116

voices outside, could not quite hear well enough to follow the conversation, but found it mattered not. She did not feel threatened. Sleep claimed her.

A low hum of voices woke her a while later. She lay and listened in the dim light. Tully and his sons, though she guessed more people had joined them. Her heartbeats quickened. What if Tully had changed his mind and considered her an unnecessary addition to his roundhouse. What if he had already given orders for her dispatch? That could not be. Her fevered mind stilled. If that had been the case she would already have been dragged from the cot she lay on, her fate sealed somewhere beyond his hearth.

A footfall approached her stall. She stiffened as she jerked upright, feeling around for the knife she belatedly remembered she did not have. Carn's soft voice called to her.

"Nara of Tarras? Awaken now. The hall fills for the gathering, you must make ready."

She subsided back under the covers as she greeted the harried young woman, then pointed to the shift at the end of the cot. "I thank you for your kindness, Carn. Do I deprive you of your clothing?"

Carn tut-tutted. "Nay. It belonged to Lorcan's mother; she was a fine weaver."

Nara considered her words before answering, fondling the soft material. "It is an excellently-made dress, but should I be given it to wear?"

"Tully commanded you be given sufficient for your needs, Princess Nara."

"Then I thank you again, Carn. I will wear it with pride."

"Make haste. Tully awaits you. Do not raise his wrath by keeping him waiting. He does not yet treat you as a prisoner, but he might if you dally too long." Carn disappeared in a flurry.

Nara rose and washed the sleep out of her eyes, the burr outside becoming louder. Cooking smells wafted along towards her, reminding her of the small amount she had eaten when they arrived. Now she was famished, and was sure she would tackle the mouth-watering smells easily. Of course that was if they fed her!

Pulling the dress on, she had only her leather thong to gather in the waist. No leather belt with special copper fastening, no finely wrought copper torque to wear around her neck, no special trappings to proclaim her princess. She did have them at the clanhold of her father, but wore them seldom. Her torque, the heavy band of precious metal worn by the nobility of her tribe, had only very rarely been donned during her maturing years.

Nara freed her hair from its confining strings and used the deer horn comb Carn had provided. As she worked through her tangles, she was aware that the noises outside were gaining in strength. Trepidation set in which she ruthlessly squashed. Lorcan would keep her safe. She had to believe it. Many brisk strokes later her long locks were free of the snags of the last days. Leaving it tumbling down her back, it hung below waist level.

When she squeaked open the leather door screen, she found the sight daunting. Many warriors were now seated around the fireside, though only a few women sat amongst them. More females hovered near the low entrance tunnel delivering a feast of platters: roasted birds, meats, fish and roots were added to the banquet set around the fireside. From the plentiful food she guessed that soon the roundhouse would be bursting full.

Full of Brigantes.

She ruthlessly tamped down the insecurity which swamped her. They would be feasting their dead to the otherworld – not welcoming her. The urge to retreat back inside and hide herself away was strong; however, she lingered at the stall door. Not knowing what was expected of her she waited, and observed, since the one person who would make her feel protected, the one person who could erase the feeling of being an interloper, was nowhere to be seen.

A moment of terrible panic engulfed her. As an acolyte, she had rarely visited the settlements of other Selgovae tribes, had rarely even been at gatherings of the Nobles of Tarras, and she had no knowledge at all of the habits of the Brigantes. She scarcely knew Lorcan, but already he was essential to boosting her confidence and reassurance that all would be well. Was she deluding herself, though? Would Lorcan protect her if faced with strong opposition from his tribe? Her stomach flipped again.

It appeared her momentary fear was inane, since no one took notice of her huddled in the shadows. Talk was highly animated around the fireside. Many different conversations were ongoing, though no particular person led the debate.

Movement near the entryway caught her glance. The leather screen of a stall moved back, and Lorcan walked out. A sigh of sheer relief hissed out, her insides settled, a measure of calm descending. He could not possibly have heard her, nonetheless, his eyes swivelled to the back of the hall where she stood in the semi-darkness.

A few strides brought him to her.

"Why do you wait, Nara?"

Lorcan's voice was hushed as she watched his eyes. They roamed over her hair, and face, lingering on her, his esteem warming her. She felt the instinctive connection between herself and this Brigante deepen, even though she did not understand it. In her abiding gratitude to see him, she was quite unaware that she stretched out her hands to him. That he was an enemy was a forgotten truth.

He clutched her fingers and stepped up close, shielding them from the gaze of those behind. Their bodies met from chin to toes and everywhere in between. Looking down on her, Lorcan's eyes blazed with appreciation. She inwardly hoped the other flicker there was of desire. Swallowing awkwardly, her fingers tightened in his grip. Yet, the noise around reminded her that she was his captive.

Reality sank in. She disengaged her fingers from his grasp and trod back a step, the leather curtain bowing behind her. She chose her words carefully.

"I linger here because I do not know your father's wishes, Lorcan of Garrigill. Your nobles gather. This is no place for me." It was a lame struggle to form the words. Barely able to meet his gaze, she was adrift once more in a sea of enemy Brigantes.

"You will sit alongside me, Nara of Tarras, at this gathering of Garrigill Nobles. You will be invited to join us as befits a visiting Selgovae princess."

His head was backlit by the firelight, his eyes adamant. She admired his resolution, even as she did not believe he could speak true. Her answer was tinged with mistrust.

"If you so wish, but your latrine calls to my needs first."

Lorcan led her behind the noisy gathering around the fireside, forging a path to the entryway. Once outside, he took her to the latrine pits, easy to locate since flambeaux in tall brackets delineated the main paths around Tully's roundhouse. Weak moonlight also shed a hazy, quivering light as transitory cloud cover flit across its path.

She was quick to return to him. Holding her lightly in his grasp, his fingers spread across her shoulders, bringing him close enough for her to inhale his unique scent. Warmth and reassurance seeped from his fingertips onto her skin for she wore no bratt, his words whispering against her cold cheeks.

"Nara, it will not be easy for you at this gathering, but know that I wish your future secure, and you must not forget your rank."

There was promise in his request which she clung to. Yet there was also a plea she could not quite interpret – tolerance, forbearance, trust? Perhaps it was all of those. She was not sure, but what she easily interpreted was what his stroking fingers did to her: they awakened the wild desire he had engendered before. There was a moment of sheer dismay when he dropped her grip and coolly ushered her back towards Tully's roundhouse.

The interior was crowded. Warriors now sat around the fully extended fire in double, and in many places triple, rows leaving little space to walk behind them as more men stood at the rear.

Striding to Tully seated close to the doorway, Lorcan greeted his father in a time honoured fashion. Tully slowly got to his feet and turned to her, wordlessly absorbing her change

120

of dress and looking at her hair hanging loose without adornment. She suppressed the fear threatening to inundate her. His glare was fierce. She frantically recalled Lorcan's words to summon the control she needed to face the swell of Brigantes: a number which had to be well over one hundred.

A hush immediately rippled around the room till all were silent, alerted by Tully's movements. A minuscule nod of his head indicated some degree of satisfaction with her, then an ancient greeting issued from his lips. Nara summoned the courage to thank him in return, in the honoured acceptance common to all Celtic tribes, praying her voice betrayed none of her alarm.

"Come, Princess Nara, daughter of Callan of Tarras, a chief of the Selgovae, sit by me here."

Tully urged her to take the coveted place beside him as he levered himself down again, Lorcan seated on her other side. She gulped at the honour rendered.

In the assembled company, she was accorded the rank of senior envoy of another tribe. Never had she been asked to sit so close by her father at a gathering. Confusion beset her, especially since a good number of the people around wore either openly hostile looks on their faces, or were offensively curious about her.

"Carn, serve our food," Tully commanded. He turned to the man at his other side and proceeded to ignore her.

Confusion reigned in Nara's heart even further.

What was she to him? She wondered as she sat in the privileged place. Neither prisoner nor hostage would be seated next to Tully. They would more likely be tied to the pole beside the entrance trophies alongside the skulls of slain enemies, a guard flanking each side. The respect and privilege being accorded her needed careful thought.

What fate did Tully have in mind for her?

Flickering firelight illuminated the gathering, some more high ranking women now seated beside their men. Plentiful food appeared to fill her hands, no hesitation over serving her, though none directly addressed her. Tully spoke to the elder on his other side, a man almost as frail as he was.

The babble grew during the feasting. Using his knife to slice off lumps of roasted meat from a skewer, Lorcan silently passed them to her as he listened to his neighbour who inquired about Gyptus. Turning to her, Lorcan gave her bread. When she had swallowed, he offered her barley beer, his bone cup held to her lips, bidding her drink deeply. His eyes were dark and watchful as he did so; the intimacy of his gesture making her feel very aware of his potency till his neighbour reclaimed his attention.

Dragging herself away from his intent gaze, she faced Brennus, on Tully's other side, a few places down in the ranking around the chief. Brennus stared at her, his frown an indication of unhappy thoughts. He was a fine-looking warrior, one she could like as a friend, but she was already sure he could be nothing more than that to her.

Lorcan distracted her, whispering into her ear. "The men all look upon you, Nara, for you are beautiful. Your hair is magnificent in the firelight, the bronze of it dancing as though it has a life of its own. Like me, I am sure Brennus wishes to run his hands through it. I believe he is jealous I sit beside you."

His words excited yet were also chilling. Jealous? Years of modest living free of vanity suppressed any urges in her to revel in the adulation.

"I do not wish to cause dissent between you and your brother, Lorcan. I do not want to be a problem to anyone, but it seems I am. Nothing is of my choosing, Brigante."

"Presently you have no choice, Nara, but it will not always be so."

The food consumed, the talks began. Clapping his hands, Tully alerted the gathering, the signal for gossip to be over. Soon, total silence descended as he stood before them.

"We have feasted my son, Arian, and his warriors, to the otherworld. All true warriors of Garrigill!"

The crowd rang their cheers of agreement round the hall, the traditional send off to the slain men.

His voice thready, Tully provided an update on the raid at Raeden and then of the Roman presence near the crannogs of

Gyptus. At this stage all listened, not yet time for debate, but Tully's voice had weakened by the time he looked down at her.

"Princess Nara, eldest child of Callan of Tarras of the Selgovae, is a visitor in our company." He allowed a slight pause to drop into the tense silence before he added more, his voice resolute. "All at Garrigill will treat her so." Then, as though his energy was spent, Nara watched him gesture Lorcan to rise before he lowered himself down onto his pile of skins.

She was conscious of everyone's concentration on her as Lorcan stood. Under their prolonged scrutiny, she refused to display fear – though it was far from how she really felt.

Lorcan's voice boomed over the gathering, his tone demanding as he confirmed the need for all Brigantes to stand united against the Roman scourge. Heads nodded in assent around the circle, yet not all were in accord. A young warrior near the back interrupted his frustration evident in his arm gestures.

"We know all Brigante leaders gather at Samhain, when the leaves colour and fall and winter drops its frigid cloak on the ground. You waste our time on that, Lorcan. What of this Selgovae woman?"

Lorcan's hand halted the man's flow of anger. "Aye, Dairmid, I come to that. We did plan to gather at Samhain, but yestreen's report means we must act much sooner than the fall of winter." Murmured cries of consternation rippled round the company.

"Our Roman enemy is hugely powerful and has already destroyed the Celtic way of life in the far south. We of the north must have more strength to our forces if we are to resist their next mighty surge. Our numbers need boosted for that. It becomes crucial we ally with tribes who have long been our enemies if we are to repel the Romans from our northern lands."

Cries of repugnance and dissent made Nara cringe at his feet as he continued to nurture the positive support of his people, his voice rising. "I propose treaties be made forthwith

with all of our tribal neighbours. Otherwise we will not eject the Roman invaders from our shores and our lands."

An outcry greeted his words. Shouts of consent, some of defiant rejection and many of derision hooted around the hall; a deafening roar. Nara's head remained bent, but she listened acutely. She had not felt threatened earlier by Tully and his sons, but she did now, for the room heaved with resentment – against her. She was not of their tribe.

An elder close by struggled to his feet commanding silence. "What do you say to us, Lorcan? Stand as one with our enemies of old? I fear madness overtakes you."

"Nay, there is no madness in me. It is the only way to defeat our common enemy, or none of us will live to see more summer suns glowing across our Brigante lands."

Lorcan's entreaty persisted, stirring their tribal passions, but Nara realised, in a contrary way, it also quieted some of those very same volatile tempers. He continued to hold the huge room in thrall.

"Bouddica of the Iceni died resisting the subsuming ways of the Romans. Her people were slaughtered, and that same carnage has been repeated over and over again, decimating the Celtic tribes in the south. Our own Queen Cartimandua could no longer maintain her agreement with the Roman hordes given that they do not keep to the words of their treaties."

His grave tones sobered those who had earlier hooted with derision. "Those southern Celts were defeated because they tried to fight their own tribe's battle. We of the north must not sit complacent for the lands of the Southern Brigantes are already well compromised, and are being assimilated into Roman culture as we sit here this eve."

Groans of protest greeted his words. Like most of her fellow Celts, Nara detested the idea. She listened keenly as Lorcan wound up his speech, his gaze straying around the whole room before settling upon her. He beseeched her cooperation...and maybe consent? She was unconvinced which, but it appeared he included her in his vision. By the degree of warmth in his eyes he, at least, did not seem to hate her.

"Since the recent fall of our Queen Cartimandua, they surge north. To repel them, we must ally with the eastern Parisi and the northern Selgovae – like Princess Nara here."

All eyes were on Lorcan as he abruptly slid to his stool allowing an outpouring to begin. That meant the eyes also fell on her. She felt overwhelmed by their demands, the room appearing to shrink to one large wellspring of hatred. No-one held the floor so all talked, shouted and gesticulated at the same time – mainly directed her way. She knew Lorcan begged her to look at him. She was aware of his eyes boring into her down bent head, but she kept her gaze averted. Staring vacantly into the fire, she mentally assessed the unstable mood. She dared not look up. If the gathering turned on her, she was doomed since there was no hope of escaping the room. Fear churned. Bile rose into her mouth as she struggled not to vomit, and icy trembles beset her body.

Lorcan's warm hand sliding over hers was unexpected; reassuring tingles spread through her whole body. It was so public a gesture. The heat of his simple touch flowed through her, the comfort enough quell the nausea, his whisper in her ear shockingly fierce.

"Raise your head up, Nara, and keep it high. Believe that I will protect you."

The elder next to Tully cranked himself up, his old bones obviously wearying him as he raised one gnarled finger to gain attention. The crowd quieted down and listened to his fragile old tones.

"I believe it inevitable we must fight the forces of the Roman Empire, Lorcan, but joining with our Celtic enemies will be no easy task. If you have a feasible plan, then share it."

Tully struggled to rise from his seat of piled up skins. "We have a Selgovae princess here with us. A captive, aye, of sorts, as you may have heard rumoured, but she can be more valuable to us than you have imagined, Dairmid."

Tully stopped as baffled murmurs circled around. Attention strayed back to Lorcan. The old chief waited till complete silence cloaked them again before declaring, "We ask no ransom for her. We request no cattle and no territory."

125

"What then?" The same question came from more than one person.

Nara felt Tully's gaze fall to her first, then he transferred it to Lorcan, and then slowly on to Brennus before he spoke again.

"This woman is eldest child of Callan of Tarras who holds a high rank in the Full Council of Selgovae Nobles."

Nods around the fire showed agreement of his words, but Tully waited till all could hear well. "Our proposal is to make use of the woman to unite our tribes in marriage, merging our bloodlines, fusing a strong bond." A gasp circulated around the assembly, some indignant cries at the proposal.

They meant to use her as a marriage bargain? Nara felt defenceless, a lone Selgovae in the midst of hundreds of Brigantes. Little did they know her father would most likely pay them huge amounts of gold to marry her off to any warrior, to have her finally out of his sight.

Tully swayed on his feet, his voice betraying the pain he could suppress no longer, yet remained determined to finish. "I propose Callan be approached without delay, our emissaries taking simple betrothal gifts as befitting a princess with a view to linking our tribes. The Selgovae worry as we do. If the Romans overwhelm us, they will then march over the high hills and attack the Selgovae next on their relentless northward progress. It is in the interest of the Selgovae to do everything necessary to stop the advancement of the Roman Empire."

So many voices called out, making it impossible to hear their comments. Tully pointed to one warrior who stood up and took the floor.

"There is need to stand united against the Romans, but why must we bring Selgovae blood into our tribe?"

Nara felt his enmity breaking over her in waves, cresting over her down bent head.

Tully sounded resigned, though she dared not check. "Many may reject the idea, but the Selgovae are fellow Celts. We have been enemies too long."

A chorus of cries continued as they debated the proposal, strident voices heated to fiery outbursts.

She thought over her earlier conversation with Lorcan. She was correct and he was wrong – she was poor bargain material. Angry resentment bridled inside. She loathed feeling so powerless and…unwanted again.

Lorcan jumped to his feet, hand held high for silence, an imperious command. "Like us, the Selgovae must swallow their spit before they fight alongside us. They, too, need good reason for making an accord with Brigantes. This woman here will merely be the device, the excuse both tribes require to convene together. Princess Nara has no husband. This we shall use to our advantage."

Her face flamed, she was barely able to suppress her anger. She was to be used as merely a device to encourage her father to parley? That plan was sure to fail.

Bitter questions roiled around, her hands fisting in her lap. She glared at Lorcan who willed all around to agree with him. His expression motivated, his voice entreated the throng, but she was not inspired by his condescending words. Yet, against her will, she found herself impressed by the way he brought around the crowd to his way of thinking. The magic of the man was not only detected by her; that thought came reluctantly, yet it was true, nonetheless. She dropped her gaze to the floor, once again unable to look at his pleading brown eyes.

"The Selgovae must also repel the might of the Roman forces. Even now they may have heard of Roman ships threatening their firth and will know their forces alone are not strong enough to withstand a determined attack. They must accept this bargain as they would not do with any other trade. They need to ally themselves with us and in so doing gain our support for them."

Nara was despondent, and truth be told, frightened. Callan would never agree to ally with his enemies of old. Madness was indeed overtaking Lorcan, and yet it seemed to her more heads were nodding than before.

"How can you be sure of this, Lorcan?" The question came from the far corner of the room as an onslaught of similar questions fired out, the noise level increasing again.

Lorcan's firm tones commanded attention. "I am confident of the outcome. I propose we approach Callan immediately. If the Romans already march north in their thousands, and simultaneously land their fleets in the north-west, we will be in a wedge we cannot escape from."

Hushed horror rippled around the room. "Our inhospitable western shoreline makes the sheltered firth of the Selgovae a convenient landing point. Each Roman ship can easily disgorge hundreds of fighting soldiers and some ships, I have heard, yet more than that. What will inevitably happen then is that the Romans will swathe a path to the north and to the south. We will all be vanquished, Selgovae and Brigante!"

Lorcan's dire words over, he sat down next to her to let the words penetrate. His eyes were reassuring, but she fumed, rejecting him for not revealing his marriage bargain to her earlier, making her believe he would be looking for gold as a ransom.

An extraordinary crushing disenchantment flooded her. Conflicting feelings tore her apart. Lorcan to be her husband? That was what he had been devising? He had been planning that throughout the whole day? Though she could not deny she continued to yearn for him he could not be her husband, and the father of her son at Beltane. A Brigante son was not what was prophesied for her.

Staring into the fire, she recalled Swatrega's declaration. Yet, when she put her mind to hear the words again, Swatrega had mentioned no details about the father. The High Priestess had never mentioned which tribe he must be from. She had only declared Nara should deliberate well before choosing the man to mate with at the Beltane rites, for he must be a mighty warrior who would beget a son who would not be forgotten easily.

Nara had assumed he would be a Selgovae warrior.

Her blood pulsed hard inside her body, a fledgling excitement tingling her skin. Could her mate be Lorcan? Turning to him, she saw his eyes were still upon her, still entreating her to believe all would be well, and he would protect her. She allowed a small smile to break the hard mould of her anger. His answering smile warmed her inside out as his fingers again snaked out and squeezed themselves around her hand, comforting her till she became aware, once again, of her surroundings.

One more time the noisy rabble was stopped by Tully's feeble attempts to clap. Unable to rise unaided, Tully used her shoulder as a lever and continued to lean on her whilst he dragged her up alongside him. Sensing his difficulty she surreptitiously supported him, mindful of his pride, and chose to ignore the irascible old man was powerful enough to call for her death in a blink. Her insides churned, but this time in heady anticipation, for maybe Lorcan was the one?

Tully gained everyone's attention. "Discussing the treaty proposals with all Brigante clanholds, north and south, will take time we do not have. The marriage alliance with Princess Nara, however, can be dealt with here with expediency."

Tully's words faded at the end, his vigour gone. Nara felt him all but collapse against her as she bore the brunt of his weight, although it may have seemed to the crowd Tully forced her in place beside him for his grip was tight, his bony arm cradling her shoulder blades.

Her eyes glanced to Lorcan, to impart to him how weakened Tully was. Lorcan looked ready to jump to her assistance, and that was all she needed. Stiffening her stance, she continued to bear Tully's load.

The old chief turned to Lorcan, looking at him across her body, his eyes rheumy with pain and with something she discerned was akin to regret. His clutch at her shoulders crunched her very bones. Something was amiss. A dread coursed through her. She did not know why, but it seemed as though Tully sent that same regret to her through his gnarled old fingers. His weary voice was as loud as he could muster though it mattered little for the whole room listened intently because his countenance was so solemn.

"At dawn, word will go to all eligible Brigante princes of the North about this marriage bargain. I will bid those who are interested to be with us by Beltane – by proxy, if not the princes themselves."

The blood drained from Nara's head at Tully's words, her body trembling as much as his feeble one. She could not be sure, but she thought Lorcan had stiffened at her other side. Tully's fingers dug tight into her as he sidled even closer to her body, yet she sensed the old chief was not attempting to control her, or harm her – rather the opposite. Knowing how much his words had caused her tremor of fear, his bony fingers appeared to be pouring the last dregs of his physical and emotional strength into her, aware of the implications to her future. The gesture strangely appealed, for Tully's touch gave her succour her own father had never, ever given her.

From that point on, Nara could not be certain if she gave the weakened Tully support, or if he supported her. What was clear to the assembled company was their chief publicly acknowledging his agreement to the marriage bargain as his arm encircled her.

"The elders of Garrigill will congregate on the morrow, to consider the wider scheme for alliances."

His voice was faint, exhausted to the point of collapse.

A nod from Tully indicated she should sit. She slipped her trembling body down to the stool as ordered but maintained the arm she had curved behind Tully's painfully thin waist. She should hate Tully. She should let him fall to the ground, or allow him to waver there on his own spindly legs till he stumbled.

Nara found she could do neither of those things. Hate his suggestions? She certainly did that, but she could not bring herself to hate the short-tempered old man next to her who had just declared yet a different fate for her. Slumping against him, her shoulder supported him even more than before to enable him to complete his speech as, yet again, she contemplated the floor rushes.

"If we ally first with the Selgovae, then I see the Parisi, Novantae and maybe even the Votadini joining, too. It takes only one stone to start a cairn. Think on it well, people of Garrigill."

As well as her own tremors, and Tully's shaking, Nara could feel the tension, even rage, emanating from Lorcan sitting alongside her. His fists clenched tight at his knees, his neck muscles straining as he stared into the blazing fire, his eyes agog with fury. Already attuned in some way to him, she sensed he repressed the urge to punch someone – almost certainly his own father, for wily old Tully had just widened the marriage alliance to include many other contenders.

Nara was appalled. Arranged marriage with a Brigante was going to be forced on her, but not necessarily with Lorcan. Escape seemed more essential than before though it was even more impossible. She, too, stared into the flames. The merest hint of protest in this company, and she would be dead.

A shout rose from a young warrior at the back of the second row, his angry finger pointing to her.

"Will retribution from her tribe befall us before we can discuss this again? Will we of the outposts of Garrigill be attacked in our very beds this night because she has been brought into our midst?"

Alarm swelled around the company at his dire words, increasingly volatile and hostile.

Tully looked to Lorcan to respond. Nara bent her head and studied the fire again, unwilling to meet the antagonistic eyes of those around. They hated her. She had been correct, but had Lorcan heeded her? Her position was even more perilous now.

Chapter Eleven

Lorcan's fierce demeanour commanded silence as he seethed beside Nara. He felt betrayed yet knew Tully could display no favouritism for such a momentous event. That his father saw the need to encourage more Brigantes to agree with the alliances stunned him, old Tully gaining even more of his respect. They would garner support more quickly.

He knew regardless of how shredded his own feelings, the assembly must accept Nara's presence among them. To ensure her safety, he needed to dispel the palpable rejection and hatred circling the room. Regardless of the outcome of the marriage bargain, he would still defend her. He felt...responsible...for her wellbeing. He would allow himself only that and would not think of his own elemental desires.

Even though Tully had just given her public support, Nara, he was certain, must detest him now. And she would reject even more what he had to do next. She would, as like as not, hate his detached manner, but it was the only way to reassure his tribe about the ultimate plan. Nara's safety during the days to come was paramount.

In his absence.

Tully would send no other to seal the bargain with Callan of Tarras. Not only had he put the idea forward, he was also the most skilled emissary his father had.

Avoiding any misinterpretations he was uncompromising. Blunt.

"Callan of Tarras will not yet realise the absence of Princess Nara. He believes her ensconced at Raeden, where she was expected to remain for some days. We have time to approach Callan before any abduction is suspected. An emissary must go immediately to Tarras, to inform him Princess Nara spends time with us as our honoured guest. In

132

this way, it will turn a hostage situation into one of practical bargaining."

Tully's words were shaky, but authoritative. "Do all of you hear this? Go easily to your bed this night, but our defence patrols must remain vigilant. We know the Roman enemy roams our lands, and they need to be watched and routed if possible. Our gathering this night is ended!"

Lorcan watched his father collapse onto his pile of skins. Once down, Tully waved his hand weakly for people to disperse, which they did with amazing speed, only a few High Council leaders lingering at Tully's behest.

Lorcan made no attempt at any kind of intimacy again with Nara; neither by touch nor eye contact. He dared not. He had indeed sealed her fate, but not how he had first envisaged. Sitting as rigidly as she beside him, he could almost taste her hurt and felt her silent agony, though he did not dare look at her. His agony was gnawing enough to deal with at that moment, remorse too simple a word for what had just occurred.

She must believe he had agreed to Tully's plan – but that was far from being true. During his talk earlier with Tully, his father had shed no hint of his declaration. In fact, Tully had only gradually warmed to the marriage idea as Lorcan persuaded him of the benefits of guarding the high heights from the north and south across its peaks with the Selgovae and Brigante tribes working together. That would be especially effective if Roman attack came from the west rather than the south.

He was disillusioned with his father, but even more dissatisfied with himself. He had not even considered that Tully would widen the marriage alliance to include other Brigante princes as suitors, and that had put Nara into an even more vulnerable position. Utter discontent, and deep regret, washed over him because he had selfishly, and mistakenly, only considered himself as the husband of this beautiful, lovable woman. Yet he could not do anything rash and endanger her even more, was trapped in the plan he had devised.

133

***

Nara was distraught, feeling like the outcast again since Lorcan sat next to her with the cold stillness of a carved effigy. Like a dead creature, unmoving and unresponsive, his gaze fixed rigidly on the glow of the fire in front of him. Irritated with everything that had happened, she tapped his arm insisting on his attention, unable, unwilling even, to mask her sense of abandonment.

"Do I require permission from you, or from Tully, every time I wish to go outside?"

"Nay, but do not go far without an escort. You are yet an enemy to many here at Garrigill, and I cannot vouch for the behaviour of all the people, even though Tully made his views clear."

"I heed your words, Brigante."

Making her way outside, she inwardly raged against Lorcan, yet she railed more so at her goddess, Rhianna, for putting her in such an appalling quandary. Locating the latrine area was simple, but on the way back she found Brennus lounging across her path. Fury beset her. Had Lorcan sent him out as guard? Again?

"So, Lorcan believes I need a keeper after all."

Brennus appeared amused by her anger, incensing her even more. His gaze bore down from his great height. "Lorcan does not direct my life. I make my own choices, Nara of the Selgovae. He did not send me after you if that is what you mean? I wished to speak with you."

"You wish to speak with me?" Her reply was every inch the arrogant princess.

Brennus casually stroked the hair at his lip, his regard frank. "The developments of this evening were very enlightening. You do realise the outcome of these proposals?"

"Aye. I do," Nara spat back, angered also by him physically preventing her from moving forward. His large hands cupped her shoulders and held her in front of him as though she weighed nothing.

Intent focus on her, he drew her nearer and whispered in her ear. "Last night Lorcan made us believe you were already his woman, but now I am not so sure. I do not believe the outcome is as inevitable as he thinks. A Brigante prince is proposed for you, but there are many eligible ones…including me. Every son of a local chief may call himself prince, as you well know."

Nara struggled to free herself from his grip, but could not prevent his cool lips clamping down to claim a kiss. Brennus did not exactly repel her, but neither did she gain any pleasure from his embrace. His relaxed laugh made her even more wary of him as he released her. "You have more to think on, Nara, than you may yet know."

She knew he spoke true, as she wended back to the roundhouse. Triply trapped was what she had come to: trapped at Garrigill without knowledge of who her Brigante husband might be; trapped she was unable to inform her father of the intelligence she had learned about the Roman movements; trapped knowing Beltane was not long hence, and she still had to choose the father of her prophesied son. A father who was not necessarily one of the contender princes put forward as her future husband?

Would Tully, or Callan, give her any choice in the matter of which Brigante prince she would marry? It seemed most unlikely.

The burden of choosing the correct mate to fulfil the Priestess Swatrega's prophecy lay at her own feet. Neither Tully, nor Callan, could influence that as they had no knowledge of it. Neither did Lorcan. Her secret was known only to Swatrega and herself. And she must keep it that way.

Her body sang when Lorcan touched her, yet how could she be certain he was the one to father her child without some better experience of men? At Raeden, she had planned to seek all possibilities, so why should it be different at Garrigill, especially when Brigantes found her beddable?

She was confused…and sick at heart.

Few warriors remained when she rejoined Lorcan at the fireside, his eyes tracking her every movement. His earlier detachment appeared turned to concern. "Has someone outside accosted you?"

"No one who gives me worry. I watch, and I wait. I see no other course to take, Brigante. You leave me no other choice, yet again." Her terse words were dismissive since she was not prepared to converse with him.

"Ah. You are annoyed at me again."

"What would make you believe that?" She was indeed annoyed; he seemed so able to capriciously turn on and off dark moods.

He whispered, his deep tones riling her even more. "You always call me *Brigante* when you are exasperated with me. Do not deny it for it is truth." His teasing defied her to declare otherwise.

It most likely was true. Her thoughts whirled, but she would not give him the satisfaction of being correct. "You assume too much, Brigante, but one day what you deserve will come to you."

"I am now not so convinced."

Lorcan's words were wry, and she had had her fill of them.

"Will Tully take offence if I retire? I wish to be alone. It would seem I have much to think on."

"Then let us ask him."

Tully's weary body was propped against the entryway whilst he took leave of the last visitors, his strength spent and the pains of life drawing him down.

"Father? Does Nara have your permission to retire?"

Tully rasped a reply. "Why do you bother me with minutiae, Lorcan? You know well what my answer will be. What ails you?"

Lorcan's laugh rang out. "Nara would have you see her good manners, Father. She wishes to show you respect."

Tully's eyes sought hers, a gleam softening his frown. "So you wish to be thought well of, princess? Even if my son is too familiar to give you your title, I am able." He gazed longer, noting her deferential air and then looked to Lorcan. "Aye. Go to bed, woman, and sleep well since there are others who will not sleep so comfortably this night."

"My thanks. The events of the evening have depleted me, Tully of Garrigill." Her answer was clipped, unable to fully guard her tongue. Though unsure of his words, and of his strange looks, she nodded and headed to her stall.

"Princess Nara?" Tully's abrupt croak made her turn back. "You have a feeble man's gratitude. You bore me up well tonight, woman...even though my actions will have repercussions you may have cause to despise. Your heart is large, and you shield your pain well. I say now, that warrior's mark you wear was well worth the branding, for you have more courage in you than many a man I have come across. And they generally do not have your compassion."

Dismissed by Tully, Lorcan walked her to the back of the hall.

"Your father speaks in riddles. What exactly did his words mean?"

"He pays you a compliment."

"I understand about his gratitude, and even about the courage he referred to...but not of the others not comfortably sleeping."

An ironic chuckle drifted to her in the gloom. "My father's body is now frail, but his wits are sharp, and his memory of coupling is good. He means your loveliness will keep many men from sleeping this night, and the next nights to come. You draw men like insects to a flame with your curtain of hair framing your pretty features."

"Lorcan?" She was surprised by his statement...and discomfited. Yet, she could not deny she liked his compliments.

He held her elbow, his voice persuasive. One finger drew her chin up, the better to see into her eyes in the gloom of the roundhouse. "I wish I was retiring with you, but I will be joining the ranks of those who will not sleep well tonight, and the next nights to come."

"The next nights to come?" She repeated, missing his meaning.

"Nara! You must know how men are the nights before Beltane?"

137

Embarrassment flustered her when she realised what he alluded to. Already past twenty winters, yet she had never been in the position of actually seeing what the warriors were like on the nights before Beltane.

"Men assiduously seek to woo their lovers before Beltane. They wish to be sure they are chosen by the one they are attracted to, on that celebratory night."

"I know of it, for it is so in my tribe too, but there are still many nights before Beltane, Lorcan," Nara whispered to the ground, unable to face him.

"All too few. Many of those present tonight who have no permanent mate will imagine your body lying beside them."

"Why me? I see many attractive women here at Garrigill."

"You are a newcomer to Garrigill, you are beautiful, but it has also been made clear tonight you are free to wed…and maybe bed before then."

His frankness shocked her, but she still dared a question. "Will you seek a lover tonight to assuage your lust?"

"The way I feel, I should." His grip on her elbow tightened. "But since you are here in my father's house, I will go to bed and dream." He pulled her closer to him.

His mouth tempted her greatly. She wanted to feel his lips on hers, did not wish to be free of his grasp as she had with Brennus, yet resentment prompted her snide reply. "The events of this night may make you dream a long time, Brigante."

He tightened his grip a little but made no attempt to kiss her. Their intent connection lingered, each asking silent questions. Nara knew what hers were but could only guess at Lorcan's. Preventing her insecure words from spilling forth was not possible. "How many other princes might be eligible for this marriage bargain?"

Lorcan's passionate brown eyes flashed sorrow and something she wanted to call desperation, yet she was not sure until his voice grit in her ear. "I do not know. Perhaps five…even ten? Nara, do not think on that now. You must put it from your mind for the moment, as I must. It troubles me too much to contemplate."

138

Her voice quieted as she spoke words which tore the heart out of her. "Rather than dream, maybe you should choose someone else to woo tonight."

Lorcan gave no answer as he stared, looking even more anguished. The strain he was under she could truly feel for his fingers twitched at her shoulders as he put her from him, her skin flaming under his scrutiny...till he groaned. Not loud, but heartfelt. His tortured grimace changed, a resolution of some sort replacing it.

The speed of his next manoeuvre caught her unawares as he whipped them both inside her stall, letting the door hide drop back into place. Warm lips slammed their way down upon hers as he toed them back onto the low cot. Urgently seeking, his hands caressed her, his questing mouth stealing her breath.

Those thrilling feelings returned, even more powerfully as the kisses deepened, his body moving against hers as he lay atop. Nothing she had ever before experienced compared to what Lorcan could make her feel. Her hands caressed him, too, wanting to return his fervour.

Almost as suddenly as he had started, he called a halt, his lips a hairsbreadth from her own.

"I must not go any further, Nara of Tarras. You are not mine, yet." He pulled back and sat at the edge of the cot, smoothing down her shift and covered the legs he had only barely exposed. He brushed her cheek with his lips before he turned away. "This is all I may offer you this night, but somehow, believe that I will protect you. Even though I know not how that may happen, I will ensure your life is not endangered."

Lorcan caressed her skin where he had placed his whisper of a kiss, then turned away. Nara watched him make his way outside, already bereft of his touch, her heart still palpitating for he had roused her so easily. As he passed Tully's stall, she heard the old chief cry out. Lorcan halted long enough to listen to his father.

"Aye, Lorcan. Leave the woman alone. She will have need of her courage in the coming days."

Inside her stall, Nara made ready for bed, dazed by the events of the evening. For the first time ever, she wished to have a man beside her when she slept: a wish which had nothing to do with her safety.

Sleep eluded her. For an age, she tossed and turned, her thoughts whirling. Had Lorcan spoken truly? Was he alone now? Could he have gone to assuage his lust on a woman well known to him, someone who welcomed him? She had noted the interested stares of many of the women who had served in the roundhouse that evening. Their glances had told her he was popular.

Jealousy ran like a burn in spate, something else to cope with in this new life of hers. It had been much simpler to be a maiden of the goddess with no prophecy to fulfil.

Eventually, she slept and slept on through the first stirrings in the roundhouse…dreaming of Lorcan.

Something touching her brow brought Nara to wakefulness. Fearing a threat, her hand dashed up.

Carn hastily apologised. "I wanted to ensure you had no fever. You have slept so long I thought you were unwell."

"I am well. I must have been overtired; it took me a long time to get to sleep last night."

"Were you kept from sleep? Did someone pursue you unwillingly?" Carn sounded horrified she might have been pestered.

The idea of Lorcan pestering her brought a smile to her lips, her heartbeat increasing in anticipation of seeing him.

"Nay." Her words admonished as Carn set down a washbowl. "You must not wait on me. I can look to my own needs."

Carn was cautious. "You are a chief's daughter. Surely you have a woman to wait on you at Tarras?"

She knew Carn had no idea why she smiled so heartily. "Perhaps some day I will tell you about my life at Tarras."

Nara readied herself, her thoughts chary since she had no idea what to expect, the events of the previous evening having been confusing. All was quiet as she completed her hair-braiding, but since she had slept so long it was no surprise that the roundhouse was empty, Carn alone hovering by the entryway.

Propped against the exterior wall, Tully sat on a pile of furs in the sunshine and greeted her with the crotchety voice she was becoming accustomed to. "Slept long enough, woman? Carn has food here to break your fast."

A bowl of oatmeal was handed to her.

"Eat quickly. Gabrond awaits your horsemanship." Tully's tone and gestures were jerky, as though any power spent on talking pained him.

"Gabrond?" Whatever did the old chief mean? Nara ate as ordered, her stomach appreciating being filled even if the rest of her balked at being commanded in such fashion.

"You met Gabrond, did you not?"

"Aye." Her reply was guarded for Tully was so tetchy, his old eyes rheumy. It did not escape her notice that a stern looking guard stood sentry a few steps away, well within hearing distance, awaiting orders from Tully.

Lorcan and Brennus, she was informed, had set off at first light for Tarras, to take the marriage bargain to her father, but Gabrond had been assigned to assess her skills.

The bright start of the day dulled, her spirits plummeted. Lorcan was no longer nearby. Swallowing the insecurity rushing through her, she reflected on her situation as she ate. She could not gauge whether Tully expected success as an outcome to Lorcan's journey as the old man looked troubled. Her insides squirmed. Lorcan was her bulwark at Garrigill – without him who would be her defensive protection? In Tully's company she had not felt a prisoner the evening before, indeed he did not appear to be threatening now, yet she felt exposed without Lorcan to shield her from the rest of Garrigill.

"So…princess." Tully's terse address claimed her attention, his glare penetrating. "Lorcan leaves me to deal with you till his return. Listen well. You will not leave Garrigill without my permission, but I will not truss you up as prisoner in my roundhouse or any other place in my settlement."

141

Nara held her tongue, she had no ready answer but since Tully gasped on there was no need to reply.

"Lorcan is a judicious man. He thinks to use you as unusual barter, Nara of Tarras, so I will use you also in similar fashion."

If Tully's words had been delivered in anger, or if his body had not been so raddled with a wasting disease, she knew she would have been quaking for his words could have had many meanings. The sick man before her was not angry, his eyes were piercingly astute though, and followed every gulp of her throat as she swallowed down alarm. She did not speak, in fact could not, but waited for Tully's plans to be revealed. No doubt he had decided a stratagem, for though his body was weak, his mind was sharp.

"I have no patience to dither. My body, which you look upon so perceptively with your expressive eyes, hampers me. Thus, since I cannot accompany you around Garrigill, I order others to do it for me. You will give them the answers you would impart to me, and you will not fail me in this, for I will know of it. I will have your knowledge as a warrior-woman of Tarras put to the test while we await Lorcan's return. By then, I will know if my opinion of you is as high as Lorcan's."

Nara maintained full eye contact with the old chief and worked out the machinations of his cunning. Her distrust of fathers ran deep.

"Why do you wait?"

Eventually she replied, unable to prevent a smile of admiration, the old man was crafty. "You expect me to find my way to Gabrond?"

"Are you incapable of smelling a horse?"

"Nay, Tully…but I smell a deer being hunted." Her eyes strayed to the sentry nearby.

Tully's cackle of laughter startled a tribeswoman out of a nearby roundhouse. When she realised Tully was not being threatened, or ill, she retreated back inside her domain.

Nara stared at him. "Chief Tully of Garrigill, I have already noticed that the horse enclosure is inside the gates of Garrigill. And the practice field is well outside the gates."

Tully's laughter ceased as quickly as it started. "Aye, woman. I had a notion last night that you were a quick thinker. I was not mistaken."

She waited, hoping the irritation she felt did not show. It was one thing to be part of a jest, but another to be an object of ridicule.

"You have my authorisation to go out with the gates of Garrigill to the practice field only, Nara of Tarras, and when Gabrond is done with you return directly to me here."

Nara became aware of two things as she left Tully's roundhouse and headed for the entrance gates she had come in at the previous day. People observed her passing them, some openly stared, but they did not attempt to speak with her...or accost her in any way. She also knew she had acquired a shadow since a warrior was following her; not entirely unexpected.

Nonetheless, she had a freedom of sorts as the man stalked at least ten paces behind her. In spite of her situation, a grin broke free. At least she was unfettered, no leash on her wrist...

The sudden thought of Lorcan made her unsure which was better. To be free of him? Or tied in some emotional way? Nonetheless, she missed him as she strode onto the practice field.

Gabrond, she soon learned, was one of Garrigill's most skilled charioteers. On the practice field, he demonstrated his skills with his spearman, Seamus, on his two-person wicker chariot. Nara was intrigued to find he preferred to do the driving, not regularly the position taken by the higher ranking warrior.

"I manage the horses better, and I drive the chariot more skilfully than any other Garrigill warrior," he boasted unreservedly. "But my spearman, Seamus, has the better aim. We work well together."

"Your brother, Lorcan, has a fine aim with his spear." Nara's comment was grudging, but it made Gabrond laugh heartily...though perhaps with far too much ribaldry for her present mood.

143

"Aye. His spearing skills are legendary. Lorcan would do as well for me as Seamus, but my brother has other duties. He is unsurpassed as emissary for our tribe."

Nara preferred not to dwell on the dangers that beset the spokesperson of a tribe, as Gabrond led her around the area. It came as a surprise when he insisted she demonstrate her skills with a spear, though she was completely aware that should she attempt anything foolhardy she was outnumbered by a whole tribe. Time spent riding a chariot alongside Gabrond was exhilarating. The vehicle was perfectly balanced for her strength and proficiency.

She had not been allowed to ride at Tarras for two long moons.

During the course of the morning she learned about many of the Garrigill practices from Gabrond, and he, in turn, learned about the usual routines at Tarras. She imparted no secret information about Callan's training strategies, since she truly had no recent knowledge. Tarras now seemed a distant memory, though she had only been away from it for mere days.

Tully had ensured his sons had all gained the skills to lead the huge settlement, though she discovered each had a particular area of expertise.

Gabrond was the horse expert, and best charioteer. His main tasks were to oversee the equine stock and to train up the horse-handlers.

Brennus was tribal champion, and overseer of the younger warriors in swordsmanship.

Lorcan was the tribe's special envoy. Nara knew that meant being a routine messenger, yet he was also the bearer of sensitive news, and often worked under dangerous and clandestine conditions.

Arian had been in charge of Garrigill's defences, and had been master of the weaponry stores.

"A replacement for Arian should be decided upon very soon given our defences must remain unvanquished in the event of Roman attack." Gabrond spoke only of Roman threat and not from another Celtic tribe.

144

"Who will be chosen?" she dared to ask, wondering who had the best knowledge and skills for the job had complex issues.

"There are many able warriors, not offspring of Tully, who will be considered by the council. In particular we have very fine warriors in Bran and Roc."

The process of choice was similar in her own tribe as the next chosen leader was not always the son or daughter, of a chief.

***

Ford of Sequanna – Selgovae territory

Lorcan had been in similar situations before, his outward appearance confident and purposeful. Accompanied by Brennus and six warriors, he had ridden hard all morning, and now approached the Ford of Sequanna. He knew the moment Raeden warriors had spotted his band, could see them making ready to attack.

Pulling his horse to a halt, he ordered his men to follow suit. He rammed his spear into the earth alongside his horse, giving the signal that weapon less, he came to the area with peaceful intent. Dismounting first, he waited for a moment before his warriors also slid from their horses, to rank themselves at his side.

The Raeden warriors halted within shouting distance. "What brings you here, Brigante?"

"I am Lorcan, son of Tully of Garrigill. I wish to speak with Rigg of Raeden regarding Princess Nara of Tarras."

He wanted no mistake about his purpose in riding their territory. He needed Rigg's permission to undertake the rest of his journey safely in Selgovae lands.

Until the Raeden messenger summoned Rigg, Lorcan's warriors rested by the ford. He sat by the banking where Nara had challenged him only days ago. He was filled with a longing he had never experienced before. She had been in his thoughts the whole ride. She was a tempestuous forest goddess, wild and challenging. He missed sparring with her,

145

missed her sharp wit, and the taste of her eager tongue wrapped around his.

He felt a measure of regret that he had not taken their lovemaking of the previous evening to a satisfactory conclusion – yet knew he would have been disappointed if he had done that. It would have been too hushed and far too hurried. He would not have been disappointed with Nara, yet he would have been dissatisfied with himself. He had a duty to his tribe. His fist slammed against the ground venting his frustration.

Nara must not be given to anyone but him.

Yet he had forced a situation he had to see through to the end. It was fortuitous that within a short time Rigg himself appeared, putting an end to the murky thoughts overtaking him.

"You have Princess Nara of Tarras captive at Garrigill?" Rigg demanded before his horse was even properly halted.

Lorcan had no desire to inflame Rigg unnecessarily, yet though the manner of the Selgovae chief's approach was abrupt and challenging, it was not truly aggressive.

"Princess Nara is an honoured guest of Tully of Garrigill. I need to speak to Callan of Tarras, regarding her future welfare, and for that I request permission to cross your lands."

He was gratified – indeed it was what he had hoped for – when Rigg insisted on Raeden warriors escorting his band across Selgovae lands since it meant no delay in reaching Tarras, the Raeden escorts knowing the swiftest route.

The incident over the recent loss of both Garrigill and Raeden warriors was skirted over in the usual way, since it was a closed matter. Yet Lorcan took the opportunity to inquire if Rigg knew anything about Cearnach, knowing how distressed Nara had been. Of Cearnach the news was good, he was alive and recovering.

Less good was the news that Rigg had already sent messengers to Tarras about the incident, warning Callan that Nara was thought to have been abducted by the raiding Brigantes. As Lorcan journeyed on to Tarras, he thought on how to tackle that supposition.

Chapter Twelve

Hillfort of Garrigill – Brigante territory

Tully was waiting for Nara inside the roundhouse, her shadow having again followed her back into the hillfort. She did not know whether to feel offended, or thankful, since she had not yet worked out Tully's full reasoning for the guard. She was certain it was not simply to ensure she did not escape.

The old chief sat atop a pile of skins even higher than the evening before. Leaning heavily to one side, his voice was feeble, but determined. "So, princess. Have you learned everything about our practice methods?"

She ignored the asperity in his words. He looked deathly tired. "Gabrond made me demonstrate the skills I possess." She tried for a bland tone yet knew she failed miserably, as she had enjoyed her time on the field.

"Your prowess down on the field passes muster, warrior-woman. It seems you have been taught well by the Selgovae."

"You have heard already?"

Though Tully moved little himself, he missed nothing at Garrigill. "Gabrond's man has already informed me. Now, let us speak of other matters, warrior-princess. You may not rest now either, for you and I will talk, though I plan to mostly listen."

Tully questioned her on her visit. Her answers seemed to please him; his nods were frequent and the tone less snippy as he went on. Having grilled her extensively, he was grudging. "Woman of the Selgovae, you look, listen and learn well, but are you aware you know perhaps too much of the Garrigill practice fields?"

Her answer was careful, her tone betraying no fear, yet no overt defiance was visible either.

147

"I have learned much today, but a person may only impart knowledge in the correct places to make it valuable."

"A good answer, princess. You are a woman who sees her situation well. Now, I would have you tell me of your clanhold, as your quick mind knows much of mine already. My son, Lorcan, must have made note of those sharp wits of yours…as well as other more obvious parts of you, which I know for sure he has studied well."

The mention of Lorcan was enough to start up those longings again. He had not yet been gone a single day, but he had been much in her thoughts. When she had been demonstrating something to Gabrond she had imagined Lorcan's appreciative brown eyes applaud her expertise. That warm feeling suffused her face again.

"I believe Lorcan has impressed you in some way, Princess Nara?"

Nara found it was not only Tully who could use sarcasm to advantage. She, too, found it was easier to mouth than admiration. "Lorcan dragged me to Garrigill as his captive. Why would that impress me, Tully?"

A faint twinkling of his eyes showed the still bright intellect striving to overcome physical dysfunctions. Changing the subject, Tully questioned her about Tarras.

"Well told, warrior-woman of the spear! You have a keen mind for telling the important. I have no time for wasted words. Callan of Tarras must be proud of your knowledge for you have a true warrior's acquaintance of what it takes to keep a hillfort's defences running smoothly."

Her candid answer, she hoped, betrayed none of her feelings about Callan's lack of pride in her, but did not care too much if it did. "My knowledge has not been relied on by Callan at all."

"Then what did you do all day, since you profess a need to be active all the time?"

Since a return to Tarras did not look likely in her near future she told Tully all.

"You were an acolyte?" Tully could not hide his amazement. "But you are a branded warrior?"

"The island *nemeton* lies near Tarras but needs particular protection. Four seasons ago, I acceded as overseer of its defences. As the only warrior-princess, and the highest ranking female apart from the High Priestess, I was in charge of its defences."

"Lorcan told the assembly you have no current husband…" Tully's gnarled fingers stroked his wiry chin as he postulated, "…therefore he knows you have never had a husband before?"

"He knows." She blushed under Tully's intense scrutiny.

"Mmm…" Tully continued to grill her. "Exactly how much does my son know about you, princess?"

Nara smiled but would not be drawn further. "Your son knows I am also a trained healer. Many practical skills learned at the *nemeton* were used for the wellbeing of my tribe."

"So gifted." Back to the irascible tones, Tully mocked her confidence in her capabilities. "You are a warrior-woman, and a healer? Contrasting skills. I wonder which you would deem to be your best." His misty eyes teased, dared her answer, but his lined face remained forbidding. "As well as having a cleverly sharp tongue."

"Then permit me to speak of another matter?"

His piercing glitter lingered before a barely perceptible jerk indicated agreement.

"At the *nemeton,* I never had a woman to tend me. May I look after myself, since it appears I have no option but to remain till Lorcan returns?"

Tully's distrustful glare would have stripped a carcass without a knife. "Is this a ploy to flay me with later? Will you declare I cannot look to the needs of a visiting princess? Woman, do you know what you are about?"

"Aye, thank you. Carn has other tasks. I am fit and healthy. If I cannot look to my own needs it is an ill day."

"So be it. You tire me, woman. Leave. Go find some useful deed to occupy you."

The meal that eve was a quiet affair, only Nara and Tully. She found it awkward being Tully's sole company, knowing so little of the old man's habits, and worked out how to assess his moods. Tully was uncommunicative, was in fact back to his distrustful expression. Something angered him anew, but she could not fathom what. She made no idle conversation, aware of his dislike for such, and ate in silence.

She wondered how Lorcan fared. If he had ridden hard, he would be at Tarras before the end of the day. How would Callan accept Lorcan's arrival? Had her father's sentries already killed him at the outposts of Tarras?

Shivers beset her even though the small fire gave off sufficient heat. The broth in her bowl no longer appealed, and she felt she would choke on the bread Carn had provided. Caressing her dry throat, she remembered how tender Lorcan had been when she had choked on the bannock.

Memories stirred: how his strong hands had stroked her hair, and how his vitality had imparted into her own body. No one had ever given her that all-encompassing care. Lorcan had given her the gift of life when he had saved her, but she was realising that he was giving her more than that.

Where was he? He was potentially in danger of losing his life, and she could do nothing about it. She fretted the bread in her hands to a pile of crumbs, eventually throwing them onto the fire.

"You waste good food, woman." She noted a tinge of sympathy lurking in Tully's eyes when he focused on her fingers. "Lorcan does not need your worry, princess of the Selgovae. He is well-skilled in announcing his arrival when he goes forth to other settlements. Instead of fretting, give him your trust, and your prayers. I have nothing but admiration for my son's judgment."

Pray?

Nara was expert at that, yet, she was not convinced Rhianna was listening to her. She willed herself to believe in Lorcan, to be confident he had found a way to approach Tarras safely. And then she prayed Callan would listen to Lorcan and his bargain. And prayed her father would not murder Lorcan afterwards, or as he slept. Never in her life had she missed anyone so much, or in fact, ever had such overpowering feelings for.

150

She pushed the bowl of broth away, surprised under Tully's urging she had managed to finish it, but it lay heavy in her stomach. To be responsible for Lorcan's death anguished her. The warrior had wormed his way into her heart.

At an abrupt wave from Tully, Nara rose uncertainly.

"Soon the council of Garrigill will meet without you at my side. Go, and remain there." Imperiously he pointed to her stall. "Watch from the door, princess, but say nothing and listen well."

Hurt by his peremptory order she stalked away, her emotions fluctuating while she took up her allotted place. Feeling every bit the vulnerable interloper she had to honestly acknowledge if she remained in the shadows, Tully's people would be less inhibited by her presence.

***

Tarras – Selgovae territory

Sundown was almost complete when the shout of a Raeden warrior brought Lorcan out of his daydream of Nara as they exited a forest onto a low plain.

"Men of Tarras heading this way."

Some five and ten warriors galloped along the flat land towards them though he was not troubled as they had already passed unchallenged through the outposts of Tarras. Undoubtedly, someone had been dispatched to warn Callan of their imminent arrival.

Then he was told it was Callan himself who rode to meet him...

Lorcan sat undeterred in the saddle, continuing on to Nara's father, the man who had given her such heartache during her life. He had not liked the man when she spoke of his mistreatment, and he could not like the blustering warrior who rode up spouting an insincere greeting before he had even got close enough to rein in his horse.

"Brigantes of Garrigill! You come with tidings? Who speaks for you?"

"I am Lorcan, son of Tully of Garrigill."

151

What followed was a parody of a welcome, not expected at all. Callan, he learned, was pleased to talk to Brigantes since it was an ill time for all Celts. They must discuss recent Roman threats – but in the comfort of his home. Lorcan was suspicious. Callan appeared too affable. Yet the man could aim to deceive. Lorcan disliked Callan's cunning streak, even though Nara's father did not directly threaten him.

Nara's name never passed Callan of Tarras' lips before he wheeled around and galloped off, leading them across the flat floodplain to the hillock where the settlement of Tarras was located.

Lorcan's Brigantes were led to Callan's roundhouse as though honoured guests. Caution sat on his shoulder. Why did Callan behave in such a manner? His daughter had been snatched and made captive, yet this scheming chief welcomed the Brigante band?

Inside the roundhouse customary greetings were proclaimed. Food was brought to them, and only after they started to eat was Lorcan able to bring up the subject of Nara.

"Nara will not enter our discussion at this time, Lorcan of the Brigantes. Roman scouts invading our territory is a much more important topic."

Callan's dismissive attitude towards Nara was difficult to work around diplomatically. He was listening to Callan rant about marauding Roman scouts when warriors of Tarras burst in with news of a Roman ship landing on the coastline not far away.

His fears were coming to fruition too soon. Callan's roundhouse became a flurry of immediate decision making.

But not about Nara.

***

Hillfort of Garrigill – Brigante territory

Tully's roundhouse filled up, representatives from the outer valley areas having arrived, eager to voice their opinions on the proposals. The discussion became animated; voices rose in

152

doubt, but most favoured alliances – given the critical circumstances.

Achingly slowly, it seemed to Nara as she watched from the back of the room, Tully stood to address the crowd.

"Now, we must decide. Is anyone not meeting this proposal with favour?" A few stood up. Tully called to the opposite end of the room. "I take it that you have a better plan for us, Finlay?"

The booming voice of the warrior standing close to her was deafening. "Nay, I have no other, but it does not meet with my favour to make peace. You propose to befriend those who days past took the life of your eldest son, a man I deemed my best friend. It defies me to understand how you can forget so easily." Finlay's angry words echoed around the room as he scowled at her.

"You do me wrong to think I could ever forget Arian." Tully's old voice sounded impassioned, heartbroken. "It is for my other sons I take these steps. I would that they all live to see their own sons born, Finlay, and for that they must not die under Roman swords."

Tully gathered his ailing strength before wearily questioning the other dissenters, though nothing proposed changed the minds of the majority.

"So be it. Garrigill will progress alliances with all Celtic neighbours, and we will expect results before Beltane."

Gradually the roundhouse emptied, only a requested few remaining. Tully looked exhausted and twisted with pain as emissaries were chosen, to be dispatched in the early morn. All departed afterwards except Gabrond.

Gabrond assisted his father into his stall, every bone of the old chief showing how utterly weary he was. Moments later, Gabrond also left.

Forgotten, Nara could have easily escaped the roundhouse, but she was not lulled into believing a complete escape from Garrigill would have been possible. Guards were on high alert, and she was nobody's fool.

Lorcan permeated her dreams…A very alive and fit Lorcan.

Next morning, Nara wore the simple, almost threadbare, pale green dress left by Carn, leaving aside her warrior clothes. She had no wish to send the wrong message to the ordinary people at Garrigill who already looked upon her with such disfavour. Her warrior clothes could await another day when she took her leave of Garrigill, but till then the faded and much worn green shift would suffice.

Lorcan had already been away for one whole long day, his return an unknown event. Insecure flutters beset her, but she resolutely quelled them, instead concentrating on regaining the self-assurance she had felt before her expulsion from the *nemeton*. She tried to persuade herself that her unfamiliarity would have been similar at Raeden...but the flaw in that thinking was that Raeden was full of Selgovae, not Brigantes.

Fulfilling Tully's orders, Carn towed her around the settlement where she met women and children of the tribe. None were friendly; some were hostile, though they did not dare to directly speak of their feelings. Though Tully had given an order, she was not accorded the welcome of a guest.

Many of the younger men were overly frank in their attention, with an overt manner she was certain they would never have dared to use, if Lorcan had been present. Again, he permeated her thoughts.

Carn was a good guide, but she would much have preferred Lorcan to have taken her around. She missed him more and more as the day waned, missed his caressing deep brown eyes, his humour, and his quirky little smile. She even missed his relentless questioning and his erratic moods.

Nara sensed Carn was angered as she escorted her around, the younger woman pretending to ignore the slights made by the tribespeople. When the sun was well through its pathway in the sky, Carn took her to the smithy roundhouse where her father, Donnal, the head smith, had been labouring long and hard fashioning new weapons. She had no notion of where her own weapons were stored, but was not surprised when no new ones were offered. She could look, even admire, but not handle.

"Have you visited your mother, Carn?" Donnal asked.

"Father, my duty has been to accompany Princess Nara around the settlement."

Donnal's annoyance was clear as he stared. It took a few moments before he spoke again tension tight across his jaw when he turned back to Carn.

"Your mother is unwell today. She has been vomiting, and is unable to properly care for your baby sister."

Carn's expression was full of conflict. It was easy to see how torn she was between her duty as directed by Tully and her concern for her mother.

"Go to your mother, Carn," Nara urged.

"I cannot leave you, Princess Nara. You do not know the settlement, yet."

Nara had to persuade Carn to see to her family. "I know the direction we came in, and I will retrace my steps to Tully's roundhouse. I will not be foolish enough to try to leave Garrigill. I know well enough how defended it is...and how well I am guarded."

The rough laugh from Donnal persuaded his daughter Nara was correct – she was not going to escape from Garrigill.

"Princess Nara will be at Tully's roundhouse when you return, Carn."

Nara's nod convinced the woman.

Carn rushed off.

Nara dawdled as she wended between the isolated storage roundhouses, curious to know what each contained as she popped her head into the openings. With no warning, a sinewy form launched at her from behind, her chin slamming to the ground before she could cry out. A bruising arm at her neck had her gasping for breath, and kept her pinned to the ground. Almost immediately, a second warrior joined the affray to help gag and blindfold. Any noise she made was instantly muffled.

Yanked to feet, she reeled at the speed of the assault. Her arms were roped behind her back before she could retaliate, and then she was thrust into motion. Her upper arms felt the chill from sunlight to shade making her certain she had been pushed into one of the stores. The unexpected blow to the back of her head sent her stumbling, then a scuffling of feet, and some muffled muttering convinced her they had fled.

"Lorcan!" Everything blackened around her. "Lorc…"

Nara awoke to see nothing but the dark of closed eyes behind the blindfold. Her head hurt as she tried to remember, her knees smarting like nettle stings. Her blood did not seem to flow properly in her legs, or her arms, and then she felt herself being dragged over rough ground, her face scraping painfully along the way. She wanted to call for help, but the tight gag proved an effective muffle. She had no memory of her legs being trussed together like the boar Lorcan had tied up days ago, but she knew she was restrained in exactly the same way as she was pulled along by the feet, her whole body bowed to one side.

Lorcan could not possibly help her.

Alone, and defenceless her heart thumped a panicked beat. Who else could help? The list contained few. Perhaps Carn, or Tully? Brennus could not since he was with Lorcan.

She prayed to her goddess, Rhianna, with all her might. Surely, she was not to die, at the hands of unknown attackers? If she died she could not bear the son Swatrega had dreamed about. She wanted Lorcan. She screamed it but only her head heard. Her thoughts became a recurring jumble.

Oblivion claimed her again.

On her next awakening, she willed herself to calm the dregs of panic, working all the while to regulate her breathing. The gag was still tight around her mouth, and when she inhaled through her nose the reek was awful. Tanning leather stenches assaulted her nostrils, overpoweringly so and a weight pinned her down: from the feel of it she was hidden underneath a pile of skins.

How would anyone find her? Was Lorcan going to be told she had suffocated? After all the trouble he had gone to dragging her to Garrigill. She felt hot…trapped…her head reeling…breathing…was no longer possible…

When she awoke next, her head thumped, the earlier nausea not much alleviated. She realised she must have been in the storage room for some time for it to affect her so strongly. The same mistake would not be made again; shallow breaths were her focus.

"Nara? Where are you?"

"Princess Nara? Where are you?"

"Gabrond? Carn?

Aye. It was definitely them. Bucking and rocking under the skins she hollered to gain their attention. Her muffled cries deafened her and robbed her of what little breath she had. Surely, if she kept it up, though, someone would hear?

Voices grew louder, all shouting her name. The weight of skins disappeared; the wrap around her eyes was removed. Carn wept as she untied Nara's feet. Someone else removed the gag and ties at her hands.

"Who did this to you, Princess Nara?" Carn sobbed. "The blame is mine. I should not have left you…"

Distraught, Carn's hands straightened out her legs and she briskly rubbed the blood back in. Lying flat on her back, Nara regarded her rescuers. Gabrond looked furious, his brows drawn together. Carn was tearful but clearly happy that Nara had been found. Others around the roundhouse looked abashed, but relieved. When she could to sit up properly, Gabrond began his interrogation. Nara was reluctant to answer till the assurance came that he was not angry with her, but with her assailants.

"Tully will have their hides when we identify them," he ranted, as he strode around the room.

She could tell him nothing, had not caught even a glimpse of her attackers.

Striding around was beyond Tully's capabilities, when Gabrond led her back to him, but it did not stop his tongue from lashing when he found the breath to do so.

"Seek the culprits of this ill deed, without delay, Gabrond. Question all at Garrigill for someone will know who is responsible. I will not have my orders flaunted in this way. Whoever did this will pay a heavy penalty!" Old Tully's gaze softened when he turned to her. "Do you have hurts not visible to me, Nara of Tarras?"

She was careful to answer; did not wish to make her situation more perilous than it already was. There had been hostility enough, that afternoon, in the looks she'd received from some of the settlement dwellers. "Any bruises I received today will fade quickly, Tully. I accept your intervention, but I do not wish to inflame further resentment."

Gabrond started with a list of those who had been most against Nara's presence at Garrigill – the warrior called Finlay, in particular, who had been so vehemently against the plans to unite Selgovae and Brigante blood.

Carn fussed over Nara's wounds though they were insignificant. Her knees, and calves, had been torn to shreds when her attackers lugged her from the first roundhouse to the one she was eventually found in. A sizeable lump at the back of her head was painful to the touch, but it had not bled. The most obvious evidence of her incident was the bruising that blossomed on her chin, from the first fall to the ground, and the subsequent grazing, and cuts to her cheek when dragged between storage huts.

"Enough!" Tully was the one who stopped Carn's mother-hen fussing with a single word and one of his ferocious glares.

In spite of the pain at her chin, Nara laughed. "Aye, Carn, enough mothering. Nothing is so bad. I have suffered much worse from one fall from a horse. Do not distress yourself."

She knew Carn blamed herself for the whole incident, though it was none of her making. Retiring to her stall for a short rest, she was glad to be under Tully's protection because Garrigill was not the safe haven Lorcan thought it was.

Chapter Thirteen

Nara's quiet introspection was shattered when Brennus erupted into the roundhouse that evening in a disturbed flurry, drawing Tully's immediate attention.

"Roman forces have overpowered more of the southernmost Brigantes, slaughter is widespread, and still the Romans march on northwards."

A trail of warriors followed him in led by a forbidding man she had not seen before.

Brennus back at Garrigill, but not Lorcan?

Her heart pounded. The contents of her stomach rebelled, so fearful was she for Lorcan's safety. Forcing down the bile rising into her mouth, she concentrated on what was happening around her.

The newcomer was almost as tall as Brennus, just as broad of shoulder, but there the similarities ended. His appearance was brutal. His hair was almost as dark as Lorcan's, but one cheekbone was marred by a poorly healed laceration from his left eye to his ear. The scarring was immaterial, but it was his eyes which disconcerted. Malice and threat emanated from him like a black aura. He strode to Tully, no stranger to the roundhouse.

Tully's typical terse orders were accompanied by weak hand gestures. "Carn! Rally the women and see to these warriors."

Nara rose to help Carn, but Tully's imperious wave had her seated again, right alongside him, his gestures allowing her no option but to remain.

She could see how exhausted Brennus was. Tully, on the other hand, appeared to have found reserves of strength, eagerness sparking his old eyes.

159

"All, be seated. Give me your news, Brennus. How do you come to return without Lorcan?"

Brennus' intent gaze did nothing to quell the terrifying fear that overtook her. By Rhianna! What had Callan done? A rush of questions flooded her mind.

"Lorcan remains at Tarras."

Brennus spoke across Tully, his eyes never leaving her face. The stare he sent her she could not read. She wondered what Callan might have said to him. But then again, perhaps the bruising and grazes at her chin, which she had earlier made light of, were disgusting to view.

Dragging his gaze back to Tully, Brennus continued. "Lorcan's mission had barely begun when Callan received information about Roman scouts infiltrating his territory, and of a Roman ship having landed off his shores. It was vital information to share with all the tribes who live anywhere near the estuary and the high hills."

Nara gasped. A Roman landing from the sea was terrible news. Again, Brennus stared at her. Why should he be so angry with her?

"Lorcan remains at Tarras, to glean more information about the Roman arrivals. He dispatched me round the firth to Ivegill, to warn Shea. As you see, Shea returned with me, Father."

Nara breathed again. Callan had not put Lorcan to the sword. Her life-blood slowed. Still, news of Roman invasion was grim, and Lorcan was far too close to their ships.

Brennus sank down, his information given. Tiredness wafted from him as he slumped over.

Shea of Ivegill – the territory lying to the north-west of Garrigill – was of the Carvetii, an associate tribe of the Brigantes. Shea's lands were close to the western shores and much closer to her own home at Tarras. She had heard tell of how ruthless he could be, and now seeing him, she did not doubt it. It did not please her to see how he ogled her and deliberately stared at her chest.

Tully questioned Shea drawing his attention from her, which was heartily gladdening.

"So how fares it with your own clanhold, Shea? Have there been recent disturbances?"

"Aye, Tully. A few of my warriors routed the Roman scouting party seen by Gyptus' men. They killed three of them, but the rest escaped into the deeper forests of Fauldsbrow." His voice was civil, but though he answered Tully, Shea's beady eyes strayed restlessly towards her. "We would have got them all, but my men were outnumbered." His calculating gaze again settled on her.

"Word lately, has not been encouraging," Tully replied, and prompted Shea for further details.

"All southern Brigante tribes are now under attack. They strengthen their defences, but the Roman force marching north-westwards at present numbers well above five thousand."

"But we Brigantes can repel those numbers. We can muster many more men than that," Tully spat back.

"That is only one of their mighty legions of troops. The tribes to the far south could not repel them." Shea's tone was menacing. "The Romans are a fierce fighting force the Catuvellauni could not match. Though we fight to the death, we have no corresponding weaponry, and their plans of attack best ours. Their head and chest amour is mighty, almost impenetrable, and their firing weapons bombard our front lines mercilessly."

Again, his watchful eyes locked onto her, making her squirm. His blatant interest repelled her so much she averted her gaze, unable to face him, though she still listened to his words.

"You sound defeatist, Shea." Tully was angry. "What would have us do? Surrender?"

"Never think that, Tully," Shea bellowed. His eyes were feverishly cruel, mirroring his intimidating presence. "We need to strengthen ourselves. The Romans fight as one unit – we must also do that, but we need to prepare ourselves much better for the fray."

"You speak like Lorcan. Do you also believe we need to make alliances with our Celtic enemies to the north?"

"Brennus has updated me, about Lorcan's proposal on our travels, and I find the scheme has much merit." Shea stroked the long whiskers around his mouth. "I like it even more so since I see the princess of the Selgovae. She may be marred at present, but that only makes her more tempting."

His salivating gaze made her cringe. Ignoring his disfiguring cheek wound was easy, yet she still could not like the warrior. A cruel twist to his lips remained, though his tone became more amenable.

"My wife of six winters recently died giving birth to my fourth son. I, therefore, seek a new wife to tend my hearthside."

Nara felt nothing but pity for the woman who took on that role.

As he greedily devoured the food offered, Shea informed them of Brigante survivors who flocked to his north-western shores. The fate of those remaining in the south-western areas, newly occupied by the *Legio II Adiutrix*, sounded grim. To be a slave of the Roman Empire was an unacceptable prospect to all present in the roundhouse. As Shea expounded, Nara gazed around her, seeing the admirable aspects of her Celtic culture displayed around the room. Under Roman dominion, she imagined her life as a slave would be in very different surroundings.

It was late before the gathering broke up.

The discussion had been extremely volatile, but this time the malice was directed at their Roman enemy. The interest being bestowed on her by Shea and Brennus was, in a way, flattering, but neither of them obtained her attention like Lorcan. They were, however, contenders for the position of husband to her, and that was very troubling.

She missed Lorcan's steadying presence, but she knew she must be more disciplined. Reality had hit her. Her future was looking less likely to include Lorcan: it looked increasingly bleak.

It was disconcerting to realise Shea was quartered in Tully's roundhouse, for his lascivious regard all evening had made her feel tainted.

"I desire a word with you, Princess Nara."

Though Shea's words were casual, his demeanour was sinister. He had intercepted her, a pathway away from Tully's roundhouse, after she had gone out for a welcome escape from the fireside talk.

"A word?" Squelching her aversion, and attempting to match his informal tone, she allowed his relaxed touch at her bare arm. It was not Lorcan's hand, but made no move to reject it.

"About you and I fulfilling the marriage bargain," Shea answered, his bold hand straying to cup her shoulder and bring her tight into him. "My clanhold lies nearer Tarras than Garrigill, much closer for you to maintain contact with your own people." Both hands now caressed her shoulders, his fingers diligently fingering her collarbones. "We would make a good union," he muttered, his gaze on her body while his hands slid lower to cup her breasts, his head bending down to kiss her.

She hated the feel of his hard lips against her own, and the touch of his hands on her skin made her squirm. Though she controlled her temper, she loathed the audacity of his invasion of her body. His pitiless intensity scared her.

Breaking free, her tone was as even as she could muster. "You may like to think so, Shea of Ivegill."

She could not countenance allowing Shea to do the things to her that Lorcan had. The thought horrified her, because if Shea had been the one to encounter her in the forest she would have been cruelly violated and then most likely killed. Shea would not have bothered to discover her status in her tribe.

Squirming away, Nara made her way swiftly to Tully's roundhouse, dipping into the low entrance tunnel just as Brennus was coming out.

"So, Princess Nara," Brennus said, forcing her to back out again to allow his own exit, his eyes teasing. "It is as I told you; there are many Brigante men eligible for you to sample. So tell me, how does Shea's kiss compare with mine?"

"If I told you about your kiss you may not like my answer. It would please me to go back and bid your father good night

163

if you would permit me to enter?" Her tone was brusque, but she had no wish to give Brennus false hope.

"I will bid you a good night, Nara of Tarras. I have heard of how you came by the bruising. If you were mine, none at Garrigill would attempt to hurt you." Brennus' regard was a conflict of apology and protection.

Nara was relieved to be told the next morning both Shea and Brennus had left the settlement. Shea had gone home, and Brennus had headed off to another Brigante clanhold.

The responsibility of Swatrega's prophecy sat heavily on her. She had considered men in Tarras and none were her choice. Now, in Garrigill, it appeared men desired her, though only Lorcan stirred her spirit. There was no word of his return, yet the discourse with Callan could not have taken so long.

As more days passed, Nara really began to worry. What had Callan done? He was capable of making deadly decisions. Many possibilities flashed through her fevered mind...but Tully gave her no respite to wallow in miserable gloom.

Tully set her further learning tasks around the hillfort and challenged her knowledge on her return. Always she had a shadow, though the warrior guard changed. She got to know her guards quite well, for rather than have them follow her she bid them walk with her.

It was a situation that served both of them well, and wily old Tully did not protest when apprised of the altered circumstances.

The next day was followed by another, and another...and still no Lorcan. She tried to block him from her mind, tried to dim the attraction she felt for him. Nothing worked. Not even her pleas to Rhianna brought forth any news.

Tully's daily tests were a tease. His irascible tone never eased, but she became inured to it. Since Tully treated Carn, and others around Garrigill, with the same disdain, she came to believe there was nothing personal to his tetchy attitude. In a very odd way, she looked forward to crossing words with the old chief, but she did not look forward to seeing his gradual decline as his health rapidly deteriorated. The circumstances of the Roman threat, and Lorcan's continued absence with no further word, Nara could see, took its toll on Tully.

Risking the consequences of his disfavour, given they were not yet what she would term friends, she waited no longer to help him. "Tully, if you were not so proud I truly believe I could help ease your pain. I am trained in the healing arts, and I have watched you well these past days."

"I know you have, Selgovae woman. I can not move without those all-knowing eyes of yours tracking my every wince. You have something to say, healer Nara?"

Nara now knew when his sarcasm was at its peak it was also when Tully showed her the greatest respect, strange though that seemed. Her gaze held his unfalteringly, her candid manner daring him to verbally attack her, for she had gleaned ways to counter his biting wit.

"Your passing will come soon – I cannot prevent that Tully – but during these next difficult days I could make your living easier. You have much to do and many hard decisions to make without the demands of your ailing body."

His faded blue eyes became little pinpoints of black, as he absorbed her words. He stared for long moments challenging her audacity, yet Nara held her ground. She would not take back her words, her pride refused to allow her to quail under his gaze. Then he laughed. A feeble old man's laugh, though jovial nonetheless.

"Nara of the spear! Only a stranger would dare address me as you do." His crotchety voice mellowed. "You are confident you could ease my pains? Your arrogance has appeal. What makes you feel you can do what others cannot?"

"Tully, something tells me you have allowed no one to help you, so far, therefore how can I not have some success? My skills are well known in Tarras, though you have left it late."

Tully tested her, rising to the confident tone of her voice. "You also see into the future like a diviner?"

"No, that I cannot as you well know, or I would not be your captive. I would not have allowed Lorcan to chance upon me in the wood."

As before, Lorcan was never far from her thoughts. His name had arisen many times in their conversation over the course of a day.

"I do not need to see like a gifted one to know we all pass over to the otherworld. I merely wish no one go sooner than is their due, or more painfully if it can be alleviated. I can but try to make your last days easier."

Tully's laugh showed appreciation of her humour. "You have spirit, girl. I will think on it. Now, go! Your confrontations exhaust me."

Nara was wretched in her heart of hearts, as the endless days succeeded each other though she was at pains to keep her feelings hidden. However, she was busy, too, as Tully ensured no time was wasted. A mellowing, of sorts, towards her had come gradually, the most important of which was he allowed her to treat him with her potions. Trust was being built steadily between them. When they discussed Lorcan, as they inevitably did each evening around the fireside, Nara knew it was a two-way thing. Tully missed Lorcan as much as she did. Empathy flowed from her. Tully's only son left at Garrigill was Gabrond.

She found herself carrying out tasks rather than learning – though she still had someone trailing her every move around Garrigill. Tully saw to that even though he had routed out and severely punished her attackers. It had not been the warrior called Finlay who had trussed her up like a boar, but two others who resented her presence at Garrigill. Their ruthless sentencing – each of them losing one hand – meant it was unlikely anyone else would try to harm her, but Lorcan's continued absence fired the flames of distrust. Until he returned she was still under suspicion by many of the tribespeople.

Other warriors of Garrigill became known quite well, but none of them stirred her emotions as Lorcan did. He was unique; only he had ever created that tingling blood-rush in her with just one look. His touch was the only one she wanted on her skin. Lorcan was still the only warrior she could contemplate siring her son.

Local matters were discussed around the fireside each evening, matters she was surprised to find she had not been excluded from. Being at Tully's side alleviated the loneliness and was especially encouraging when she was permitted to voice an opinion. Tully increasingly allowed this as it appeared he valued her judgments. She had become familiar with the two warriors who were favoured to become chief if none of Tully's sons were elected. Bran and Roc, older than Lorcan, were battle hardy warriors who both possessed good organizational skills, though the elders all agreed they were not as subtle in negotiation as Lorcan was.

"Nara of Tarras!" Tully's rasping bark caught her attention. Her concentration had wavered again. The mere mention of Lorcan's name by someone around the fireside made it happen. "I have no further need of your presence."

Summarily dismissed, she walked over to her stall, contented to be alone with her sad thoughts. On closing her door screen, a noisy flurry at the entryway drew her attention.

Carn rushed in with news that delegates from Tarras had arrived.

Flustered and uncertain her hand trembled on the leather. Lorcan was back? Would he be glad to see her? It had been nine long days since she had seen him. Drawing aside her door hanging, she knelt on the ground. To wait…and watch.

Chapter Fourteen

"Let them enter!" Tully boomed, a matter of formality that they be so announced.

Nara was startled when Shea of Ivegill entered with her father in his wake. Callan blustered in followed by three of his most high ranking tribesmen, her ailing brother Niall, and a gaggle of other warriors behind them.

But no Lorcan.

Her hand clutched at the door frame, her knees unable to support her, dread filling her heart. Callan was here, but not Lorcan?

Shea headed directly to Tully, arrogantly confirming the visitor was indeed Nara's father. "I know Callan from before though not in cordial circumstances, as we expect these to be."

Nara heard the underlying malice in his tone and knew their previous meetings to have been border skirmishes. The refrain churned over and over. Where was Lorcan? Her fingers fretted the leather door skin, tiny bits of hide peeling off under her nails.

Tully struggled to his feet, his movements a little easier since taking her mixture a short while ago, though she knew the effects of each potion were short-lived.

"Welcome to Garrigill, Callan of Tarras. You honour me with your own presence. This way is better: it means no delays in our dealings." As Tully spoke the spaces immediately beside him were vacated.

Callan dragged her brother forward.

"This is my son, Niall. It is time he attends important negotiations."

She felt for her awkward brother as Niall returned Tully's formal greeting, an embarrassed flush pinking his ashen skin before he slunk back behind Callan.

"Where is my son, Lorcan?" Tully questioned as he scanned around.

"I am here!"

Lorcan entered the roundhouse and made his way through the throng of people to his father's side. Sheer relief made Nara sink to the ground; her knees unable to support her any longer. Lorcan looked in good health. He was safe. She drank in his tall strong body standing beside Tully and watched as Lorcan placed his hand at Tully's shoulder, giving his father support and reassurance. She wanted to feel that strong hand supporting her own shoulder...as he had done before.

Lorcan's gaze travelled to the back of the room to where she slumped on the floor. She raised herself a little, but did not dare rise to her feet as everyone would have noticed. A smile widened Lorcan's beard, his teeth shining white in the gloom of the roundhouse.

Tully nodded approval of Lorcan's presence then turned back to Callan. "You come to discuss proposals regarding your daughter?"

Callan looked displeased her name had been brought up so soon though his reaction was no surprise. His abrupt answer was also not unexpected. "Aye, but we have more important matters to discuss first."

"We do have matters of import to talk about, Callan of Tarras. But you have just arrived. Let us see to your comfort before we begin negotiations."

Nara thought Tully circumspect: she had heard sufficient of his greetings now to notice the difference.

"I prefer we talk now." Callan's harangue and inflexible glare was resolute. Nara had a good idea of his mood.

"If you so wish then be seated." Tully indicated the space next to him.

One Selgovae warrior remained standing behind Callan, in a customary position as the others ranked themselves on Callan's side.

The Brigantes, in turn, positioned themselves to the side of Tully: Lorcan, Shea as a chief in his own right, and then Brennus. Before sitting down Nara was sure Lorcan's gaze

169

strayed to her once more before others marred her view. A few other warriors ordered themselves after Brennus, but she had never seen them before. From their seating positions, she wondered if they were also sons of Brigante chiefs, and decided they most likely were.

When all were settled, Tully began. "Do you agree, Callan of Tarras, to the marriage proposal of a son of the Brigantes to your daughter? To strengthen our future relations and enable our mutual repulsion of the invidious Roman hordes."

Callan was silent. Even from the back of the room Nara could see his lips set in a sneer as his gaze encompassed the men arranged alongside Tully. Then, he deliberately looked all around the huge roundhouse. Nara imagined her father to be making a comparison with his own abode and was finding his own lacking the sheer size of Tully's. Eventually, his answer came.

"I too have problems with the relentless surge of Romans, Tully of Garrigill. We require this discourse to be in amity over the Roman threat, but the future of my daughter, Nara, is inconsequential."

She was not surprised when Tully's head swung to the back of the room where she knelt watching the proceedings. His frown was deep, the glare of his eyes penetrating before his aggravated voice answered her father.

"A marriage between your daughter, and a prince of the Brigantes, will forever reinforce a bond. But if you prefer it, Callan of the Selgovae, we do not have to speak of that just yet. We can turn to the other pressing matters though I cannot speak for the whole of the Brigantes confederation of tribes. At present, I can only speak for my own here at Garrigill, and the other Brigante princes here speak for themselves."

Callan was equally blunt. "I do not speak for the whole of the Selgovae either, but I do speak for Tarras. Our Roman enemy comes at us with a terrible might. We must make assurances now over how we can protect our mutual borders."

Tully waited for questions concerning her, but it was obvious Callan had totally dismissed her from the conversation. At the back of the room, she knew well how to remain invisible, this conduct typical of Callan whenever it concerned her. To go to him right now would force him to acknowledge her presence, but she knew from his fierce disposition that would be disastrous. When Callan was set on something he allowed no interference, and he was not interested in her future.

Callan's bluster continued. "It is imperative we join forces with you, for reports tell me many of your Brigante brothers are already overrun by both the *Legio IX* and the *Legio II Adiutrix* Roman Legions. They make temporary marching camps each evening as they forge rapid progress over our Celtic lands."

Tully nodded. "I, too, have received this devastating news."

Callan's lines of communication were well established, if he knew of this. Even if she had escaped Lorcan at the crannog settlement of Gyptus, she might have been taking old news to him. She could not prevent a bitter smile because Callan would have made cruel fun of her.

Callan continued, heated with aggression. "Two days ago, my druid informer told me the Roman Governor, Petilius Cerialis, has re-mobilised forces at the settlement they name *Eboracum*. Their halt at that base, which they have used as a temporary encampment for a few summers, is now in doubt since the breakdown of your Brigante Queen Cartimandua's negotiations." Even under the scowls of the Brigantes present Callan carried on regardless. "Those Roman scouting forces now in our lands establish the most direct route for the legions to follow. We can expect them to surge northward any day now."

"Aye. They plan to disembark on our coastlines too."

Lorcan's interruption earned a fierce glare from Callan. Nara was so pleased to hear Lorcan's voice tears welled in her eyes, and was even more pleased to hear Lorcan carry on, not cowed by Callan's threatening demeanour.

"They plan to land their ships at strategic points, to the west and to the east. The Roman ship that landed on Callan's shores was a small exploratory vessel, disembarking only long enough to information gather. It sailed south again with much knowledge of our coastlines."

Shea intervened, his voice an angry snarl. "The southwestern mountainous territory of the Ordovices, and the Deceangli, hold the Romans back on the land to the west, but even there Roman attacks from the sea are now more frequent. Guarding our western coast is crucial."

Shea's cruel tones no longer had power to frighten her; he was consigned to being just another tribesman. Lorcan had returned and would protect her.

Tully's voice betrayed a tired resignation; his pain seeming to have returned. It was clear to her Tully was struggling to maintain control in front of her father when he said, "So…now we must plan to defend all our lands ferociously. What is your update, Lorcan?"

"I have not only been to Tarras during these last days. With some of Callan's warriors, I have been to the lands of Mochrum which lie north-west of Tarras. Word came to them that a fleet of at least ten Roman ships, on the far southwestern shore, is being outfitted for raiding northwards." Lorcan's tones intensified as his gaze spanned the room. "They will arrive soon, probably before mid-summer's day. This means they will arrive in their thousands, even before further movement on land by the *Legio IX*. If they simultaneously attack, from sea and land, we will be wedged in."

"This is dire news, Lorcan," Tully said.

"It worsens." The assembled crowd held their breath as Lorcan pointed to a Brigante two down from Brennus in the ranking. "Murton tells me ships are also expected to make landfall on his east coast, too."

As Murton stood up, Nara saw Grond slip in place beside Brennus. Grond looked as though he had ridden long and hard to reach Garrigill for these talks, a small nod and a little smile from Lorcan acknowledging his arrival.

The slight interruption was just sufficient for Lorcan's glance to settle on her. Though fleeting, it was enough for her to believe he assured himself she was still there.

Murton's voice echoed. "My information came from a reliable trader who regularly sails our seas to the far shores of Gaul. I spoke to him yestreen before he sailed to the northern lands of the Celtic Votadini. The Roman ships he claims sail northwards will spew out many well-equipped soldiers and crush those Celts who dwell closest to their landing point."

A despondent hush fell.

Callan's arrogance broke the intense silence. "I will not contemplate Brigantes fleeing to my lands as my enemies; therefore, we must put our hands together as allies to repel the invaders."

Nara had been completely correct in her assessment of her worth in her father's eyes. He was not at Garrigill because she had been captured. He was in Tully's roundhouse because he would not allow Brigantes to overrun Tarras. Her abduction had given him a cunning excuse to meet with Tully and reinforce it.

Again she felt Lorcan's angry eyes flick to the back of the room where she huddled. He looked furious.

She would not allow the tears to fall. Callan had hurt her enough, and she would not allow him to wound her again. She wanted Lorcan to cradle her in his protective arms, but that was not possible. She hated Callan for the control he still had over her, and over her future. By her goddess, Rhianna, if she could not have Lorcan, she wished to be married anywhere away from her father's hearth. Swatrega's dream was too much a burden now. She wanted to flee the roundhouse, but that was not possible either.

Tully's exhausted voice commanded attention, breaking the low murmurs rippling through the assembled congregation. "I, Tully of Garrigill, give my agreement to join forces with Callan of the Selgovae."

Callan stood again to address everyone from a higher vantage point. "As soon as I return to Tarras I will amass a force to patrol our border lands alongside warriors of the Brigantes. Is this acceptable?"

Tully in turn stood up, with as much dignity as he could muster, to accept the proposal which, by the noise of consent, was clearly accepted by the Brigantes present in the roundhouse. "It is settled. From the morrow, our warriors will man the high hills in amity."

So saying, the chiefs clasped wrists, their sign of agreement. When they were both re-seated Tully turned the conversation back to the issue of Nara and marriage with a Brigante.

"Whoever you deem to be the best suitor, will be acceptable." Callan's blurt indicated he was already disinterested in the new topic.

"Six sons of chiefs sit alongside me. Perhaps you should ask which strengths each would bring as husband to your daughter."

Callan's reply was offhand. "If you deem I must, I will listen to their credentials."

Sending an intense glare of dislike to Callan – who ignored it – Tully named the qualities Lorcan and Brennus would bring to a joining with her. When he finished his speech, Nara felt his eyes seek her at the back of the room. Tully, she noticed, had lost all vitality and appeared disgusted. His contemptuous head twitching, she had already learned, meant he wished the visit to be over.

Tully gave the other candidates an opportunity to prove their worth.

Shea stressed his advantage in being the nearest settlement to Tarras, talked at length about his prowess as a begetter of children, already having four sons. Callan's glower deepened, Shea's boasts doing nothing to impress. It did nothing to redeem Shea in her eyes either as all Shea created were shivers of apprehension. He was not a man she ever wanted to mate with.

In contrast, Grond added his father's crannog settlement was extremely well-protected, and he would be well able to look after her if a Roman attack should take place. At the back of the room, Nara disagreed even though she had experience of the inhospitable land around the settlement. If the Romans invaded in great numbers, the local tribespeople would be routed out, even if it took a long time. The Romans were known for being relentless in finding their quarry. Grond then put forward a strong case for having the greatest admiration for her – not a feeling she reciprocated since she knew he was motivated by pure desire.

The two other Brigante suitors, one from further south and the other from the east, echoed much the same qualities raised by the first four. Though she had not yet spoken to them, she was convinced they would not be men she would wish to be wedded to.

Tully finalised the merits of all the suitors. "If none of these are suitable to you, Callan of Tarras, it will take time before other Brigante princes can be brought to a meeting."

By this time it was clear that Tully had worked out Callan was interested in none of the candidates, and would not be if there were hundreds to choose from.

"Not necessary. She will do as she is bid!" Callan's tone expected no resistance from his daughter.

Tully's anger was barely repressed as he countered. "Your daughter should have some say in the matter, Callan of Tarras. We will have her join us."

"Again, not necessary. The woman will do as she is told." Callan barked his answer, clearly determined to end the conversation. "I am ready now to accept your gestures of hospitality, Tully of Garrigill. And after I eat, if I must…" Callan scanned the whole roundhouse as though bored with the topic. She could not be totally sure, but she thought he had recognised her at the back of the room before he grudgingly finished. "I will choose your Brigante."

Tully's bellow for Carn echoed resoundingly. Women hovering at the entrance door with food and drink readily complied, immediately proffering it to the visitors from Tarras, and the other newcomers who had not yet eaten.

***

Lorcan seethed beside Tully on hearing Callan's callous words. Though suspicious of the man, he had not realised how malicious Callan was over Nara's future. Now he knew exactly what she had had to live through these past two moons, and before that. Refusing the food offered, he pushed his way through the throng around the fireside to reach her at the back. He had wanted to seek her out the moment he had entered the roundhouse, but it had not been possible. Now, he would wait no longer.

He pulled her inside her stall regardless of who might notice and yanked the leather door curtain closed. Setting her down on to the bed, he knelt beside her, his arms cradling her tight, absorbing some of her hurt into his own rigid body. "Do not allow his callous words and his uncaring indifference to wound, Nara." He waited no longer to take her mouth in a fierce kiss full of sympathy and anger. Her response was just as passionate as she burrowed into him. Only with extreme reluctance did he stop.

"We must take our places. Remember this, my desire for you remains steadfast."

He pushed his way through the throng to stand by Tully and Callan, Nara tight in behind him.

"Come. Sit by me, Princess Nara." Tully's reply was the most pleasant greeting, startlingly different from his usual, as he encouraged them both to squeeze into place. Lorcan had never been more proud of his father. In formal terms it was a rebuke which pointed out Callan's neglect of her. She should have had the ranking next to Callan, however, Tully had pre-empted Nara being publicly rejected by Callan. Tully was making it clear, in advance of an actual ceremony, he considered her a suitable Brigante wife.

Lorcan's anger knew no bounds when an indifferent Callan did not even greet his daughter before he launched into details of patrolling the high hills. Nara had had to live with this treatment her whole life. Lorcan's avowal that her life would improve went deep.

The food arrived in a flurry of movement through the entrance tunnel. A fine array of stripped meats were offered to the visitors, Callan being served first. Nara did not look surprised to see her father rifle around the platter with his knife choosing the finest cuts. She plucked a piece of bread from the bannock he shared with her but he guessed she would not do justice to the hearty barley broth given to her, misery breathed out of her.

"Your women make an acceptable ale," Callan declared after a raucous burp, his mouth still full of the salted fish he was chewing down with alacrity.

As they ate, Tully steered negotiations back to the betrothal, though again Callan showed disinterest in negotiating. Lorcan tightened his hand on the cloth of Nara's dress, the closest he could come to touching her. Her back straight, she sat rigid beside him on their shared bench.

"If you do not want animals or gold, do you seek something else?" Tully ventured once more, his voice sharpening, diplomacy long gone.

Callan's reply was impassive. "These troubled times demand new betrothal requirements."

New requirements? Lorcan wondered what Callan meant as he looked over at Nara's emotionless father who sat picking fish bones from his teeth.

The roundhouse was so quiet the single rustle of a piece of moving straw would have been heard. Callan scanned the gathering before bursting his venom.

"My only stipulation is that Nara, and the Brigante she marries, both live at Tarras."

No-one dared breathe. The implications were vast.

Lorcan's hand fisted the material of Nara's dress into a tighter bunch. He glared at the fiery flames in front of him. He saw nothing but disaster, his blood boiling as hot as the orange-red flickers that licked up from the blazing logs. Tarras? Her father insisted her husband would live in Tarras? The odious fiend!

It would be a hostage situation all over again, but one which would last a lifetime for him – or whichever Brigante she married.

By Taranis! Callan of Tarras had to be stopped. Though exactly how he could not fathom, his mind thrown into turmoil. He needed to calm down, to think his way through this impossible situation. There must be some answer? The floor in front of him consumed all his focus. He dared not look over to Callan because one smug, or calculating, smirk would have him slay the man right at his father's hearthside.

Surely Taranis could help him find a way? His pleas came fast and furious.

He picked up a piece of bread from the platter in front of him. Not because he wanted to eat it – it was merely to occupy his twitching fingers as he twirled it around and around.

Tully eventually broke the stunned silence pervading the roundhouse, his voice strung tight as his old teeth grit together. "We Brigantes need to consider your fundamental new terms. We will inform you of our decision in a short while."

With great difficulty Tully struggled to rise, Nara's shoulder a necessary support as his father's tired eyes sought Carn in her habitual place by the roundhouse door. At Carn's nod, his father addressed Callan with grim determination. Lorcan could see the tension of Tully's fingers around Nara's neck betrayed the temper his father sought to keep from view. "Stalls can be prepared for you here in my roundhouse. Or, we can make a separate roundhouse available for you."

Callan did not even blink. "Is Nara quartered elsewhere?"

"She certainly is not!" Tully's reply was a harsh bark, his eyes icy blue shards. "Your daughter has honoured me with her presence in my own roundhouse since her arrival. This is the most fitting place for her rank."

A sneer appeared on Callan's face as he viewed Nara.

Lorcan wanted to kill the man. The now almost ruined bread in his fingers shattered into a pile of crumbs as his fist squeezed it to oblivion. The last remnants he fired into the flames, his fingers flicking like sling shot. Drawing in some deep breaths, he willed himself calm, his jaw firmed as rigid as the rock of the high hills. A momentary closing of his eyes and he was ready. Looking across at Callan, he refused to allow the man to rule his temper.

"Then I also accept hospitality in your roundhouse; it is very accommodating." A twitch barely lifted the corners of Callan's lips. "It meets with my approval, but you will understand if I have one of my warriors remaining on guard?"

178

If Tully was taken aback by the request, it was not discernible in his answer. Again, Lorcan was proud of how Tully reined in his considerable fury.

"I, too, always have someone on watch." Tully's face was grave, his angry brows lowered. "Your other warriors will already have been quartered. You may prefer to check on their welfare, Callan of Tarras, while we discuss your demand?"

If Callan took umbrage at Tully's antipathy, he did not show it as he prepared to sweep his warriors out of the room.

"Nara. Come!" Callan commanded. "You will talk with me outside."

They were the first words Callan had spoken to Nara that evening, and Lorcan knew it for an order Nara could not refuse. As she rose to join Callan, he again tugged the cloth of her shift, his eyes briefly seeking hers before she followed her father. His tight fist slowly released the cloth, reluctant to let go. His eyes, he hoped, expressed everything he felt – disgust, confidence, and trust they would find some solution to the problems presented by her wicked father.

***

Outside, Nara trailed behind a striding Callan who made his expectations clear. She could not even see his face since, as soon as she drew level with him, he strode all the harder, refusing to meet her eyes. Understanding his tactic was easy. Encouraging her to feel subservient was his aim. Though she said nothing, she kept up with his fast pace around the walkways, lit by smoking and sputtering tallow flames set in high metal brackets outside the roundhouse entrances.

"Whichever Brigante you marry matters not a whit to me. I know none of them, save Shea of Ivegill, but I will have your husband close at Tarras, where I can monitor him." He halted and turned to her. "Do I make that clear?"

She refused to deign him with an answer, the slightest of nods all she was prepared to give. Callan either ignored her slight, or did not care enough to fuss. In her heart, she knew it was the latter.

"The presence of your Brigante husband at Tarras will deter any uninvited surge north to my lands, if the Roman scourge wipes them clear of this settlement."

Callan's mordant smirk she did not miss. She knew he would follow out his threat and kill any husband she may have if that situation prevailed. If she were assessing the plan in strategic terms, she might be applauding Callan's scheme. But she was not. Any husband she may have would be as dispensable as he had recently claimed she was to him. Callan had compassion for nobody.

"No one will overrun my settlement!"

Not for the first time she wondered what it could have been that had attracted Brynna to Callan all those years ago. She remembered just how devoted Brynna had been to this wicked man. There was nothing at all lovable about Callan. Yet Brynna had been the gentlest woman who had savoured his every word.

"Do you favour any of these Brigantes?"

Callan's question was unexpected. That he should even ask her startled Nara.

"Would it make any matter if I did?" Her question sounded disconsolate, even to her own ears.

"Choose an agreeable one. One who will do my bidding is what you need. Two of them are too fond of their own control, but any of the others would do."

Callan strode off to stretch his legs after the long sitting at the fireside, and without a backward glance at his oldest child, he disappeared. His warriors trailed in his wake, followed in turn by Garrigill guards.

Nara stumbled off in the opposite direction unwilling to talk to anyone, not even Lorcan, the pain of Callan's cruelty eating at her heart. She knew which two candidates he referred to – Lorcan and Shea. Both had proved themselves formidable and were well respected warriors. The heated conversation she conducted was to an absent Callan, an exchange she would never dare to have in his presence as she stomped on.

"No, indeed…Father! I know what is in your mind. I have learned too much of your twisted way of thinking during my lifetime. Lorcan of Garrigill would be far too much competition for you. By Taranis, he would not bow to your cruelty." Further curses drifted into the night as she wandered, without aim, till she skirted a roundhouse and saw Shea in the distance surrounded by some of his warriors. In her ire, her finger pointed in the dim light. "And look you there, Father! That man, I will never marry, though I will also say that he, too, would be far too much his own man for you to tolerate as a hearth-son."

When Shea caught sight of her, she scurried around the nearest roundhouse and melted into the gloom. She would not talk to Shea either.

Despondency suffocated her. She may not want Shea as a husband but how could any Brigante warrior meet Callan's demand? It was impossible. She needed a strong warrior to be her husband, the father of her prophesied son – but not someone who would be her father's underling.

Chapter Fifteen

"How is it feasible to send a Brigante to live at Tarras?" Tiernan, the candidate from the south, was adamant it was not going to be him. "The princess has many charms but not enough for me to live with Callan of Tarras. I remove myself from the offering."

Brennus' answer to Tiernan was contemptuous when he championed Nara. "Nara will make a fine wife, and I would be proud to call her mine."

Lorcan could not say a word, his throat constricted. His nails dug deep channels into his palms, his eyes staring at nothing. He could not even look at Brennus as fierce jealousy engulfed him, still devastated as he was by Callan's demand.

Callan had just made the whole situation unattainable. He had never guessed a stipulation like this could be requested. How could he – a candidate for Tully's successor – live at Tarras? His father weakened by the moment, not the day, or moon. The tribespeople of Garrigill depended on strong leadership. His honour and duty was to his tribe…yet how could the prophecy foretelling of his rise to power as a negotiator be fulfilled if he went to live at Tarras?

But…give up Nara? Suffocating guilt engulfed him for, by Taranis, he had made a mighty mess of the whole circumstance. Why had he not thought through every possibility? The mood settling over him was a black pit, a quagmire that sucked his very spirit in deep. What had he done to her? What kind of future would she be subjected to?

Shea butted in. "I am already chief. I cannot leave Ivegill to live at Tarras, though the princess tempts me greatly. She has a ripe and luscious body, but I also have to pass on the marriage…though I would couple with her in an instant."

Further lewd comments reignited the spark of jealousy in Lorcan to the point he wanted to smash his fist to Shea's mouth so much the man would never speak again. It was as well that Shea chose at that moment to excuse himself, his exit salutation so curt Tully would not have accepted it in normal circumstances.

The Brigante from the south east was equally sure he did not want to live with Callan at Tarras.

That left Grond.

"What do you say, Grond?" Tully addressed the last contender. "Are you prepared to live at Tarras?"

"It would please me to marry Princess Nara, but I have no authority to make such a decision this eve. My father depends on me already. Like Shea, I could not lead my tribe and live at Tarras at the same time."

Lorcan's untold frustration deepened even more when Tully spoke again.

"You speak for more than your own situation, Grond. I am not the man I was. Garrigill also needs a new leader."

He felt the soothing touch of his father's hand on his shoulder.

Tully looked to the senior nobles and elders of Garrigill. "You cannot tarry any longer to decide on my successor. Your new leader must be elected now."

The Brigante visitors quit the roundhouse, leaving only Garrigill High Council members. The already discussed list of candidates was small. A quick consensus narrowed it down to three men who had the maturity, abilities, knowledge and strength to do the job. Lorcan, Bran and Roc. Though Brennus was their tribal champion, they agreed, he was yet young for the burden of leadership. Bran and Roc were not sons of a chief, nor contenders for marriage to Nara, but though they would be good choices to lead Garrigill they lacked the emissary skills Lorcan had. The council settled on him as their preferred choice.

However, the elders were not prepared to declare him their new leader that evening with Callan of Tarras in their midst; they wished for no sign of chieftainship weakness in the presence of the Selgovae. Tully was to remain chief till after the feast of Beltane.

Lorcan sat stunned, unable to participate as their words washed over him. He wanted very much to be the leader of his tribe, but that meant he could not leave Garrigill. He could not marry Nara. He barely felt the reassuring squeeze from his father's fingers on his shoulder.

Yet, she could not be lost to him, there had to be another way. He still took no part in the discussions, his eyes locked on the dancing fire in the centre of the room as the elders droned on. They were reluctant for a warrior-champion like Brennus to leave Garrigill, but Brennus was ultimately deemed their choice to marry Princess Nara.

Brennus? Lorcan had almost forgotten his brother's eligibility.

He knew well how Brennus desired Nara. He had watched his brother's hungry gaze follow her at every opportunity. How could the gods be so cruel to bring him Nara, and then give her to his brother? He loved Brennus, but right then the burning hatred swamping him surpassed all brotherly affection. It was as well he looked only to the flickering fire for if he had caught sight of Brennus that moment, he knew he would surge up and kill him. The murderous rage inside continued to find sustenance. Beside him, he heard Tully's weak voice, the words separated by pained breathing pauses. "It is a huge sacrifice we ask you to make, Brennus, living at Tarras as Princess Nara's husband."

"I had not considered such a thing would be required of anyone, but I confess Princess Nara is a prize worth having."

Brennus' words were doubtful but Lorcan would not look up.

The breath left his body. His head ached, his heart even more. Crushing guilt sucked out even more of his spirit since he had also just, to all effect, banished his brother.

Tully's voice was fading, his reserves of strength depleted. "If you accept this stricture, Brennus, think on it as you being our representative who lives outside of Garrigill. If you keep our tribes at peace I will be everlastingly proud of you, my son. For make no mistake, Callan of Tarras is a very shrewd man who will test your allegiance at every turn."

"I know this. I will marry Nara and be our eyes and ears at Tarras." Brennus' voice sounded forced to Lorcan's ears, but he could say nothing because his whole being had stalled.

***

Gutted by Callan's pitiless treatment, Nara went back to the roundhouse where Tully hobbled around in severe pain. There was an almost deathly silence in the dwelling as she approached him.

"Woman of the Selgovae, I know nothing about your relationship with your father, but let me say I will be very proud to call you daughter, though I have only known you a matter of days."

She felt his awkward shoulder pat as he circled her protectively. His eyes were conspiratorial, his bony fingers reassuring.

"Callan need never know this. Your potion has kept me going well this distressing evening. You have my heartfelt gratitude."

"Tully of Garrigill, you may be pleased to know Carn sees well to your needs." She was marginally cheered by Tully's support.

"Carn? You instructed Carn? You were sure she would give me the correct dose at the appropriate time?"

"Carn looks to your needs much better than you give her credit for, Tully of the Brigantes. She learns well with instructions. If you are very fortunate she will ensure you have another drink before bed – a drink for you alone."

Tully's burst of laughter surprised the men still seated around the fireside. "Nara, I thank you." Drawing her very close he whispered in her ear. "Do you not have a little potion that would make your father sleep the sleep of the very dead?"

It was Nara's turn to laugh. "I would not dare. He would rather not have me anywhere near him, thinking for sure I sought to poison him if I approached with a drink. If I even attempted it, he would likely give it to my brother to taste first!" Her bitterness could not be put aside.

"Go and rest. The decisions made tonight are profound. Lorcan has just cause to regret he brought you into this situation, but you must have realised I was honour bound to do what I did. I deeply regret any discontent you feel over the outcome of this eventful night's work."

Biting back the wounding tears, she looked around for Lorcan, but he was nowhere to be seen, nor were the other major contenders.

None of those around the fireside noticed Nara's walk to her stall for they were deep in discussion of how any Brigante could possibly tolerate living at a Selgovae settlement. Pulling back the curtain, she blundered inside, her vision clouded with stinging tears. A familiar hand covered her mouth.

Lorcan.

She fell into his arms as he drew her down to the mattress. His lips were on hers immediately. His first kiss of comfort led to silent ones of desperation. Keeping his fingers on her lips when he disengaged from their embrace, Lorcan's whisper feathered her ear. "Nara. How could he treat you so?"

She had no answers.

In his eyes she could see the turmoil Lorcan felt inside, his anger a different frustration from her own.

"I want to be the man who takes you to wife. I need to be him…yet I cannot. Believe me, you are the one I crave. The elders deem me our new chief of Garrigill. Though, since your father is here, they do not declare me yet. They do not wish Callan to detect any sign of instability, or weakness, at Garrigill. They will pronounce me new leader after Beltane. Therefore, I cannot be your husband at Tarras."

Nara could not condemn anyone to a life sentence of living with Callan. How could her goddess, Rhianna, bring her to Lorcan then take him from her? She dreaded to ask, yet had to, silent tears leaking down her cheeks.

"Who, then, has been chosen?"

Lorcan's voice was a cracking whisper at her cheek. "My brother, Brennus." His forehead bent to meet with hers in silent communication, their noses aligned, and their breaths mingling. "On my honour, and my duty to my tribe, I must not ever touch you again." Lorcan wrenched himself away, turned and walked out of her stall.

Sagging to the floor, Nara continued her silent weep where she lay and awaited her fate. She did not dislike Brennus, but she did not love him. How could she live with Brennus and bear him children? She knew in her heart a marriage to Brennus would destroy any brotherly love between them. Huge and strong as Brennus was, she did not want him to be the man who would father her prophesied son.

Silent tears trickled past her ears. Her future looked even bleaker now than when she had first left Tarras. Why had Rhianna mocked her future? It had been much easier when promised to the goddess only, and no man. That had been a time of no heart-pain. Being promised now to the wrong man was surely not what Swatrega had seen in the entrails?

Nara had no answers to such endless questions, for Rhianna did not listen to her entreaties.

Sounds of her father returning to the roundhouse filtered to the back of the room, the hum of conversation continuing around the fireside a while longer. Most details were unheard as there was no heated element to the talks. But she did hear Callan being told of the Brigante choice for her husband and Callan's grunting dismissal that it was a good enough choice but did not really matter to him.

After a while, she heard her father's companions being allotted stalls close by, and the bustling of Carn tending to their needs, but Callan made no attempt to speak to her.

Hardly moving from the position she had laid down in, muscles tense as a harp string, she listened to the noises punctuating the night – the shuffling around, finding comfortable positions on the straw pads, the soft snores.

From the next stall she heard the splutters of her brother Niall, perennially riddled with a wracking cough. No matter the concoctions she fed him, it always returned. Niall's debilitating breathing problem angered Callan as much as she did.

Children…she fell into a very disturbed slumber, dreaming about her impossible role at Beltane.

Before daybreak, Nara wakened. She had fitfully slept for short spells yet, though exhausted, she was ready to face the day, resolute about facing her future. If she could not have Lorcan, what mattered? Her fevered mind had worked through all the possibilities she could come up with, and none altered the inevitable.

She could refuse to marry. She and Lorcan could flee the settlements of their birth. They could create her prophesied son, but where would they live to rear the child – they would surely be denied at Tarras or Garrigill.

Nothing made sense, or gave her hope.

Her fate was sealed around marriage to Brennus.

She was out of her stall before the others were awake, with the exception of the guards. A mere nod to the Garrigill sentry was sufficient to acknowledge her exit, the Selgovae sentry saying nothing as she passed by. Vaguely aware of other early risers exiting their roundhouses, she wandered aimlessly. By the time she returned to Tully's roundhouse, her turbulent thoughts had eased, an acceptance of her fate having dropped like a soaking bratt on her shoulders.

Acceptance of her marriage, maybe? But the prophecy? Nay! She was now resolved on that. How to contrive it she did not know, but somehow she would make it happen.

After breaking her fast, she ensured Tully had potions prepared for several days. The strength of the brew would have to be increased as his condition worsened. The last days of a disease like this one came swiftly upon the sufferer. The decline was drastic, and Tully neared the end. Carn was tutored well. She knew exactly whichever method, food or drink, would be most appropriate to surreptitiously administer the potion.

"When Tully asks, and I am convinced he will, say with confidence you know what you are about."

"Will he make trouble?"

Nara handed Carn the mixture she had prepared and filled into a small flask. "I am perfectly sure when you offer him drinks today he will accept them...but being Tully, he will make acerbic comments. Ignore rudeness, for the sickness makes him testy."

"Tully has always been testy. He just has even more bite than he used to." Carn's words made her smile.

Nara was relieved Callan intended to leave immediately. Called back into the roundhouse as the Selgovae broke their fast, she found Brennus in the coveted next place beside Tully, but Lorcan was absent.

"Come. Sit here," Callan demanded, without even greeting her, indicating a position next to him. Nara knew it to be all show and bluster.

"You will marry Brennus. He will come to Tarras four days after Beltane. I insist your marriage ceremony be there." His jaw was set, decision made.

She could not look anywhere but at the ground as she rallied thoughts and feelings. "Am I to have no say in the matter of my future husband?" Eventually she sought out Callan's eyes when no reply came.

His features set like hard clay, without dropping eye-contact, he impatiently pointed to the stool alongside him. A gesture she interpreted as a belated counter to Tully's slight of the previous evening. "Why would you have any say in this matter! It is decided. You will marry Brennus." His tone of voice held great contempt, the bite to it a flay against her bruised feelings.

Callan turned to Tully. "I will take my leave of you now. We will meet again before the summer solstice." After a formal appreciation for hospitality received, Callan nodded and strode off.

Tully's shout halted his progress. "Since you have not ordered your daughter to accompany you, I take it you are leaving her with me, till after Beltane?"

"She will slow me down," Callan said without turning around. His parting words were delivered with a menacing undertone. "Since you saw fit to capture and bring her here, you may have the pleasure of escorting her to Tarras yourselves."

189

No-one spoke as he and his warriors swept out of the roundhouse, all stunned by his attitude.

Brennus jumped up, to rush out after them, his temper wild.

"Brennus," Tully remonstrated, "do nothing rash!"

Brennus gave a brief nod before he stomped out.

Tully beckoned Nara to help him shift to a more comfortable position. "Believe this, Nara. The nobles would not countenance Lorcan living at Tarras since we need him as new chief. Brennus will be a good husband, though he is young. He thinks ill of living at Tarras, yet he is a strong warrior who will endure this unusual circumstance, and he will protect you well."

Nara felt Tully's gnarled fingers curl around hers, his very weakness of body giving her a strange succour. Looking deeply into her eyes, he willed her to accept his words. "He will see to your protection and to any children you might have. He will do it better than any other Brigante prince who was proposed last night…except Lorcan…who would also have made you a fine husband had Callan not insisted on you living at Tarras."

Tully was not deceived by her silence, and she knew it. His glazed eyes emitted sympathy for her plight which she realised he could not put into words – he too was losing Brennus to Tarras, subjecting his son to the formidable iron will of Callan.

She was not the only one suffering. The decision having been made she could see no way to challenge it, though it left her bereft.

"I promised Carn help with preparations." Her wooden-sounding words Tully more than understood.

"Go, then. Work is an answer to a bleeding heart."

Fleeing the roundhouse, Brennus intercepted her, his body blocking her exit. Reaching for her hands, he held them gently. "Nara, we must talk."

Her eyes filled with unshed tears, her pride keeping them hovering on her lashes. His fingers linked with hers as he sought the best words to convey the importance of his vow.

"I promise you I will try to be the husband you need. I will look after you, and maybe in time you will come to love me."

Nara's heart was breaking, as was her voice. Tears ran down her cheeks. "I know you will try, Brennus, but I cannot talk…" She fled.

Railing at her fate, Nara mindlessly ground emmer seeds with the quern stone, and helped prepare the evening meal. Wandering without direction, a while later, she found she had gravitated to the practice field where she watched the youngsters train. Brennus would normally have presided over the training, but he was nowhere to be seen.

Neither was Lorcan.

She felt so alone.

Strangely even more alone, since she no longer had a shadow dogging her every move. Since Callan's visit it appeared she was no longer deemed under threat of attack from Garrigill warriors. Fleeing the settlement was also known to be pointless since everyone knew Callan had journeyed home without her – publicly rejecting her.

Worthless.

Four days later, she still felt alone in amongst a steady stream of Brigantes from other settlements who arrived for the Garrigill Beltane festivities. Around her, happy women prepared the Beltane victuals. Normally a cheerful time for Celtic tribes, it marked the coming of better weather, into summer and longer days, the time when the cattle were sent out after the purification rites to graze in the far fields, away from the winter feeding and closer protection around the settlement.

Tension and excitement built throughout the day as down in the lower fields, close to the riverside, the warriors prepared the large bonfire stacks of wood. They laid bonfires in two long lines, a walkway between them. Through the fire-lit walkway the farmers would drive the cattle, in a symbol of belief that forcing the beasts through the Beltane fires would protect them from disease, purify them and would keep them healthy throughout the coming months – fertility abounding in beast…and man.

191

Fertility and a new beginning, it was a happy time for most of the women, but not for her. After the purification rituals, feasting and dancing over, the women of the tribe would slip off with their chosen lover to find a quiet spot.

As the day progressed, the prophecy lay heavy on her heart. She wanted only to make love to Lorcan. He was the one man whose touch had stirred her desires, and melted the bones now telling her that her son should indeed be conceived that night, and that Swatrega's premonition would be fulfilled. But how could it happen? Lorcan had not returned to Garrigill. Brennus – soon to be her husband – was expected to be chosen by her, since he had returned as the sun moved overhead in the clear sky. As part of the rites, the officiating druid would expect her to be at Brennus' side…all through the eve and into the night.

Her heart ached for Lorcan.

***

Lorcan strode to Tully's roundhouse. After many setbacks over the last days in meeting Liam the Bard, he had returned later than intended. The Beltane proceedings were starting imminently and he still had preparations to make. Tully's urgent request to speak with him he pretended not to hear. He was not yet ready for talk, not convinced he would remain strong. Fearing he might lash out at his father, he avoided that happening by steering clear of Tully. His mood was dire, his heart heavy. Duty to the tribe had never been a burden before.

That was not how he felt now.

Hurriedly washing, he donned better clothing, fit for a prince of the Brigantes. His tunic was new, the dark red of it smooth against his chest, the weave very fine. Lorcan replaced his worn belt with his newest one, decorated with bronze enamelling that glinted in the firelight. He only possessed one gold torque, but that denoted his status as no other would. Finally, he plucked a gold ring from the small leather pouch that hung next to his bed. The knotwork ring had belonged to his mother, and only barely fit his smallest finger, but he vowed to wear it that night. There was only one finger he truly wanted to see it grace, but, since he could not give it to Nara as a betrothal gift, he would wear it. He squeezed it into place.

No longer capable of the long walk, a makeshift litter arrived to carry Tully down to the bonfires. Lorcan heard them leave; calling out to his father that he would see him on the field…soon.

But he was not in a hurry. There was nothing to revel in, no joy to celebrate. A future without Nara was bleak, and no other woman would do as wife. Gone from Garrigill, he would never look on her lovely face again. He could never contemplate visiting her at Tarras as Brennus' wife.

Reluctant to appear at all he dawdled to the field since he would not totally shirk his obligations. He did not join Tully at the top of the avenue as was expected, but slipped to the back of the five-deep lines of revellers; knowing he was likely to be the only person not delighted by the prospect of Beltane feasting. It was only his above average height which enabled him to glimpse his brother Brennus.

A woman walked alongside him.

Nara?

Lorcan's heart lurched before the rhythm of it pounded loud in his chest. How could she still be here? Callan had surely taken her home with him? As he stared, beads of sweat trickled down his temples. His palms felt clammy, too, as he rubbed them on his tunic.

Brennus and Nara walked to the end of the pathway of bonfire stacks where the Chief Druid awaited them. The crowd quickly quieted, the front rows hushed at the command of their religious leader when Brennus and Nara joined him. The druid's boom intoned over the crowd.

"People of Garrigill. Take heed. Soon, Brennus, son of Tully, will marry this Selgovae Princess, Nara of Tarras." The commanding voice paused. The hush continued. When no expected sounds of celebration came from the assembled crowd, he ploughed on. "Brennus, our fellow brother of Garrigill, will remain at the hillfort of Tarras after the marriage rites four days hence. He will be our eyes and ears in the lands of the Selgovae. Fear not, people of Garrigill, he will still be one of us."

Those words seemed to mollify the doubts that Lorcan could see on the faces of his people. A resounding cheer rang out. Nara might still be suspect in the eyes of some of the people, but Brennus was the tribal champion of Garrigill. He would be sorely missed from that role, but the mass of people around the fires knew him to be a formidable young warrior who would represent them well.

Lorcan was torn between sheer joy at seeing her, and anguish on hearing the betrothal announcement.

Creeping behind the lines till he was closer to Tully, he watched Brennus and Nara take their places at his father's side. The elders also moved forward, ranking around Tully, as the druid spoke of the end of Tully's chieftainship. He could no longer remain concealed.

"Come, Lorcan." Tully beckoned him forward. "Take your place beside me."

Before the Chief Druid could proclaim him new leader, Lorcan held his hands high and addressed the crowd.

"People of Garrigill, listen well. My time to be your new leader will come soon, but I ask our Chief Druid to postpone that ritual this evening. I bring back dire news to Garrigill, which must first be imparted to Tully." He waited till the noise of panic settled, till he had everyone's full attention. "The news will likely mean, as emissary, I must leave again at first light. For that reason I ask that Tully remains your chief for a short while longer. Are you in agreement, tribespeople of Garrigill?" Roars of noisy assent rang around the area. "Our Beltane rites will continue, though, for you are not at risk this night."

Further calls rent the air, the crowd delighted to hear they were not in immediate danger.

Tully was propped onto a high stool. Lorcan felt his father's feeble fingers clutch at his belt for balance when he drew alongside, the Chief Druid commencing the Beltane rituals without delay.

The loud caw-crowing hoot of the calf-headed carnyx rent the air – the call of the battle horn symbolizing the advance of summer. The pounding of feet grew louder as the tribespeople of Garrigill began the rituals to welcome Beltane. As the stamp of feet grew louder the chant started low. Soon the ripple of soft chanting increased, steadily increasing till it became a deafening holler.

The flash of bluish light spiking from the Chief Druid's staff halted the thunderous roar. The crowd instantly quieted and all watched for the Chief Druid's signal, as his subordinate druid bore a burning brand aloft to the nearest fire stack.

The first pyre was lit with noisy ceremony, the sparks and shards of its driest wood crackling and flaking up into the air above it. Then, one after the other, the whole avenue of bonfires was set ablaze, the purplish-blue light of dusk filled with increasingly blinding yellow-orange warmth, the tribespeople of Garrigill appreciating the gathering speed of the burning. A huge cheer resounded, for the gods and goddesses were looking on Garrigill with favour when it was so successful.

Soon the bellowing of cattle being mustered near to the fires drowned out the sounds of cracking and popping wood and the cheers of the hundreds of tribespeople gathered around. The wood smoke, and flashes of burning bark, rose gracefully into the dusky deep blue sky, the stars having recently begun their twinkling. Early moonlight illuminated the whole scene.

Lorcan, unlike everyone around him, was desperately miserable. He stood rigid alongside Tully, unable to dart a glance over to Nara. He could not be sure to control his feelings if he even caught a glimpse of her face. He wanted to be the one standing so close he'd feel the warmth of her body – even just to hold her hand at such a heartbreaking time. She wanted him as husband. Not his brother, Brennus.

He knew it in his soul.

As he supported his weakening father, who slumped further into his side, other devastating feelings swamped him as well. Hatred. His eyes blazed ahead, seeing little but the red burn of anger. How he detested Callan of Tarras! His jaw clenched even more. Callan had left her behind. Publicly humiliated her. Nara must have been devastated at that, and he hadn't been around to console her. His guilt increased even further.

In some ways, he wished he had never set eyes upon her, never brought this terrible fate to befall her.

He could not look at his brother, either, in case the murderous wrath he felt inside set his feet and fists into motion. He couldn't match the strength of his brother normally, but the blood lust he felt right that moment would lend fiercer power to his blows.

Lorcan fought to control his temper as he watched the cattle being driven up the avenue between the flames. He had witnessed this ritual over the years, but had never truly appreciated the significance of a Beltane coupling with a chosen mate. He had always been chosen, and had mated with the woman – sometimes a maiden.

For the first time in his life, he realised what it must mean to couple with the one love of your heart, and spread your seed on her fertile ground. But Nara was not his. His seed would not be sown that night. He would have no other woman.

A rustling alongside made him aware of Brennus moving behind Tully, but the whisper was for him, not his father.

"I must talk with you, Lorcan. I cannot live the life now mapped out for me, if I do not share words with you."

Jealous hatred consumed him, but he knew he must listen to Brennus as he loped away from the lines of people.

"I am in a poor position, Lorcan. I desire Nara like you do, but anger between you and I is unproductive. I know she returns none of my feelings beyond that of a friend, therefore I will not act on my lust while we are all here at Garrigill."

Lorcan whirled round to face his brother, not at all sure what Brennus meant.

Brennus' voice was a sad whisper as his hands locked onto Lorcan's shoulders, holding him in place as though he feared

Lorcan would not listen to his words. Brennus' eyes beseeched him. "The crowd expects her to choose me as her mate this night, but on this you have my word. I will make Nara my wife in every sense after our marriage at Tarras four days from now, but I will not do that tonight. I will put no such pressure on her, Lorcan. You have my promise."

Lorcan fought against his baser feelings. He had been a hair's breadth away from pounding his fists into his well-loved brother's face, and Brennus knew, understood it. He wanted to shrug off the restraining fingers but did not, for in his heart he appreciated what it took for Brennus to confront him.

"I cannot countenance losing you as my brother, Lorcan."

Brennus was the emotional younger brother that he had always loved, his words betraying his strength of feeling. He valued his brother's need to reveal his intent.

"You cannot be her husband, Lorcan. Garrigill needs you, more than me. Yet, if I do not marry Nara, her repulsive father will trade her off to some ingratiating feeble warrior who will do Callan's bidding. I cannot condemn her to that fate, and neither can you."

They both knew Brennus' words were profound, and nauseatingly true.

"Though I must go and take my place beside Nara for the rest of the feasting, and though I regret this badly, I tell you now that she will not be my woman tonight. She will not willingly choose me to bed her this night, and I will not force her."

Lorcan felt the tension of Brennus' fingertips at his shoulder blades, knew how much control it was taking for Brennus to even contemplate what he was proposing.

For a number of heartbeats, no-one else existed around them as they silently communicated, each wanting to say more, each wanting to have more, yet each knowing they were as trapped in an uninviting future as the other.

"Look after her well in the days to come, Brennus, or you will answer to me!" Lorcan vowed as he gathered Brennus into fierce embrace, his fists pummelling his brother's back, the fury he felt inside restrained to a pounding he knew his brother would accept. He did not wish to cross swords with Brennus but could speak to him no longer.

He quit the Beltane gathering and strode back up the rampart defences to the settlement, unable to watch the proceedings. Unable to wait and watch the women choose their lovers of the evening.

Chapter Sixteen

Nara knew Brennus hovered at her side as she watched the last of the dancing around the dying bonfires, the feasting long past, most of the gathering having slipped away.

"Nara?" His hesitant voice broke their silence. "You cannot remain under the scrutiny of those watching your every move."

Brennus was trying so hard to be kind to her, but she could not bear to move. One silent tear escaped. Lorcan had disappeared again, though it was impossible to have publicly chosen him anyway.

Nothing about this Beltane prophecy was falling into place. It seemed her goddess, Rhianna, was displeased with her. She had made mistakes, but she had not betrayed Rhianna. She was still a maiden, ready to fulfil the prophecy – but only with Lorcan. Her heart bled as silently as her tears fell. Rhianna had deserted her, so she must make up her own mind now.

"Nara?"

The entreaty in Brennus' voice she could no longer ignore for she had no doubt of his sincerity. If he could try then so could she, she vowed, though it was so hurtful to her heart.

"Nara. I promise I will not touch you tonight, but I must ensure you are safely to Tully's roundhouse. Let us go now."

Brennus' plea was enough to nudge her out of her stupor. She could not go straight back to Tully – it would make Brennus a failure in the eyes of the tribespeople – and he would appear shunned by her. She could not countenance the mockery.

"Nay! I would not have the tribespeople call you less than a man if we return directly to your father now. May we find somewhere other than Tully's roundhouse for a while? To make it seem…"

199

They left the fading light of the bonfires and walked down to the riverside, the moonlight making it bright and clear as they picked their way along the banking. Eventually, they stopped by a small ford, the sound of rushing water soothing as they sat.

"Thank you." She sighed. "I do appreciate your compassion, Brennus. After our marriage, I promise I will be a wife to you, but I cannot be that person tonight. Can you understand?"

Brennus' cheerless answer sounded resigned. "For all our sakes, I will not touch you tonight as I want to, but let me hold your hand, only to comfort for you are so dispirited. I request no more of you just now."

"The sons of Tully are truly honourable men."

Brennus' fingers clenched around her hand, his grunt of frustration belying her statement.

"Make no mistake, Nara. I lust after you, but I love my brother. I look forward to being your husband and, I believe, love will come later but I am greedy, not honourable. Lorcan and I share a strong bond of brotherly love I do not ever wish to break. What I do this night is more for Lorcan than for either of us, because I know how the decisions made lie heavy on him."

"To think of others is a truly noble quality, Brennus."

Brennus' brown eyes twinkled, a hint of sarcastic humour returning to break the tension. "With Tully as father how could we grow up to be otherwise? He would allow nothing less."

They sat in uncomfortable silence, Nara unable to make conversation, drowned in deep thoughts…of Lorcan, where he was, and what he was doing. If he had already gone off with another woman she would want to die. Prophecy or no prophecy.

A silent tear tracked down her cheek, then another.

"Why is your father so unfeeling? How can he be so indifferent to you?"

Dashing the tears away, she struggled an answer. "I have no answer for that riddle, save he has always been that way."

"He has no interest in your life at all."

"I may have grown used to it, but that does not mean, I will ever like it," she said, a spark of anger breaking through before apology replaced it. "Brennus, I really fear for how he will treat you, as my husband, when we live at Tarras. He will either be vindictive towards you, or totally ignore you and treat you as someone of no consequence."

Brennus' fingers loosened their grip. His arm curved protectively around her shoulders, the support of a friend, drawing her into his chest. "I am not worried about how I will deal with your father. I will manage however he treats me, but I will not be his inferior." His free hand touched her chin to bring her eyes back into contact. "I am more worried about how you and I will deal together."

A small smile broke free from her as they regarded each other. "If I had not fallen in love with Lorcan, I am sure you would have been my choice of the other contenders. As brothers you are not alike but...there is much to like about you, too."

There was no more to say as they made their way back to the settlement, couples drifting across their path in both directions. Near the entryway to Tully's roundhouse Brennus stopped. No guard stood sentinel since it was Beltane. Many people would still be awake and around late into the night.

"I go no further. I promise you, I will not seek the arms of another woman, but I cannot enter the dwelling with you. You will be safe since Tully will already be abed."

Brennus strode into the darkness. Knowing he would look after her well in the future should have made her feel better...but it did not.

As she stooped to enter the entrance tunnel, a shadow detached itself from a hiding place behind the roundhouse. A warm and well-loved hand, the skin scent of it familiar, covered her mouth, dragging her body backwards to brush against him, merging them back into the shadows.

Lorcan.

Her whisper was immediately insistent, her hand tugging on his as she turned in his arms.

"Lorcan!" Their kiss was frantic before she wrenched her lips away. "Come with me now! I must be with you." Urgent kisses peppered his mouth as she pleaded with him. "We must be together."

"Nara..."

"I can have no other lover this night." Her whispering was frantic as she drew her bratt over her head, pulled him away from the shadows of the roundhouse, and back down towards the palisade.

Her utter desperation seemed to confuse him. He pulled her to a stop, his breath ragged. "Nara, you are promised to my brother."

"This night is not part of that agreement. You must be mine, now. Do you no longer want me?" Her eyes pleaded with him, her tears shining them. She knew when all resistance fled, could feel his need. It mirrored her own.

Hooked into his arm, she pulled him out of the settlement, avoiding been seen by others, her pace speedy till she reached nearby woods. Lorcan halted their flight when they came to an empty copse. The first touch of their lips set off a conflagration, mimicking the fires of Beltane earlier that evening, licking and crackling with an untamed energy that needed to be released – immediately.

"I followed you," he gasped as his lips tracked a path from her earlobe under her chin, gently nibbling. "I could not bear to think what my brother would to do to you, yet I could not keep away." His hands framed her face. "I do not know what I would have done if he had made love to you, Nara. I believe I would have killed him. I do not know…"

"We did nothing; he did not even pressure me for a kiss."

"I know. I watched. I know he wants you very much, but he waited." His eyes sought her answer. "What did you say to him?"

"I said nothing." Nara held his face between her hands. "Your brother is a very honourable man. He hopes I will eventually come to love him."

"Can that happen?"

"No. His touch does nothing for me."

Lorcan grasped her shoulders, holding her a little back from him. "How can you know that?"

"He kissed me some nights ago, when you were away from Garrigill."

Lorcan pushed away from her, pacing around in his agitation. "If I had known, I would have killed him." His vehemence made her chuckle, jealousy so apparent.

"Then I believe you must also kill Shea."

"Shea kissed you?"

"One kiss." Nara pulled him back to her. "A trial."

"A trial?"

"I have no experience of men. I needed to prove they do not affect me the way you do. Now, no more talking. Please, love me properly?"

"You are promised to my brother, but our fire burns brightly and needs feeding. If I can only ever have you once, let it be now."

"This night I really do have the choosing, Lorcan. My Beltane choice is you!" She was more than ready for him. She had already done her penance to her goddess, Rhianna, having been given the task of choosing her mate. Lorcan was the choice of her heart – the only choice she could have this Beltane night.

He freed her long hair and spread it out before him. "You are like fire, Nara, you burn me, and you truly are a Beltane gift."

"I was born nine moons after Beltane, yet, I was no gift to my mother or father."

They both knew many children were born around nine moons after the Beltane festival, considered to be children favoured by the goddess of fertility, regarded as privileged.

His mouth closed around hers and stopped any further talking, the kiss expressing every need and full of the love they shared. "I cannot wait any longer."

Her waist belt and short bratt dropped to the ground. Lorcan wasted no time removing her dress, his hands sliding over her breasts. Clutching his long thin side braids, pressing him against her, she moaned for more. Without breaking their kiss, he worked off his braccae and boots as she pushed his tunic free.

She had never yet seen him bared. As he had caressed her breasts, she kissed him, before Lorcan slid them both down onto the forest floor. Naked, atop their pile of clothes on a bed of dry leaves, Nara was lost to the surfeit of sensations Lorcan brought her…making her soul fill to overflowing. Her sighs of pleasure turned to even more excited moans as he explored every last part of her.

Astonished cries were accompanied by delighted squirms when his clever fingers sought out her secret places, not ceasing their torment till her body tensed in anticipation of the satisfaction she'd never yet experienced. His tongue mating with hers, he broke through the barrier, absorbing her small cry of discomfort. Soon the surges were ever increasing, her responsive body following his lead, enwrapped in the all engrossing tide of intensity that gripped her.

He tore his mouth from hers. "I cannot hold back any longer. My seed comes…"

He began to pull out.

"Nay!" Her anguished cries beseeched him. "You must not leave me. I must share all with you. You have shown me the beginning, now give me the end. The goddess has willed it so."

Lost in his desires, he groaned into her mouth. "I cannot deny you anything, Nara."

"Nor I, you." Her breathing erratic, she pushed herself against him. "No more talk, Lorcan. I must know it all…"

Lorcan picked up the pace, ensuring she reached the same fulfilment, as one with him.

For endless moments they lay entwined, waiting for their breathing to return to normal, for their heartbeats to settle. She never wanted him to ever let her go.

"Oh, Lorcan. You are truly my lover, now." Her voice was husky, her laughter bubbling. "I did not realise what joys I have missed during all those acolyte years."

Lorcan chuckled. His breath fanned her cheek and gently blew stray strands of hair from her face. "Do not be deluded.

Mating is not always so tumultuously fulfilling. That was my body truly calling to yours." A series of tender kisses punctuated his words.

Neither wanted to speak of the realities. All they had was the night...not ceasing till the first hints of dawn. She savoured every touch, kiss and feeling, and sealed the sensations into her heart. Reluctantly, they rose and dressed, knowing they must return while the light was faint.

"I have to leave again this morning. Can you understand I cannot bear to watch Brennus take you hence to Tarras?"

Nara was unable to respond for her heart was already breaking.

Feverishly clutching hands, they ambled back to the settlement, stopping for a last poignant kiss near the defensive ramparts. Then, without a word, Lorcan turned back the way he had come, without another look. Nara was relieved. She could not have walked away from him.

Buried deep in her bratt, she headed for Tully's roundhouse. She did not regret one single moment of the time spent with Lorcan as those memories had to go with her into her future.

In her heart she was certain they had created her son, but her life had to go on for that son to be born.

Later that day, Nara was helping Gabrond down at the horse enclosure.

"I am going back with Gyptus and Grond to their crannog settlement. Would you like to ride with us?" Brennus' question was tentative.

His offer was made to distract her, to make her forget Lorcan had again left the settlement, to go to Owton on the east coast. She would have to bear the company of Brennus soon – just not quite so soon.

"I do not know when I will return." Concern spilled from his regard.

A weak smile was his reward. Reaching for his hand, she squeezed his fingers. "I wish to remain with Tully, for his time is short."

Brennus knew that, too, but Tully had tasked him with gathering fresh information from the west, in the same way he had sent Lorcan eastwards.

Mid-morning, two days later, Nara was urgently summoned to Tully's roundhouse. Fearing for his health, she ran all the way from the training field where she had been overlooking the instruction of the younger warriors in Brennus' stead. Bursting through the entrance tunnel, her call echoed.

"Carn, is Tully worsened?"

Tully's voice was weak, but his spirit still had fire. He sat propped up against the wall near the doorway, his answer halting her headlong rush. "Stop fussing, woman, and sit here. I have gifts for you."

Nara was torn between delight and dismay as she sank down onto the stool beside him, her heartbeats settling to a normal rhythm. His old, rheumy eyes softened, even though his tone of voice still had gruff edges.

"I ordered that to be made for you." His bony finger pointed to Carn. "She has ensured the best weaver at Garrigill has made it a dress fit for a princess to wear for her marriage rites."

"This is for me?" Nara found her voice breaking, tears threatening. Feelings of gratitude swamped her as much as tears of regret. She'd tried to put the prospect of her marriage to the back of her mind, had purposely not allowed herself to think on it. But here was Tully, and Carn, too, ensuring she went to the hand-fasting ceremony with proper rights accorded to her.

"The cloth is perfect, Tully. Thank you." Tears leaked and dripped off her chin, her smile tremulous as she leaned over to hug his shoulders in a light embrace, her kiss the barest of touches on his sunken cheek. Cool fingers crept up to cradle her elbow and tapped gently, the closest Tully had ever got to showing full emotions to her.

"This darkest and lightest of green checks is the perfect contrast for your deep auburn hair, Nara." Carn sounded emotional, as well, as she encouraged Nara to stand before her. The younger woman held the soft weave to her shoulders, allowing it to settle over her curves. "A perfect length, too."

The dress was beautiful, though the occasion was not. Tully and Carn had given her more than the material gift. Their support – and she was sure their respect – was in it as well.

She felt Tully's old eyes drift appreciatively over her. "You came to us with no adornments. Do you have trappings of a princess?"

"I do. At Tarras, a bronze torque and copper arm bands belonging to my mother, are stored for me, but I rarely wore them. As an acolyte I wore no jewellery." She laughed at Carn's expression of dismay. "When hunting, the torque chafes my neck."

Carn found her voice, her eyes wide with curiosity. "You were an acolyte?"

"Aye, Carn." Her reply was soft.

"Carn, you will leave us now if you continue with your nosey questions." The irascible Tully had returned. "If Nara wishes to share her life with you, she will tell you another time. We have more to do today."

Nara was pleased to see Carn was not upset by Tully's rebuke that would have made most people mute. An ornate, wide leather belt lay alongside him, the copper studs over it winking a beautiful scrolling design.

His tone still gruff, his eyes had considerably softened when his shaking hands passed it to her. "The dress and this new belt are from Garrigill."

Nara could form no words to thank him. That the belt was from Garrigill meant it came from him, and had been fashioned at his behest. The studded design represented a series of stars across its length.

"I do not know how to thank you." Gifts for her alone had been few in her life. Her eyes filled with moisture, she reached for Tully's old hands. "Thank you, Tully, they are beautiful, and I will wear them proudly."

"I am not done yet, woman. You still have more to be grateful for."

A thin golden rope with copper end finials, and two narrow armbands, one of gold and one of copper, were placed into her hands.

"These are for me?" Only a squeak passed her lips. They were narrower versions of the ones Lorcan wore, the carved designs on the armbands similar to his. Fat tears dripped from her eyes and dropped off her chin.

"Aye, they are for you, Nara."

When she made no answer, Tully patted her hand.

"Lorcan had our smiths fashion them for you. I am told, as soon as you arrived at Garrigill, he deemed it necessary for them to be wrought specially for you – since you came with no trappings of your rank. They have been formed from gold he has garnered, earned from making useful trade with other tribes." Tully waited to give her time to gain control again. "It will be difficult for you to wear these as Brennus' wife, but for Lorcan's sake I hope you will manage to do this, daughter-to-be."

Nara removed the leather thong at her waist and wrapped the new belt on, slipping her still empty knife sheath on to it. Closing her eyes, she slid the torque around her neck, imagining Lorcan was placing it there. As she slipped the arm bands on, the strident sound of the carnyx broke into her dream and widened her eyes.

Chapter Seventeen

The carnyx?

There was a moment of sheer silence before alarm ensued for the battle horn was rarely sounded except during celebrations. Or to herald war. Beltane well over, it was an alarm call, an impending threat to Garrigill. Warriors burst into the roundhouse, two exhausted messengers limping in behind them to deliver their devastating news.

"The Romans marched north-west from their base at *Eboracum*. They mobilised the whole legion, and swamped the warriors of Swale the day of Beltane. Their Roman leader, Governor Petilius Cerialis, is determined to subdue the whole of the Brigante tribes and continues north."

His companion continued. "They stop only to make overnight marching camps while the weather stays fair. They will be on the move again today. The hillfort at Whorl is now in their sight." The man collapsed in a heap at Tully's side, unable to stand any longer. "Rode the first part of our journey…ambushed by a scouting party close to Whorl…we came the rest on foot."

With Lorcan and Brennus both gone from home, Gabrond and the top ranking warriors flooded the roundhouse. Nara made to leave them but was halted by Tully's peremptory commands.

"Nara, you will take the place of my son."

The others took up their positions. Which son Tully meant was not important. At a nod from her, Carn passed Tully a potion before he issued a breathless stream of orders.

Support for the Brigantes under attack was planned. Messengers were dispatched to nearby settlements requesting aid. Bran and Roc took over the mobilization of battle-ready warriors from Garrigill, as many as possible to support their besieged tribespeople of the southern areas.

That decision made, Tully turned to her.

"Make haste to the weapon store. Make sure all is well with the distributing of weapons, and fit yourself out. You can only do the work of a branded-warrior when kitted out properly."

Tully's words croaked with the suffering he attempted to suppress, for now he was pained in body and in heart; powerless to do anything physical to help his people.

Dashing to the weapon store, Carn's father had already laid out every possible weapon that was in their armoury, alongside all the new ones lately fashioned. A sense of purposeful urgency dominated the movements of everyone around as Nara selected new weapons for herself.

Where was Lorcan? Was he safe?

"This short sword and that shield are likely to be a good weight for you, princess," Donnal said as he selected weapons from the stockpile, handing them over to her as she hefted a spear of her choice to check its balance. A quick pick at the pile of small knives and she was ready.

The long curved ended rectangular shield was indeed just right for her. Though she had never fought and killed in a real battle, she was well-trained and knew how to defend her body with the barrier.

Lorcan was an experienced warrior. Wherever he was he would be safe. Yet, her heart still fretted.

Since all was well with their organization at the weapon store, Nara headed to the horse enclosure. Gabrond and Feargus had selected which horses would go, and they were being made battle-ready. Though not yet twenty summers old, Feargus was a most competent horseman and would travel with the herd.

"Eachna will remain at Garrigill," Feargus told her. "Your filly will be available to you if you need her, but you must take over her daily care."

His speech halted for a moment to clutch Carn to his side as she rushed to him, silent tears coursing down her cheeks, her arms circling his waist, almost squeezing the breath out of him.

"Why has Rowan not been allocated?" She was surprised to see the bold stallion still in the far field of the horse enclosures.

"Tully ordered he be left for Lorcan when he returns to Garrigill."

"The horses will be seen to, Feargus. I pray the gods to stand with you."

Nara mouthed the words, meaning them from the heart, but her mind was on Lorcan. She had no warrior to wrap her arms around, or say farewell to, as Carn was doing with her Feargus. Lorcan's absence was a wound in her heart. What if he had gone south-east rather than east to Owton? He could be in the middle of the battle, and she would not know.

Over five hundred male and female warriors, including many untried youngsters, left Garrigill for battle, their weapons glinting in the sun, their mid-blue woad-decorated faces and bodies fierce to the eye. Determined battle cries accompanied their pounding feet.

A mounted force of senior warriors, led by Roc and Gabrond, accompanied the battle chariots, the horses and chariot wheels hammering the ground as they quit the settlement. Those on foot were led by Bran.

Tully was litter-carried down to the settlement gateway to bid them on their way. Nara stood cantankerously at his side along with the wives of Arian and Gabrond. Tully had refused to allow her to join the war-band. Understanding why did not make it easier. The most able warriors were gone, leaving the hillfort guarded by older veterans and young untried bloods. With dread in their hearts, they watched the force of Garrigill go forth to battle.

"You must be my eyes and ears, daughter-to-be. Your expertise and your quick brain I cannot do without. If a second wave of attack happens you may need to lead us for who do I have left, who is trained and is fit for the purpose?"

Nara empathised with Tully's pain. In his debilitated state he was a liability to the clan.

The hillfort of Garrigill did not settle to bed as normal, nor was it expected to. People worked in the dusk, and into the dark, to continue to prepare weapons, and to replenish supplies of easily stored food. Nobody could settle to sleep when they knew their loved ones would be active in battle in the coming days, not knowing if they would return. She eventually lay down.

Where was Lorcan? The words had been playing in her head all day.

Thinking about the safety of Brennus was an afterthought Nara was briefly ashamed of.

Just after dawn, a messenger staggered into Garrigill. The *Legio IX* had indeed surged forward again from their marching camp near Swale, sending their usual scouting parties ahead to assess the terrain. The warriors of Garrigill, joined to the forces of Whorl, were expected to do battle later that day as the territory of northern Brigantes was seriously compromised.

A short while later, another messenger arrived from Gyptus. "When news of the Roman attack at Swale came to us Grond and Brennus left with as many warriors as we could muster to meet the Garrigill contingent at Whorl," the courier informed them. "We have had no reports since then."

Two dreadful days passed with no updates from the battlefields. Tully had heard by then that Callan had rallied up Selgovae and Novantae hillforts north of the high hills. They were battle-ready should there be an attack from ships to the east or west.

No word from Lorcan meant Nara was frantic about his safety, but she was trapped at Garrigill and could do nothing but wait. Tully relied heavily on her now as war preparations at Garrigill continued. She checked the progress of their new weapons stocks at the reduced smithy and saw to the depleted herd of horses.

She worked tirelessly, like all the others at the settlement, including the children who now had even more daily chores to see to. Darting back and forth to Tully's roundhouse, she tended to a visibly shrunken chief who rapidly deteriorated. He was no longer able to make the sharp assessments necessary, so Nara helped him make decisions, though she managed to make it appear as though he still led the community. The remaining high-ranking elders who visited Tully accepted her assistance – too old to make wise decisions themselves.

She fretted more and more for Lorcan and, in smaller measure, for Brennus, but as a warrior she strained at the leash. She wanted to take up her weapons to do more to help her fellow Celts…but at Lorcan's side.

Eventually, a small group of wounded warriors made their painful way back to Garrigill. It had been no small skirmish with the Roman *Legio IX*. The Garrigill warriors had arrived at Whorl, exhausted from their fast paced march south. They had plunged into battle but the Roman attack was ferocious, the resulting casualty list from Garrigill high.

"We had no chance of defeating them, Tully. Although their number was fewer than ours, we could not penetrate their front lines. They came and came, swiping through us as though a blade was cutting our emmer wheat at harvest."

"All the territory north of Whorl is now under Roman occupation," one of the survivors rasped, his thrice-broken arm in a makeshift sling not supporting much at all. His injuries were so bad Nara feared he would lose his whole arm. "They have set up a marching camp north of Whorl to re-group. Garrigill is the next biggest settlement on their northwards progress."

Another herald arrived later with worse news. "Two auxiliary cohorts, each with five hundred men, came north to give support to the *Legio IX*. And now they all move northwards."

He also brought the most devastating news, yet.

Brennus was lost!

Brennus and Grond had both been felled, at Whorl. The Celtic spears, even raining in their thousands, had minimal impact when the Romans formed their protective tortoise formation. The Celtic warriors had no strategies coming anywhere near the discipline of the Roman army.

No one knew anything about Lorcan.

A blinding, howling grief encompassed Garrigill that night. Nara assumed even more duties for there were few others to lead Garrigill. Gabrond, she had learned, was still alive, though he had been seriously wounded.

Tully was devastated.

"Two of my sons dead, Nara. Gabrond wounded. Lorcan? My son, Lorcan? I do not remember…"

Nara did not even want to think about Tully's younger sons and daughters, as they were all fostered in Brigante strongholds south of Garrigill.

Tully wailed his grief, unable to support his body upright any more. His bony fingers gripped hers in a desperate clutch, his mind now drifting since clarity was a thing of the past. Her hand clutched Tully's weak fingers and put them over her stomach.

"Lorcan is not dead, Tully. The father of my son is not dead…he will come back to us."

Tully's eyes closed, as though satisfied with her answer, sinking into another place again, the last potion numbing his acute pain.

That evening, Nara used her *nemeton* training to proclaim the correct rites and incantations for the dead, since there was no druid present at Garrigill. Feting their bravery was vital, even though their physical bodies were elsewhere, for those who died gloriously in battle were sent festively to the otherworld. None at Garrigill challenged her right, or her decision to conduct the ceremonies – though the feasting did not happen as normal.

The following morning, she was tending the horses when the alert came that two Selgovae warriors had approached the settlement. As they came into view, Nara felt the happiest she had been since her night spent with Lorcan.

"Cearnach!" She ran to the warrior who vaulted down from his horse with the ease of someone fit and healthy. "You are well?"

Cearnach laughed as he hugged her, wincing as their bodies made contact. "I am not completely healed, but I have ridden here to support you at Garrigill. When news of you reached Raeden, I begged leave to come to aid you." He introduced his companion, a young warrior from Raeden, called Ailin.

Nara was overjoyed to see Cearnach, and towed him and Ailin along to Tully's roundhouse.

"So, this is the warrior we thought at first might be dead." Tully's breath was raspy but welcoming, his mind for that moment in tune with his surroundings. "In my name, Garrigill apologises for wounding you, warrior of Tarras. I am glad to see that you are hale. Attend to Nara's safety as you did before and if you believe that you need more help, I will find it for you. Look after her well for she is a daughter to me already, and will be the mother of my grandson."

Cearnach declared he needed no urging to look after her, though asked no questions.

"He comes, Nara!"

The shout went up around mid-morning of the following day. Nara's heart lurched into an unnaturally fast rhythm. Lorcan? Returned? Jumping to her feet, from Tully's side, she sped to the entrance gates, her feelings in turmoil.

It was not Lorcan who was driven into Garrigill on the floor of a battle-scarred chariot. Her eyes alighted on the prostrate body of the warrior laid out on the planking, gutted that it was not him, but also heart-sore for the warrior.

Gabrond's leg wound was severe. The slice of a sharp Roman sword had taken its toll, no main blood flow had been severed but infection had set in. Nara was fearful her healing skills might not be enough to save his life, never mind his damaged limb.

Tully was lucid when informed of Gabrond's arrival. "Gabrond returns?" His thready voice showed a hint of its former arrogance. "Nara, you will do what you can...and if the gods will it he will walk again."

She wiped Gabrond's wound, slapped on a thick honey poultice and bound his leg tight. Gabrond was delirious, slipping between fevered consciousness and disorientation,

215

though she had administered a strong sleeping draught. He cried out to Lorcan, his mumbles incoherent and confusing. "Lorcan is alive." Nara found her hand seized in an iron grip and pulled close to Gabrond's face. His eyes were glassy, his speech low but his words were frantic. "Lorcan is alive."

Her heart stuttered. "You know this?"

"Wounded…" His speech drifted off, restarting only when Gabrond suppressed the crushing spasms of pain. "Lorcan fought close to me when I fell…find Seamus."

Where was Lorcan?

Seamus did not know where Lorcan was. He had removed Gabrond from the battlefield and set himself to the perilous task of getting him back home on their war-torn chariot. The return journey had been a problematic quandary to remain undetected by marauding Roman soldiers who now patrolled the lands of the Brigantes.

He could only confirm Lorcan had arrived at the fray with warriors from Owton, and had been wounded.

Nara was frantic. She had to find Lorcan, but she feared Tully would not countenance her journey. Heavy of heart she sought his permission.

"You must do as your heart tells you, Nara." Tully's thready voice was resigned but supportive. "I am a greedy old man. If my son Lorcan is alive I wish him home. I wish both of you home as we know now the gods have deemed Brennus was not the husband for you."

Fully-weaponed and dressed in her warrior clothes, she prepared to leave Garrigill, accompanied by Cearnach and Ailin, taking Rowan on a lead rein. None of them had ever trodden such southerly paths before, so a young Garrigill guide, Aanghos, was enlisted to lead the way to Whorl.

Warriors returning to Garrigill passed them along the way, but none of them had news of Lorcan. The going was easy for a while since the Romans had entrenched themselves near Whorl, and no known scouting parties were encroaching to the north. Though still needing to remain undetected, they were able to keep to main tracks, covering the distance quickly on horseback.

***

"The hillfort of Whorl is that way, but to reach it we must cross through the Forest of Kinninvie," their young guide informed them, pointing out its direction. "A small village lies to the east. We can reach there by dusk end, but not Whorl, that would be too far before dark sets in."

Shelter was necessary as heavy cloud cover meant no moonlight to guide them. Approaching the roundhouse village, there were no guards posted at the outer fringes. That was not a good sign. On alert, they tethered their horses and crept closer on foot. A deathly quiet lay around, only the sounds of an occasional hen rooting around and the bleating of an un-milked goat penetrated the silence. No human sounds could be heard, but evidence Romans had swept the area recently was clear to see. Looms and work areas had been smashed; tools and other items scattered around. Devastation abounded. The villagers had fled.

They rose after some snatched sleep at the first faint signs of dawn, Aanghos leading them back to the main trail. Barely into the Forest of Kinninvie, their progress was halted by the sounds of neighing horses and the tumultuous pounding of marching feet in the distance. The might of the Roman army was heading towards them.

Sufficiently forewarned, changing direction, they fled to the east. The sounds of pursuing Roman cavalry terrified her as their young guide pushed them on faster through the trees, but leading Rowan meant Cearnach dipped behind. Roman cries of attack came louder to her ears as a band of at least ten mounted soldiers pursued them. A Roman javelin flew alongside as the young Garrigill lad changed direction, yet again, choosing the best pathway through the thickets for the small Celtic horses.

Nara yelled at Cearnach. "Let Rowan go free. Save yourself, Cearnach! I will not lose you to the Romans."

217

Digging her heels into Eachna's flanks to spur her on, she had no idea if Cearnach heard her, or did as he was bid.

A howling cry came from Ailin at the same time as they heard a sound not unlike their carnyx ringing through the trees.

The tone of the Roman *cornu* was higher, but she was sure it must mean the same thing to the Roman soldiers as it would to Celts if sounded during battle or during a skirmish. Rally to arms or sounding the retreat was universal; or so it seemed. Nara saw one last *pilum* hurtle towards them before the Romans wheeled around and sped off after their legion. The javelin had missed Aanghos by a hairsbreadth.

Only when they were sure the Romans had all disappeared behind them did Cearnach pull up his horse and gather in the terrified Rowan as they approached a small stream near the edge of the woods. That was also when she realised Ailin had been pierced by the first pilum throw.

Jumping down from Eachna, she rushed towards Ailin who lay slumped over his horse. The javelin tip was in his lower leg in such a way it almost pinned him to his mount. With Cearnach's help, she pulled him down to lay him flat on the ground.

The blood was flowing fast from the wound, but when she examined it the javelin tip had not crushed the bone, though it was directly though the muscle. The pain had rendered Ailin unconscious, which was good: Nara was able to remove the weapon easily after Cearnach had snapped the shaft close to the top join. The javelin tip was sharp and with careful manoeuvring she was able to pull it free without causing further damage.

She reached for the pouches on Eachna which were bulging with supplies for wound tending. By the time she had dealt with it the best she could, and bound the wound, Ailin had recovered his senses. Embarrassed at having fallen unconscious, he declared himself ready to move on.

They had no choice but to mount, and ride off, since they had no idea if the Romans would return and pursue them again.

"Where does this way lead to, Aanghos?" Nara's shout was barely discernible over the pounding of their horses' hooves as they sped across open ground heading due east.

"Going east for a half day's ride, we will pass three small hamlets. Beyond that there is nothing till the settlement of Owton near the coast."

"Owton? Gabrond said Owton warriors fought alongside Lorcan."

"Then Owton should have news of him, Nara," Cearnach shouted, sounding convinced about it. "If he is still alive."

"He is alive." Nara's determined answer interrupted him.

The first hamlet was empty, the tribespeople having abandoned it. The second village, Mordon, was not deserted because guards had intercepted them very effectively, well outside the hamlet perimeter, saying although the Romans had been quite close they had not ventured into their village, but they had no news of Lorcan.

After leaving Mordon, in the distance fleeing Celts headed across a ford to denser tree cover on the other bank. They were escaping tribespeople, women and children supporting weaker relatives, covering the ground as fast as their feet would carry them.

Nara and her band galloped on to them.

One of them cried out, "The Roman fleet landed on the coast near Owton. Two whole cohorts disgorged to subdue everyone around here. We are heading north to the Votadini. We pray they will shelter us even though we are Brigantes."

"Nay!" Nara urged them. "Avoid the Votadini, they sympathise too much with our Roman enemy. Go to the Selgovae. They will take you in."

"Lorcan of Garrigill told us already. He said we should flee there," a young boy confirmed.

219

Chapter Eighteen

Hamlet of Skerne – Brigante territory

Lorcan? Nara's heart was pounding from more than the fast gallop. "Lorcan? We seek Lorcan of Garrigill. Where is he?"

The boy pointed back the way he had come from. "Back in the hamlet of Skerne, at the far end of those woods."

"He is wounded?" Cearnach asked.

"Aye, a chest wound, but he determines to get our chief's son, Keirnan, back to his family."

"To Owton?" She was terrified, knowing the danger Lorcan was heading towards. "Even though he knows the Romans have landed?"

"Nay, he goes not to Owton. Our chief has fled, too. Lorcan followed him."

The boy's harried words sent a rush of relief to her thumping heart.

At the edge of the village of Skerne, a stripling rushed to them having heard their approach, the lad distraught.

"I have tried to waken him…but he will not." The crackling of his immature voice was wretched, matching his ghostly exhausted pallor. Having recently lived through a bloody battle, the boy's collapse was imminent as he slumped against Cearnach's horse. "I do not know what else to do."

Nara slid from Eachna's back to support the boy's wilting, gangly frame. "Tell me slowly," she soothed. "What is your name?"

"I am Egan…my cousin, Keirnan of Owton, is dead." The boy sobbed, pointing to one of the roundhouses, no longer able to suppress his anguish. "We got him into that abandoned roundhouse, but he died."

His wail of grief was heartbreaking. Nara's sympathy soothed him as she stroked his back and encouraged him to give more details. She willed his strength to last, desperate to hear about Lorcan. "Lorcan of Garrigill? What of him?"

"Lorcan? I cannot get him to waken up. He is maybe dead, too. He lies in there."

Nara took to her heels and fled in the direction pointing to a different roundhouse, her heart hammering, and tears of relief flooding her eyes. The boy said he was asleep. She was not even going to think about his other words.

Lorcan's naked body was stretched out on a bed in the last small roundhouse. Even from the entryway she saw the shining flush of fever on his skin. He thrashed about, fighting off some foe in his delirium. Flying across to him, she held his writhing head still as she inspected his glazed eyes.

"Lorcan?" she whispered. "Lorcan, can you hear me?"

His eyes were open, but there was no recognition.

"Have you given him anything for his pain?" Nara asked Egan who hovered behind her.

"Nay." His head shook rapidly. "Some stream water only from my pouch, but that was a long while since. He coughed most of it out."

"How long has he been hot like this?" She felt the high fever on his forehead then uncovered the dirty blood-stained wrap covering his chest wound.

"Since first light today." Egan slumped to the floor beside them. "I tried using cold cloths to wipe him, but it does not work. He still burns up."

Nara reassured the lad he had been doing the correct thing for Lorcan. She ushered him to lie down and rest, for he truly was weary and she feared he was too near to collapse. Looking around the small dwelling, she gave thanks to Rhianna because the boy had managed to light a small fire.

Dipping a small pot she found at the hearth into a tub of water that lay over by the door, she set it quickly on the flames to heat. Rushing back outside, she collected her herbs from a pouch on Eachna believing that cleaning the wound was essential. Her relief soon exhaled in a huge sigh because

221

although the wound was ragged it was not deep. It was already scabbing well; it no longer bled; and best of all there were no signs of suppuration. Lorcan moaned and thrashed around but it did not seem that his wound was causing the fever. Whatever weakness beset him, it was not that. Yet, her experience gave her no guidance to what the cause could be.

When sufficient water had boiled she infused a mixture of herbs to reduce the heat gripping Lorcan and set it aside to cool down. Able to do little more at present, she went to find the others.

"What of Keirnan?" She did not really doubt the young lad Egan but needed to be sure.

Cearnach confirmed that the warrior in the next roundhouse was definitely dead.

"Lorcan looks to have dragged Keirnan for a long, long way. The deep and bloody tracks go well outside the village."

"Do you think that is why Lorcan is so weakened?" Young Aanghos's question was hesitant.

Nara agreed. It could easily have been a combination of the effort made, perhaps some blood loss from his own wound, and maybe also because he had had no sustenance for a long while.

Over the next while, she managed to get sips of her infusion past his lips and maintained the cooling of his body. Eventually, the cup was empty. Rhianna had many prayers while Nara impatiently waited.

When Egan woke up, he confirmed they had carried Keirnan most of the way from Whorl, Lorcan shouldering most of the burden. He told her that his cousin Keirnan and Lorcan had both been fostered by Gyptus at the same time and they had remained firm friends. Though he was wounded himself, Lorcan refused to abandon him.

Late in the evening, Lorcan stirred, the fever almost broken. In the dimness of the weak firelight, his eyes opened and raked around. "Nara?" His keening cry echoed in the roundhouse.

Kneeling beside him, she grasped his hand, her voice a hush in the silence. "I am here."

Lorcan flailed around, his flapping arm pushing her away, his yowl of agony piercing her ears. "Nay! Nay! I wish for Nara..." His voice rose to a crescendo. "I need you, Nara...where are you?"

"Lorcan." Nara's lips touched his still warm cheeks, before settling on his lips. "I really am here. I am here..." Her tears mingled with the sweat beaded on his skin.

"You are no dream?" His body froze, before shudders rocked his huge frame. She climbed onto the mattress beside him and held him tight to make him believe she really was with him. "I thought I would never hold you again." His voice tapered off and his lids closed only to jerk open again in anguish. "Nay! You belong to Brennus..." His rambles reflected his troubled conscience. "You are my brother's wife."

"Lorcan." Her tears dripped freely off her cheeks, as she held his head steady, willing his eyes to focus on her and for his mind to be clear enough to understand what she told him. "I bear sad tidings. Brennus was lost on the battlefield. He was never my husband."

"Dead?" The black centres of Lorcan's eyes lost shape, as he struggled to make sense of her words. "My brother gone? No marriage?"

His eyes lost clarity, drifted shut, and his body relaxed in her arms. Sleep claimed him again.

The fever eventually broke. Lying alongside him, clutching his body close, Nara felt the calm descend upon him as he slept peacefully. She too slept, exhausted by the recent days.

When Lorcan next awoke, she was on her knees at the bedside, her hand on his brow checking for fever. He snuggled against her arm, his eyes flickering. "Nara? I do not imagine you?"

"I am never going to leave you." Her fierce avowal radiated through her glistening eyelashes.

His face contorted, his whisper barely audible. His hand gripped hers tight enough for it to be painful. "If you are here that means Brennus is dead? I want you as my wife Nara...but I never wished Brennus dead."

223

"I know." She climbed onto the bed and lay beside him, slowly turning him round to face her. Careful of his wound, she clasped him to her chest. "The gods have willed this, Lorcan. You are meant for me, and I am meant for you. You are the father of my son."

"You are with child?"

Her voice was soft with conviction. "I am sure. The goddess willed it. I was sent from the *nemeton* because it was prophesied I will bear a son who will be a great leader of the Celtic tribes. You have given me that son."

"Nara?" His voice was full of awe. "Just before Arian's death the druids prophesied I would rise to greatness. I would become a spokesperson for all Brigantes – a skill which would eventually pass on to my first-born son."

"Then both the gods and the goddess have willed our union.

***

Lorcan felt much recovered, due to the deep sleep, aye, but more so because he now knew Nara was his. She redressed his wound and helped him stand. His arms locked around her for long moments; not because he needed support, but because he was unwilling to let her go. Sitting down at the fireside he was introduced to Cearnach – an awkward meeting as neither could forget the original circumstances of their first encounter.

Cearnach grasped his arm in an arm lock. "If you do not look after Nara, I will hunt you down and kill you!"

Lorcan knew then he would deal well with Cearnach.

Filling in details of the days since he had left Garrigill took a while. It was as well that Cearnach and the others had gone hunting and though the fare was not exceptional it was sufficient to ward off hunger. They supped a hare broth thickened with some barley that Nara had found in the roundhouse and picked the meat from the carcasses.

"The battle at Whorl was almost at an end when I reached it with the Owton warriors," Lorcan said. "Even though the battle had raged for some time, the Roman forces were still fresher than we were since we had travelled from Owton with no rest. I was fighting alongside Keirnan when he was struck down. Those Roman swords hew a mighty wound, but it was even worse when the Roman soldier slashed a second time and almost sliced his leg apart. I rushed to Keirnan's aid but I was taken unawares. An auxiliary soldier whipped me around and had his *gladius* at my chest before I could repel him. A few blows from his shield knocked me to the ground, where I fell on top of another slain warrior."

Nara's grip on his hand was strong enough to reduce the blood flow to his fingers. He patted her tense fingers with his other hand.

Catching Egan's attention, he continued, "Young Egan, here, had been stunned by the flat blade of a sword and another warrior had fallen dead on top of him. The Romans assumed Egan was also dead during their bloody sweep of the battlefield after the end of the fighting."

Egan had been sitting desperate to add to the conversation, his expression showing how keen he was to join in. At Lorcan's nod he took up the tale. "When I came to it was moonlit dark, not easy to see anything on the bloody battlefield. I knew the warrior above me was long dead when I pushed at the arm that locked over my neck. So many slain warriors lay silently around me after I struggled free. Thankfully, the Romans had left by then. Through the darkness of night I staggered back on the northerly path. It surprised me to find I was stronger than most of those unfortunate souls I passed by, my forced sleep having fortified my strength. Dawn had already broken when I reached the next bedraggled warriors on that path." The boy looked to him. "Lorcan had my cousin Keirnan draped over his shoulder."

Lorcan patted the boy's back. "Egan came at the best of times. I struggled even then with Keirnan's weight. Without this valiant warrior's help I would never have reached this place."

"The gods were looking after you," Nara said after Lorcan had finished his story.

"What of your King Venutius? Has he fled, too?" Cearnach wanted to know.

Lorcan had no idea but word had gone around the survivors that Venutius was feared dead. That was as bitter a blow for the Brigantes being overrun by the Roman armies of Governor Cerialis.

They set off for Garrigill as soon as he had given Keirnan the best rites to the otherworld that Nara could manage. The hamlet of Skerne was not the home that he had wanted to return Keirnan to but it was close enough – it was too dangerous to risk taking the body back to Owton which would likely be swarming with the detested *Ceigean Ròmanach*.

Nara shared Rowan with him; a good pairing since he was still frail. At least, he allowed her to think he needed her support but it was more he did not want to let her be anywhere except in his arms. Since they had no idea where Egan's family had fled to he journeyed with them on Eachna.

Forceful winds blew. No rain fell, though the sky was dark and heavy when Lorcan looked up. They were traversing the flatlands bordering a dried-up riverbed, trees swathing both sides, when Cearnach's warning alerted them to immediate danger. Romans! A small troop of them were approaching quickly.

Carrying two weights, Rowan lingered behind the other horses as they sped into the nearest trees. Nara had ridden at his back, but barely into the woods he heard a faint cry behind him and felt her lurch from Rowan's flanks. Pulling the horse up as quickly as he could, he circled back to find her. When he spied her his ferocious cry rang out across the glade.

"Cearnach!"

Nara lay pinned to the ground, a Roman spear thrust through her upper arm. Two Roman auxiliaries were swiftly dismounting and hurrying towards her.

"*Diùbhadh!*"

Cearnach's spear caught the first Roman in the throat where the earflaps of his helmet parted and his chest amour had not yet begun. The soldier thudded to the ground. Nara's bodyguard had whipped back to help him, both of them

226

launching upon the second Roman before he could wing his *pilum* or raise his sword.

When the soldier lay dead at their feet Cearnach' satisfied grunt was breathless. "Scum truly is what they are."

Lorcan surged back to Nara.

"Nara! Do not dare die on me now."

"Lorcan?"

Her cry was feeble. She lay slumped on her side but she was not dead. The spear was embedded in her upper arm, pinning her to the ground, making her unable to move. He had seen many warriors fall, in many skirmishes, but none had ever mattered as much as Nara.

He slid to the earth cradling her body to him as close as he could get. As he clutched her, Cearnach's strong hands reached below to pull the spear point out of the soil. Carefully bringing her up to her knees, Lorcan slid round to take her head in his hands, supporting her upper body. Nodding to Cearnach, an unspoken command given, he kissed her, absorbing her cry of agony as Cearnach snapped the spear shaft as close to her arm as he could.

"Nara?" Lorcan's voice sounded calm, but he far from felt that. Her pain was an agony in his heart. "We must clean off the splintered edges before we withdraw the shaft. Do you understand?"

He knew Nara had removed more than one spear shaft from a warrior in her times of being a healer, indeed had done it recently. Though it would be utter agony, she knew what they had to do – and do quickly. Other Romans might still be around.

Gripping her body tightly, trying to hold her completely still, Lorcan again took her lips, less desperately but forcefully enough to make her focus on their kiss while Cearnach trimmed the wooden shaft.

With no delay, Cearnach slowly pulled out the spear, tip first. Once the weapon was fully free, he applied pads of cloth, swiftly cut from the bottom of her tunic, to both openings of the wound. Withdrawing a leather thong from his waist, Lorcan tied it close to the top of her arm to minimise the blood flow and used another one to tie around the makeshift bandages Cearnach held in place for him.

Nara was barely conscious of the sounds made by Ailin as he and Aanghos felled a third Roman soldier who suddenly appeared on foot near them. Cearnach lifted her almost unconscious body onto Rowan, and then Lorcan climbed up behind.

Hillfort of Garrigill – Brigante Territory

Garrigill.

Nothing looked finer than Garrigill in the distance as they came down off the hill. It had taken them two long days to trek there after Nara's injury. They had had to stop and rest in the forests, to set a fire for searing heat to cauterise her wound. She was able to indicate which herbs in her stores should be used for packing the wound, and which should be used to dull her pain.

All were battled scarred in some form as they trudged on, but though Cearnach offered, Lorcan would not let him ride with Nara.

Their welcome home was ecstatic, though only from a small amount of tribespeople, since many of the Garrigill warriors had not made it back. His dying father was overjoyed to welcome them home, knowing he, Nara and Gabrond were all safe. Gabrond managed to hobble along to join them in Tully's roundhouse to tell them the latest news.

"For the moment, Garrigill does not seem to be under threat. The Romans have pulled away from Whorl and are headed back to their camp at *Eboracum*."

A light meal later, they had shared their stories. By then Lorcan ached, and he was sure Nara felt likewise. He was more than ready to slip into the stall at the back and sleep – with her by his side. Nobody was going to part them. Shedding their footwear and filthy *braccae*, they stretched out alongside each other and snuggled under the bed skins. Making sure neither wound was chafed Lorcan touched his lips to hers, sweetly and softly. "Tomorrow."

***

Before dawn, Nara felt a whisper at her cheek. Turning over to clasp Lorcan, her wound screamed at her, making her gasp with pain and him hiss with his own discomfort when her withdrawing palm bumped his chest. Small pained laughs shook them. He reached for her hand and gently squeezed. "Maybe we can work this out." His words turned to a whisper of what they might manage.

"Me above?" She was intrigued. She used her sound arm to nudge him gently, her laughter not so quiet. "There is so much for me to learn, Brigante!"

When she eventually sobered up, she heard a loud throat clearing from outside their stall. "If you can manage to get up, Tully would like to speak to you." Carn's words were greeted with their quiet gurgles.

Tully lay outside in the late afternoon sunshine, on top of a raised pallet piled up with many skins to comfort his aching body. The warmth of the day lingered, yet Nara could see he shivered underneath the woollen blankets. His body was now a shrunken shell, though there was still a sparkle of wit in the weary eyes as Lorcan slid down beside his father. She knelt on his other side.

Lifting the old man's fingers, she felt the tiniest of squeezes at her palm. Her lips touching the briefest caress at Tully's emaciated cheek was rewarded with a hint of a smile and a twinkle in the glazed eyes. Carn had done a fine job to keep Tully alive this long.

His feeble voice whispered, the effort too much to do otherwise. "My son, Lorcan. I am still able to give orders around this hillfort."

Lorcan's laugh gave Tully the opportunity to regain his breath. "I know you are, Father, and it pleases me greatly."

Tully attempted a laugh, but it came out as a croak. "Arrangements have been made. Carn, give them the details, for I have no breath…"

Carn stepped forward from her place at the entrance.

"A very fine dress, a new belt and some beautiful jewellery await you in your old stall, Princess Nara."

Nara refused to acknowledge Carn's disdainful look at the ragged clothing she was wearing.

In a hurry to talk to Tully she had not taken time to change; she had merely pulled on the mud- and blood-crusted *braccae* she'd worn for days. What was left of her tunic was in an even worse state, pieces having been hacked off by Cearnach to mend her wound.

When Carn's cheeky smile appeared, she knew the girl had only been toying with her.

Tully recovered sufficiently to speak again. "Lorcan…new garments in that same stall, for you. They would have been delivered…"

Carn finished for the old man. "You were too occupied earlier to receive them, Lorcan."

Nara felt her cheeks heat. The look Lorcan sent her was blatant. He answered Carn but his gaze lingered on her. "We were."

Carn's eyes danced in merriment while she delivered the rest of her chief's instructions. "As well as ordering new clothing, Tully will wait no longer to have the marriage rites performed for you. He was so sure of your success in finding Lorcan that our chief druid responded quickly to Tully's summons, sent for when Nara left to find you. He has arrived at Garrigill this afternoon. The rites will be performed tonight."

"Nara? Where will the ceremony be…?" Tully's words faltered as a spasm of agony hit.

Nara's thoughts whirled. She was already Lorcan's woman, but this would seal their future together. Her eyes drifted over the prone body of Tully. The smile on Lorcan's face told her everything she needed to know. He knew exactly where she wanted their rites to take place and he answered for her.

"There is only one place for us, Father."

"Water for bathing has been placed in your stall, Lorcan," Carn said.

Nara looked at the younger woman, the glint in her eyes a hint of what was to come.

"Aye, my son," Tully rasped. "Tidy yourself up. You…stink of battle."

Lorcan disappeared. Carn towed Nara to the back of Tully's roundhouse, to her old stall. Warm water for bathing had already been put there, too, by Carn's helpers. After many days of hectic travel, the prospect of being properly clean was a delight, and Nara needed every drop of the water that had been set out for her. Her laughter rang out, echoing around the almost empty roundhouse.

"I do not need to be told that I stink, too?"

Carn laughed along with her but had the manners not to confirm. She lingered around to help wash her hair and body clear of the grime and blood of the previous days and to rebind her wound.

All was going smoothly till Nara tried to don the new dress that had hung in the stall, awaiting her return. Carn held the neck slit above her head ready to slip her arms up into it.

"I cannot raise my arm so high, Carn." She was despondent, her happy expression disappearing into a sad frown. "I will not be able to wriggle into that lovely garment."

"I know what will work." Carn smiled before disappearing from her stall.

Disappointment weakened her knees. So much so, she had to rest on the bed as she fingered the fine weave on her lap. The weave was beautiful, and she really wanted to wear the simple shift for her marriage rites to Lorcan. He did not even know Tully had gifted it to her. Tears of disenchantment leaked, and tracked a pathway down her newly washed cheeks. She was too exhausted to think clearly. She had not envisaged any kind of marriage ceremony earlier that day, but now that Tully had set it in motion, she wanted to look her best.

"No tears, Nara." Carn sounded almost like Tully as she entered the stall, though her huge grin softened the rebuke.

She had returned with a simple answer.

When Carn lifted the dress from her fingers and whipped out the knife at her belt, Nara squealed. "What are you doing?"

One clean cut and one opened shoulder seam hung loose.

A few minutes later, her new dress fit perfectly, having acquired yet another jewel to enhance it. She now wore a simple penannular bronze pin, one that had originally belonged to Tully. It held the opened seam in place, the bindings around her arm mostly disguised by Carn's clever arrangement.

"There," Carn said, as she patted the sharp tip of the brooch pin in place at exactly the edge of the circular bronze loop. There was going to be no danger of the tip stabbing her. "Your dress looks perfect, now."

After brushing her long hair to a gleaming curtain, which hung to her waist, Carn placed a thin silver circlet on her head, to hold her wavy hair in place. It was another gift. Again from Tully, it had belonged to Lorcan's mother.

"Nara! We must go. I have no wish to keep Tully waiting, and more than that, I want nothing to stop this event from happening." Lorcan's cry from the roundhouse doorway sounded impatient.

Carn stood back to admire her. Nara was touched by her wobbling lips; Carn had been such a mothering hen she felt like one of her chicks, suitably brought into order.

"I will not weep," Carn bubbled, her fingers brushing the hint of tears from her lids. "Now you look as a princess should, for her marriage rites."

Nara's eyes also filled with tears. "Thank you, Carn. You will not believe this till I relate more of my story, but I have had few friends in my life. I would very much like to continue to be your friend, as well as the princess who now goes to marry a prince of your tribe."

Her star-studded belt glinted in the last vestiges of the evening's sunlight, neat around her waist, as she trekked beside Lorcan to the place she had chosen for the ceremony. Her torque, with its shiny copper finials, matched the one

232

Lorcan wore. Her armbands likewise corresponding to Lorcan's as their arms brushed together.

Now thoroughly clean, his hair gleamed. His side-braids were kept in place by new leather thongs, and his chin shaved.

Lorcan looked down at her. "Do I match up to you, Nara of the Selgovae?"

"I could not have chosen a better man to be my husband; you know that, Lorcan of the Brigantes. You will be the finest looking man at our ceremony."

"Tully's doing. He tells me he ordered this tunic made, after you fled in search of me. He believed your claim that I still lived, and had the weaver make me this garment to match yours."

The same yarns had been used in Lorcan's tunic, though the checks of his were smaller, and his *braccae* had been fashioned from dark green yarn.

By the time she and Lorcan reached the nearby woods, the same woods where they had fled to the night of Beltane, Tully's litter had already been carefully carried there. The old chief had insisted he join them, and would not have the location changed when she protested it was too far for him to be conveyed.

Dusk had already fallen, the lighter blue of the day replaced by the darkest silvery-blue hues of the night when she stood with Lorcan, in front of the Chief Druid. Behind the druid was the oldest oak in the small clearing – an important aspect of the ceremony.

Alongside, Tully's litter was slightly elevated, a temporary framework having been constructed to ensure he missed nothing, with Carn beside him seeing to his needs.

Behind the old chief were gathered those elders and important people of Garrigill who still lived. On Carn's other side, Gabrond stood with his wife, Fionnah, and his brood of small children. It was not as large a crowd as at Beltane, but substantial.

The Chief Druid swept his arms aloft. "Taranis, hear us this night!"

His deep boom rang out over the darkening copse. The moon shone brightly in a sky clear of cloud cover, the same as the last time she had been in this spot with her Beltane choice. But so many things had changed since then.

Lorcan's tight grip held Nara's hand. Not hurtful, but possessive. His dark eyes reflected tenderness and love in the growing moonlight. They could have been the only two souls around; though she was glad others were there to witness her pledge to Lorcan.

The druid called back her attention from Lorcan's mesmerising eyes.

> *"Long life and the fair days of Lugh*
> *Look upon these two,*
> *May their souls not go to that place of valour,*
> *That place beyond living,*
> *Till their own children*
> *Look upon their children's children."*

Lorcan drew her towards him. Mindful of their wounds, his lips touched hers. A fleeting kiss before he set her back a little. Her two hands were clasped in his, their arms outstretched as much as she could manage. Pride radiated as he displayed her to the assembled crowd. Then his voice resounded clear and loud, his gaze never wavering.

> *"You are the star of my every night,*
> *You are my brightness, every morn,*
> *You are deep in my heart,*
> *You are the face, of my light.*
> *You are the mother of my children,*
> *The gods have willed this."*

Tears dripped silently, and made neat little furrows down her cheeks, though the smile she wore demonstrated they were tears of happiness. She made her voice strong, and spoke her vows with pride.

> *"You are the first story my guests will ever hear,*
> *You are the start and end of all my music,*
> *You are the keeper of my company.*
> *And with the blessing of the goddess Rhianna,*
> *You are the only father of my children."*

In unison, on the nod of the Chief Druid, Lorcan and Nara turned and chanted to the crowd,

"Heart to heart, hand in hand. Together."

"Look!" All heads turned upwards when someone gasped. A shooting star flashed its sparkling path across the night black.

The Chief Druid's voice rang out again after the last hints of the star had vanished into the blackness above. "The god Taranis has truly given you his Brigante blessing, Lorcan of Garrigill."

But so had Tully whose fragile hold on life had just slipped away. Carn wept by his side, claiming her chief had died with a small smile of happiness on his gnarled old face.

***

Lorcan took over as Chief of Garrigill.

Time slipped past and the settlement carried on as normally as possible given their huge losses, but it was a shadow of its former self. The Roman threat was not going to go away...but at least it was in abeyance for the foreseeable future.

Callan had sent word that Nara should consider coming back to Tarras with Lorcan, and any other Brigantes who wished to come north to safer pastures.

But Nara could not bring herself to trust her father. "His request cannot be genuine; I will not go. Callan must have some devious plan in mind."

Lorcan believed her fears. Whether there was a conniving plan or not, they stayed at Garrigill.

Word reached him at the hillfort that some of Governor Petilius Cerialis' forces had gone south from the temporary camp at *Eboracum*, returning to their huge fortress *Lindum*. Those left at *Eboracum* looked to be building a permanent fortress, but they no longer seemed to be on an aggressive offensive across Brigantia and Parisi territories.

Rumour also went that the extra cohorts who had arrived by sea before the battlegrounds at Whorl were recalled back across the water to Gaul.

The crushing thing was that the Romans still had left enough forces to control the whole of Brigantia.

"For the good of our people I must do it, Nara." Lorcan grated the words out as he restlessly paced around the roundhouse some moons after their return to Garrigill. "I have to swallow my spit and make treaties with the Romans; otherwise none of the Brigante survivors will live any longer. If we retaliate like Shea of Ivegill wants us to do, we will all be annihilated. We have no resources to win against them."

"I know you are correct, Lorcan." Nara cringed at the notion, but acknowledged they had no real choice any more.

Thus, after weeks of negotiations, he made a pact with the emissaries of the Roman Governor, Petilius Cerialis. So long as his northern Brigantes did not attack the Roman forces at *Eboracum,* or at any of the other nearby Roman forts, then his tribe would be allowed to continue with their lives more or less as before. The Roman Empire demanded some of his harvests but there were no other moves to force his northern Brigantes to adopt Roman ways of life. His negotiations did not include a human tax to Rome in the form of young blood.

It was a co-existence that lasted for almost seven winters. Lorcan became the finest negotiator with the Romans and was proud to have it acknowledged. New agreements were made with the next Governor of Britannia, Sextus Julius Frontinus, and the fragile peace continued. It caused him pain to know that Frontinus spent much of his time subduing southern tribes like the Silures, but selfishly that meant they were not interested in attacking his own Brigantes.

The elders of Garrigill continued to favour him as the chief, with Nara sharing his decisions. Together, they protected and continued their Celtic way of life, assiduously resisting Roman influence. His son, Beathan, who had been conceived that long-ago Beltane night, was joined by two little sisters – children born of his great love for Nara.

But the inevitable day came when the newest Roman Governor of Britannia, General Gnaeus Julius Agricola, began his campaigns to conquer the whole of the island of Britannia, and only total domination of all of the Iron Age Britain tribes would satisfy.

It was with a heavy heart that Lorcan heard about the decimation of the Ordovices and of further expulsions of the last of the Druids on the island of Mona. Sufficiently advance news of his campaign reached them at Garrigill, and they set their long made contingency plans into motion. Lorcan ordered a gathering of the nobles and paced the roundhouse till they mustered.

"If we want our children to survive we have to go over the high hills to Tarras." He stopped striding to gather her into his arms, almost crushing her in his desperate embrace.

"I know. It is time, though I am loathe to return to Callan's machinations."

"Our people of Garrigill need a safe harbour; it is our duty to lead them to safety."

There was no more to be said, only a hasty packing for a swift departure. They needed to be well ahead of General Agricola's forces.

With deep sadness, the Brigantes abandoned Garrigill.

They stopped at the top of the hill where Nara had had her first sight of Garrigill and took a last look at the deserted settlement. "When I first saw Garrigill all those years ago, I did not have a place I could call home." Tears running down her cheeks accompanied her words. "And now I am back to the same."

"You do have a home." His tones were just as determined as they had been all those years before. His arms enclosed her and their children. "It does not matter where we actually stay, so long as we are all together we can call anywhere home."

At Tarras, an extremely frail Callan had not completely mellowed, but he was particularly pleased with his grandson, Beathan, who was a very bright and strong lad for his age.

Nara's brother, Niall, had died of his wasting lung disease a long time before, so soon after arrival, Lorcan found himself stepping naturally into the role of Callan's second-in-command, and surprisingly found that he could share the trappings of leadership remarkably well with Callan –

probably because he learned how to predict the ways the old chief's mind worked.

Nara had recently given birth to their fourth child, the summer after their arrival at Tarras, when he was alerted that Callan had collapsed. The old chief was barely conscious when he arrived with his reluctant wife. Callan's dying words were an explanation...of sorts.

"Your mother took a lover soon after I married her. He was young, like her. I hated him, for he was able to give her children."

"Me?" Nara's question was more of a squeak. "And you knew this?"

Lorcan saw that the wizened hand found some untapped strength to grip her. "I could not sire children, but neither could I love you, or your brother, knowing you were not mine. But I needed the standing that having offspring gave me in the tribe."

Callan's voice faded again, the effort too great for much more. "Your young sister is the product of a fleeting Beltane night's coupling, since by then your mother's lover was dead. I could love your sister...I had no idea who her father was...but she was not his."

Nara could only look at the barely living remains of the man she had never ever understood. Over the last moons at Tarras, Lorcan knew that she had not grown to love the man she named father, but she had got to know him better. In his last words he was at least honest, his reasoning exposed since he no longer had anything to gain from lies, or twisted dealings.

He could see that Callan's parting from life saddened her as much, and no more than, any other Tarras resident she had taken some fleeting care of. Her reaction entirely summoned up her feelings for the man called Callan, whose eyes closed for the last time.

At his side, Beathan cried: strong and loud. He watched his son drop to kneel at the side of the cot Callan lay on, to take one last hold of the old man's hand. For her son's sake he could see that Nara expressed some sorrow for Callan, her only public display. For some strange reason, he knew that Beathan had loved the cantankerous old chief.

After Callan's death, he insisted that he and Nara both became joint chief of Tarras when the council asked him to be their leader. This was entirely appropriate as they always made all their decisions together.

His burning love and desire for Nara, the deep affection that had started abruptly in the forest many springs before, had never waned. She boasted out on the practise field while sparring with him – Beathan watching their performance. "I may not wield my sword as often as I used to, Brigante, but I can still bring you to your knees!"

He threw down his sword and grappled her to the ground, his strong arms and legs entwining with hers. Laughing into her face, he kissed her wildly. "Nara, my love, you can bring me to my knees anytime you want."

"Lorcan." She blushed. "Our son listens."

His long kisses were enough to send Beathan off in search of a different kind of action.

~~~

*The stories of the Garrigill clan continue in Book 2 of the Celtic Fervour Series **After Whorl: Bran Reborn** where we learn of the fate of Brennus, after the bloody battle-field of Whorl.*

Glossary

Gaelic terms
An cù!—The pig! /the bastard!
A ghlaoic!—You fool!
Athair!—Father!
Ceigean Ròmanach!—Roman turds!
Ciamar a tha thu?—How are you?
Dé thu a déanamh?—What are you doing?
Diùbhadh!—Scum!
Tapadh leat—Thank you

Dating Terms
Time mainly in moons/ half-moons before or after…

Imbolc—Feb 1st
Beltane—May 1st
Lughnasadh—Aug 1st
Samhain—Oct 1st

The above are the quarter year main Celtic Festivals

Roman Legions mentioned
Legio IX
Legio XX
Legio II Adiutrix (new legion raised for Governor Petilius Cerialis in Britannia)

Historical Context

After Emperor Claudius invaded Britannia in AD 43, the Ancient Roman focus was on subduing more of the southernmost Britannic tribes, and absorbing them into the Roman Empire. Their method of setting up Client Kingdoms, where possible, was continued which meant swathes of land were largely administered by the local ruler, who complied with Roman laws and was directly answerable to the Roman Administration in Britannia. These Client Rulers encouraged the development of Roman culture and customs, and compelled their subjects to adopt Roman habits into their daily lives. In turn for paying taxes to Rome, in goods and in man power for the armies, the ruler was given assurance of help from Rome's armies should they be involved in confrontation with a rival local tribe.

It's likely they were also given a sweetener; perhaps call it a bribe, as in Queen Cartimandua of the Brigantes Federation becoming gold-rich. So long as the Client tribe (as in the case of Cartimandua) instigated no major aggression against Rome, it is thought that they continued to, more or less, carry on with their normal daily traditions.

Queen Cartimandua of the Brigantes Federation became a Client Queen of Rome in approximately AD 50. During the period from AD 50 to the late AD 60s, Cartimandua's dealings with Rome meant her Brigante territory did not suffer the large scale invasion, and often destruction, that befell many other resisting tribes. So, it can be said that, in a way, her dealings with Rome brought a sense of security to her people for many years.

However, this situation came to an end when her relationship with her consort, King Venutius, broke down. When Cartimandua divorced Venutius (and declared a relationship with Vellocatus, Venutius' standard bearer) civil war ensued across Brigantia, though Cartimandua still had the official backing of Rome.

Following the death of Emperor Nero in AD 68, by suicide or assisted suicide, civil war also ensued across the Roman Empire. Consensus amongst the Senate, and the ruling elite in Rome, about the next ruler could not be found. Within the legions, including those stationed in Britannia, there was volatile disagreement over who should step into the role of Emperor of Rome. The Year of the Four Emperors (AD 68/69) saw a quick succession of short term military rule of the Roman Empire – first Galba, Otho, and then Vitellius who lasted eight months. Next to be proclaimed emperor was Vespasian in AD 69, who ruled for the next decade.

The turmoil of the succession of the Roman Empire in AD 68/69 caused ripples within the Roman Army in Britannia, and this unrest, in part, enabled King Venutius to rise up and confront Cartimandua's loyal warriors. Many of the Brigantes fighting alongside Venutius, rebelling against Roman domination, were lost in skirmishes and battles fought against Cartimandua, backed by Roman troops.

In AD 69, Cartimandua disappears from the scant records. It's not known whether she died during a conflict with Venutius; or if she fled to Rome after being rescued by the Roman Governor Bolanus, as is described by the Roman writer, Tacitus. Perhaps some other scenario occurred regarding Cartimandua, and will be revealed in the future.

King Venutius took up the reins in Brigantia in AD 69. It seems that small battles and skirmishes continued for some time against the forces of Rome who infiltrated Brigantia and stamped their presence in the form of forts, fortlets and signal stations (watchtowers).

In AD 69, Vettius Bolanus became Governor of Britannia followed by Quintus Petillius Cerialis in AD 71, and Sextus Julius Frontinus c. AD 73/74. It's not clear yet which of those governors were responsible for invading and settling troops on parts of Brigantia – even on a temporary basis. Cerialis was nominally given credit for some campaign successes in northern Britannia, but the most recent archaeological records are indicating that Bolanus may have had more incursions in the north than he has formerly been credited with.

It is into this historical backdrop that my Garrigill Brigantes and Selgovae find themselves, in the Beltane Choice.

Author's note

Though I always make a conscious effort to make my settings as credible as possible, it has to be said that this is my fictional interpretation of what life was like amongst the tribes of northern Iron Age Britain.

There are very few written sources to research for first century AD (CE) northern Roman Britain, and what I've found to date can only be used in a broad context. I believe there will always be ongoing views of the work of Cornelius Tacitus, the map maker Ptolemy, and fellow Roman writers of those early centuries AD—as in how much of the writing is hyped up propaganda, and how much can be considered to be realistic.

During the writing of my *Celtic Fervour Series,* I've continued to research Iron Age Roman Britain. I've acquired new knowledge over the years about the circumstances of late first century northern Roman Britain, and some of my earlier conceptions, as I wrote *The Beltane Choice* in 2011, have become modified slightly as I write this note in 2018.

Why would this be so?

Archaeology is an organic process. My reliance on particular archaeological findings has to be judiciously used since they, too, are an interpretation of what might have been. Some archaeological interpretations of the 1970s are slightly different from the current beliefs, often due to more sophisticated scientific analysis being used today, which can alter dates estimated from earlier excavations. In terms of the Ancient Roman campaigns of northern Roman Britain, it may become a new question of which Governor of Britannia was in place, or which General commanded the armies during the 'altered' time of occupation.

Thus, interpretations of what happened when, in northern Roman Britain are constantly fluid. I find that this variability is one of the most fascinating aspects of writing about a time and place that is essentially in a pre-historic context. Keeping up with the newest findings about the conquest of northern Roman Britain is a time consuming passion.

The decision to use the word 'CELTIC' in the title of my series has been made with great deliberation. During the past few years, I've avoided arguments with people who believe that all of the Iron Age tribes of Britannia should be named Britons – and that the word Celts should only be used for the Iron Age tribes of Central Europe. The use of the word Celt to describe the cultural aspects of broad set of people is something still being debated in the halls of academia, and exhibitions have been mounted to try to display an answer to 'Who Were the Celts?'

Archaeological interpretations can demonstrate that the tribes of northern Britannia had similar patterns of living to other peoples loosely named Celtic, for example as in evidence of roundhouse dwelling. Other findings of horse 'helmet' decoration, or the remains of a carnyx found in northern Scotland indicate a (possible) similar culture to other parts of Europe. Therefore, I've used the word Celt loosely, mainly to distinguish between an indigenous Iron Age tribal character and a usurping Ancient Roman in my novels.

And when used in dialogue, indigenous Iron Age Briton is so much more long-winded, than Celt!

Another aspect I deliberated over is my use of the Ancient Roman names for the tribes of Britannia. The indigenous tribes left no definitive record of what they termed themselves. I could have invented new tribal names for my fiction, but by using those as given down to us by the map maker, *Claudius Ptolemaeus* (c. AD 120-150) my hope is that it's easier for my readers to imagine the geography involved in the tribal territories that I've described.

I've also deliberately chosen contemporary place names in northern England because I like the cadences of them, and because they lie close to places thought to be Iron Age settlements. Whorl was deliberately chosen as the battle site at the end of *The Beltane Choice* because the topography of the hilly area at Whorlton would have been suitable for battle chariots, and for ranked layers of Celtic warriors on the slope above the plain. It's also relatively close to Stanwick which is thought to have been a settlement of either King Venutius of the Brigantes, or of Queen Cartimandua.

Character names are also chosen with deliberation because I take great delight in finding a name that fits my characters and are ones which I hope also give a sense of relevance and authenticity.

The first edition of *The Beltane Choice* in 2012 (initially in ebook format) had no maps with locations or tribal names. It was as a result of a comment made in a customer review that maps were made for the subsequent books. This new edition of *The Beltane Choice* has maps to make the territory covered easier for the reader to envisage.

I'm completely fascinated by the era and hope you will be, too, as you read *The Beltane Choice*.

The *Celtic Fervour Series*

Book 1 The Beltane Choice
Book 2 After Whorl: Bran Reborn
Book 3 After Whorl: Donning Double Cloaks
Book 4 Agricola's Bane (coming in 2018)

Ocelot Press

Thank you for reading this Ocelot Press book. If you enjoyed it, we'd greatly appreciate it if you could take a moment to write a short review on the website where you bought the book (e.g. Amazon), and/or on Goodreads, or recommend it to a friend. Sharing your thoughts helps other readers to choose good books, and authors to keep writing.

You might like to try books by other Ocelot Press authors. We cover a range of genres, with a focus on historical fiction (including historical mystery and paranormal), romance and fantasy. To find out more, please don't hesitate to connect with us on:

Email: ocelotpress@gmail.com
Twitter: @OcelotPress
Facebook: https://www.facebook.com/OcelotPress/

Other novels by Nancy Jardine

Ancestral/ family tree based mystery/thrillers:
Monogamy Twist
Topaz Eyes

Romantic comedy Mystery
Take Me Now

Time Travel Historical Adventure
The Taexali Game –suitable for ages 10+ to adult.

Email: nan_jar@btinternet.com
Website: www.nancyjardineauthor.com
Blog: https://nancyjardine.blogspot.com

The next part of the Garrigill adventures continues…

Book 2 – After Whorl Bran Reborn

AD 71 After Beltane—Whorl

"*Fóghnaidh mi dhut!* I really will finish you! I have you now, invading scum!"

Another couple of whacks would have the shield gone. The Roman auxiliary's arm already showed signs of fatigue as Brennus slashed below the man's chain link protection, his full power backing each blow of his long Celtic sword. The man was brawny, a practised opponent at the edge of the tight cluster of Roman bodies, but was much smaller than he was and rapidly weakened. Brennus knew the advantage he had. A drained grin slid into a grimace of pain as his sword jarred on the Roman gladius when the soldier's stab interrupted another of his blows, the impact juddering his weakened elbow, an injury sustained with a previous combatant.

"*Diùbhadh!* Scum!"

The gladius flashed upwards. To reach his head the angle of the auxiliary's attack had to be higher than the usual, demanding a different force to succeed, and the Roman just did not have the strength any more. A cry of frustration emerged from the Roman, the clenched teeth an indicator of the man's tenacity as the gladius prodded forward yet again. Brennus understood none of the man's tongue, the battle ground not the place for meaningful talk, but the intent was clear.

"Come! Come forward! *A ghlaoic!* You fool!" Brennus' hollering taunts and crude gestures gained him a little ground as the auxiliary broke free of the rigid formation, desperate to gain conquest over yet another Celtic adversary, the shorter gladius slashing and nipping at his chest but not quite breaking the skin.

The tight group of Roman soldiers had been impossible to breach; their raised cover of shields an impenetrable barrier. He had been toying with and provoking this particular soldier for long moments. Yet, even with his superior strength, he knew he could not sustain such weighty combat for much longer either before he would need to retreat to regain his reserves of vigour—though only a little more wearing down of the man's resistance should be enough. He knew that from an earlier experience. Drawing breath from deep inside he slipped back a pace, and then another as if giving up the pursuit.

"Come forward, you piece of Roman horse dung! You demand the blood of the Celts? Let it be so! Have mine!"

Powerless to resist the lure the Roman soldier surged at his bidding, his shield swinging, his gladius jabbing. One last twisted swipe of Brennus' longer Celtic sword detached the blade-nicked shield from his foe and sent it sailing aside. Abruptly unguarded, the auxiliary pulled his gladius in front of his rippling mail in a futile attempt to cover his chest.

"Too late!" Brennus' snort rang out as he whacked the soldier's fist with his shield when his opponent readied his blade for another stab. It was enough: all the leverage needed to topple his foe. Witnessing the Roman's slithering attempts to right himself he allowed an exultant smirk to break free, knowing victory would be his over this particular rival. "Death to all of the invaders!"

***

You can buy the next books in the *Celtic Fervour Series* in ebook, or in paperback versions, from suppliers like Amazon (https://www.amazon.co.uk/Nancy-Jardine/e/B005IDBIYG/) and other websites across the internet. Or, buy signed paperback versions directly from the author, and locally at various venues across Aberdeenshire, Scotland – mainly at FOCUS Craft Fair Events.